THE ENCHAN

*

Sir Hector Stanyon commands Melinda, his niece and the poor relation in his house, to marry an elderly suitor and when she refuses he tries to beat her into submission. That night Melinda creeps out of the house and escapes to London in search of work.

Frightened and not knowing where to go, she is grateful to a middle-aged lady who offers her accommodation for the night. But she is alarmed by the house and its occupants although she overcomes her fear when she is offered an opportunity to earn far more money than she thought possible. For this she must go through a pretence marriage with the notorious Marquis of Chard. . ..

Also in Arrow Books by Barbara Cartland

Again This Rapture
The Black Panther
Blue Heather
The Captive Heart
The Coin of Love
Cupid Rides Pillion
Desire of the Heart
The Dream Within
Elizabethan Lover
The Enchanted Moment
The Fire of Love
A Ghost in Monte Carlo
The Golden Gondola
A Hazard of Hearts
The Hidden Evil
The Hidden Heart
The Kiss of the Devil
The Knave of Hearts
Lights of Love
Love Holds the Cards
Love in Hiding
Love is an Eagle
Love is Dangerous
Love on the Run
Love to the Rescue
Love Under Fire
No Heart is Free
The Smuggled Heart
Sweet Punishment
Theft of a Heart
Unpredictable Bride
A Virgin in Paris
The Wings of Love
Wings on my Heart

Barbara Cartland

The Enchanting Evil

ARROW BOOKS

ARROW BOOKS LTD
178–202 Great Portland Street, London W1

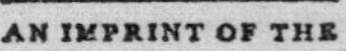

AN IMPRINT OF THE HUTCHINSON GROUP

London Melbourne Sydney
Auckland Bombay Toronto
Johannesburg New York

First published by
Hutchinson & Co (*Publishers*) Ltd 1968
Arrow edition 1970

Made and printed in Great Britain
by The Anchor Press Ltd,
Tiptree, Essex

09 002650 0

1

The schoolroom door burst open.

'Haven't you finished mending my dress yet?' Charlotte enquired in a sharp voice.

Her cousin, Melinda, looked up from the window-seat where the sinking sun cast the last rays of light on the delicate pattern she was embroidering on a ball-gown of pink taffeta.

'I've nearly finished, Charlotte,' she said in a soft voice. 'I could not start until late.'

'You didn't start because you were messing about at the stables with that horse of yours,' Charlotte retorted angrily. 'Really, Melinda, if you go on like this I shall ask Papa if he will stop you from riding so that you will have more time to attend to your household duties.'

'Oh, Charlotte, you could not do anything so cruel!' Melinda cried.

'Cruel!' her cousin retorted. 'You can hardly say we are cruel to you. Why, Sarah Ovington was telling me only this week how the poor relation who lives with them is never allowed downstairs to luncheon or dinner, and when they go driving she always has to sit with her back to the horses. You know as well as I do, Melinda, that I let you sit beside me when we go out in the brougham.'

'You are very kind, Charlotte,' Melinda said quietly, 'and I am sorry if I was delayed in mending your dress. It was only because Ned sent a message to say that Flash was off his food. Of course, when I went to feed him he ate his oats immediately.'

'You are quite nonsensical over that ridiculous horse,' Charlotte said crushingly. 'I cannot think why Papa allows you the stable space when there is hardly enough room for our own horses.'

'Oh, please, Charlotte, please do not mention it to Uncle Hector,' Melinda begged. 'I will do anything, anything you like—sit up all night to mend your gowns, or embroider them from neck to hem. But do not put the idea into your father's head that poor Flash is an encumbrance.'

There were tears in Melinda's blue eyes and her voice broke a little with the passion of her feelings.

For a moment her cousin stared at her in a hostile manner; then suddenly she relented.

'I'm sorry, Melinda. I'm being a beast to you. I didn't mean it. Papa has been scolding me again.'

'What was it this time?' Melinda asked sympathetically.

'It was you,' Charlotte said.

'Me?' Melinda ejaculated.

'Yes, you!' her cousin repeated, and mimicking her father's voice she asked ' "Why can't you look neat and tidy like Melinda? Why does that dress fall so badly on you, while Melinda's, old though it is, looks so elegant?" '

'I cannot believe Uncle Hector says things like that!' Melinda exclaimed.

'Indeed, he does,' Charlotte asserted. 'And, what

is more, Mamma has been saying much the same. You know she dislikes you, Melinda.'

'Yes, I know,' Melinda agreed with a little sigh. 'I have tried so hard to please Aunt Margaret, but everything I do seems to be wrong.'

'It is not what you do,' Charlotte said bluntly, 'it is how you look. Oh, I'm not so stupid that I can't understand why Mamma resents your being here. She wants me to get married, and if ever a gentleman comes to the house he has eyes only for you.'

Melinda laughed.

'That is the most foolish notion, Charlotte. You are imagining things. Why, Captain Parry was all attention to you last week. You said yourself that he never left your side at the garden party.'

'That was before he saw you,' Charlotte replied sulkily.

Quite suddenly she put out her hand and taking hold of her cousin's arm pulled her to her feet.

'Come here and see what I mean,' she said.

'Whatever are you doing?' Melinda ejaculated. 'Oh, do be careful of your gown! There will not be time to mend another tear.'

But the pink taffeta dress fell to the floor and Charlotte pulled her cousin across the room to a long mirror framed in heavy mahogany. Charlotte pushed Melinda in front of it and stood beside her.

'Now look!' she bade her. 'Just look!'

Almost fearfully Melinda did as she was told. She would have been very stupid indeed if she had not realised the poignant difference between herself and her cousin.

Charlotte was big-boned and inclined to fat. She

had a sallow, spotty complexion due to the inordinate amount of puddings and chocolates she consumed. Her hair was a mousy brown and so limp that not even the ceaseless ministrations of Lady Stanyon's lady's-maid could do anything but make it look an untidy mess. Charlotte had good features, but there was a frown of disagreeableness between her eyes and her mouth turned down at the corners because she was continually complaining. She was not a bad-humoured girl but she would, indeed, have been inhuman if she had not been jealous of her cousin.

Melinda was small, slender, with thin, white hands and long fingers. When she moved she had an innate grace which made her seem almost ethereal. There was, too, something spiritual about her tiny, heart-shaped face. She had huge, blue eyes fringed with dark lashes, a legacy from an Irish forbear, and her hair, the colour of ripened corn, fell in soft, natural curls on either side of her face.

'Do you see what I mean?' Charlotte asked harshly.

Melinda turned hastily away from the mirror because she could see all too clearly why, in a burst of temper, Charlotte had recently called her 'the cuckoo in the nest'.

'My mother always said that comparisons were odious,' Melinda said in her gentle voice. 'Everybody is different; everybody has her own particular good qualities. Look how well you speak foreign languages. And your water-colours are far better than mine.'

'Who wants a water-colour?' Charlotte asked bitterly.

Melinda went back to the window-seat and picked up the fallen gown.

'This will be finished in five minutes,' she said soothingly. 'You will look charming tonight when you dine with Lady Withering. Perhaps Captain Parry will be there, and you know I am not included in the invitation.'

'You were,' Charlotte replied gruffly, 'but Mamma said you would be away from home.'

For one moment Melinda's soft lips tightened. Then she said:

'Aunt Margaret was quite right to refuse on my behalf. You know I have nothing to wear.'

'You could ask Papa to let you have a new evening gown.'

'I am still in mourning,' Melinda replied.

'That's untrue and you know it,' Charlotte protested. 'You have had to go on wearing your greys and mauves because Mamma is frightened that if you branch out into colours she will have to take you to the parties that I go to, and then no one will look at me.'

'Oh, Charlotte, dear, I am so sorry,' Melinda exclaimed. 'You know I do not do anything intentionally to call attention to myself.'

'I know, and that is what makes it worse,' Charlotte answered. She turned again to the mirror. 'I ought to get thinner! But I hate giving up the delicious puddings that chef makes and his crisp, newly baked bread for breakfast. I sometimes wonder if it's worth bothering so much to attract a man—and yet what else can we do but get married?'

'I do not suppose I shall ever find a husband,'

Melinda smiled. 'Who would want a poor relation without even a fourpenny piece to bless herself with? —as Aunt Margaret always reminds me!'

'I cannot think why your father was so extravagant,' Charlotte said. 'What did you all live on anyway, before he and your mother were killed in the carriage accident?'

'There always seemed to be a little money,' Melinda answered. 'And, of course, there was the house and the garden and the servants who had been with us for years. We never thought of ourselves as being poor—but then darling, careless Papa had never paid his bills.'

'I remember how shocked my Papa and Mamma were when they learned of the extent to which he was in debt,' Charlotte said frankly. 'It was then they decided that you would have to come and live with us. "No one else will take her," Papa said, "without even a pittance." '

'I should have been more independent,' Melinda sighed. 'I should have insisted on taking a position as a governess or a companion.'

'Papa would never have let you do that!' Charlotte asserted. 'The neighbours would think it stingy of him not to look after his only niece. Papa is very sensitive about what the County says about him. It is just a pity, Melinda, that you're so pretty.'

'I do not think I am really pretty,' Melinda interposed quickly, 'it is just that I am smaller than you, Charlotte.'

'You're lovely!' Charlotte contradicted. 'Do you know what I heard Lord Ovington say the other day?'

'No, what did he say?' Melinda asked, stitching away as she spoke, her fair head bent over her work.

'Of course, he didn't know I was listening,' Charlotte explained, 'but he said to Colonel Gillingham: "That niece of Hector's is going to be a beauty. He'll have a lot of trouble with her if he doesn't look out." '

'Did Lord Ovington really say that?' Melinda asked in an astonished voice.

'He did, and I wasn't going to tell you,' Charlotte said, 'but somehow you've wormed it out of me. I never can keep any secrets from you, Melinda.'

'What did Colonel Gillingham reply?' Melinda enquired. 'There is something horrible about that man, Charlotte. Last time he dined here I saw him watching me. I do not know why, but it sent a cold shiver down my back. I think he is perhaps a devil in human guise.'

'Really, Melinda! How you do exaggerate!' Charlotte exclaimed. 'Colonel Gillingham's only a crotchety old crony of Papa's. He shoots with him and they sit in the smoking-room until all hours of the night, which annoys Mamma. But he's as dull as ditch-water, like all Papa's friends.'

'I really do dislike him,' Melinda reaffirmed, 'and you haven't told me how he answered Lord Ovington.'

'I'm not quite certain that I heard aright,' Charlotte answered, 'but I think he said: "Just what I had thought myself—a high-stepping filly if given the chance!" '

'How dare he speak of me like that?' Melinda ejaculated, the colour coming into her cheeks. When she was angry it seemed as if there were sparks in her eyes.

'Don't worry about it!' Charlotte laughed. 'I'm sorry I told you. I only wish I could overhear some compliments about myself.'

'I am sure you will tonight,' Melinda suggested soothingly. 'There, the dress is finished and you know, Charlotte, it becomes you better than any other gown you possess.'

'Mamma always says there is nothing like a colour to make a girl stand out in a ballroom,' Charlotte agreed. She was silent for a moment and then added wistfully: 'I wonder if Captain Parry likes pink?'

'I am sure he will like you in it,' Melinda assured her.

'I do hope so,' Charlotte said uncertainly. 'And I think it's a very good thing, Melinda, that you are not going to be there.'

There was a knock at the door.

'Come in!' Melinda called.

The door opened and one of the younger housemaids appeared, her white, starched mob-cap slightly awry as she said breathlessly:

'Sir Hector wants Miss Melinda downstairs in the Library at once.'

The two girls turned to look at each other in consternation.

'What can I have done now?' Melinda asked. 'Charlotte! You didn't say anything to him about Flash?'

'No, of course I didn't,' Charlotte answered. 'I was only teasing you.'

'Then why does he want to see me,' Melinda asked,

'at this time of day? It is very unusual.'

She glanced at the clock over the mantelpiece and saw that the hands stood at six o'clock.

'Well, I had best go and start dressing for the party,' Charlotte said. 'Come up and tell me what he wanted. I do hope it is nothing that concerns me.'

Melinda did not answer. Her little face was pale and worried as she glanced at herself swiftly in the mirror to tidy her hair and adjust the prim white collar that she wore at the neck of her grey cotton dress. It was a drab, dreary cotton cut in unfashionable lines and without the crinoline which made Charlotte's dresses stand out elegantly and gave them a swing. But somehow, ordinary though it was, Melinda invested it with an air of grace as she ran almost silently down the thick-carpeted stairway and across the marble hall towards the library.

Just for a moment, as she grasped the handle of the Library door, she paused and drew a deep breath. Then her chin went up and she told herself she must not be afraid.

'You sent for me, Uncle Hector?'

Her voice seemed very small and somehow lost in the heavy pomposity of the great, high-ceilinged room, with its velvet curtains, huge Chippendale book-cases and leather-covered furniture.

Sir Hector Stanyon rose from the desk at which he had been writing and stood in front of the fireplace. He was a heavily built man of over fifty. He had dark, beetling eyebrows and hair that had just begun turning grey. His deep, booming voice seemed almost to shake the crystals of the chandelier as he replied:

'Come in, Melinda. I wish to speak to you.'

Melinda shut the door and moved across the Persian rugs to stand respectfully in front of her uncle, her hands clasped together, her eyes raised to his. He stared down at her with an almost inscrutable expression on his face.

'How old are you, Melinda?' he enquired.

'Eighteen . . . Uncle Hector.'

'And you have lived here now for nearly a year.'

'Y . . . yes, Uncle Hector. After Papa and Mamma . . . died, you most generously gave me a home.'

'I have sometimes regretted it,' Sir Hector replied. 'I won't pretend to you, Melinda, that I have not, several times during this past year, thought it a mistake. You are not exactly the companion I should have chosen for Charlotte.'

'I . . . I am sorry about that,' Melinda said, 'because I am f . . . fond of Charlotte and I . . . think she is fond of . . . me.'

'You put ideas into her head,' Sir Hector boomed accusingly. 'Yesterday she answered me back. She would not have done that a year ago. That is your influence, Melinda. You have too much spirit, too much impertinence.'

'I try to . . . to be . . . unassuming,' Melinda faltered, groping for what she thought would be the right word.

'Not very successfully,' Sir Hector said grimly.

'I am sorry,' Melinda said. 'I have tried to . . . please you and Aunt Margaret.'

'And so you should! So, indeed, you should!' Sir Hector snapped. 'Do you realise that profligate brother of mine left you without a penny? Without a penny! In fact, the sale of the house hardly covered his debts.'

'I know,' Melinda said meekly.

She had heard this many times before and always she longed to throw up her head and defy her uncle, to tell him that somehow, by some method, she would pay back everything that he had done for her. But she knew that she was helpless; knew that she could only murmur, as she had murmured before, her gratitude at receiving the crumbs that fell from the rich man's table.

'I don't blame only my brother,' Sir Hector went on. 'Your mother did not influence him as she should have. She may have been the grand-daughter of a duke, but there's bad blood in the Melchesters and always has been—too wild, too undisciplined! They need to be curbed, just as you need to be, Melinda.'

'Yes, Uncle Hector,' Melinda murmured.

She wondered how long this harangue would go on. She had been subjected to many such exhortations since she came to live in her uncle's house. At first, with blind stupidity, she had thought she was to be treated as an equal. It was only after many lectures, corrections and punishments that she began to learn her place; to know that poor relations had no privileges and, least of all, the privilege of having pride. She had to force herself to be humble, to apologise for things she had not done, to be contrite for having an opinion of her own or, at least, for voicing it.

Now, almost automatically, she muttered:

'I am sorry, Uncle Hector. You have been very kind.'

'But, now, I have news for you,' Sir Hector said unexpectedly. 'And may I say, Melinda, I consider you a very fortunate girl! Very fortunate indeed!'

An answer seemed to be expected of her and Melinda automatically said:

'Yes, indeed, Uncle Hector. And I am very grateful.'

'You don't know yet what you are to be grateful for,' Sir Hector said. 'In fact, I have something of great importance to impart to you, Melinda. Something which will doubtless surprise you, and which, as I have said, is excessively fortunate for someone in your position.'

He paused and then said in a stentorian voice:

'You have received an offer of marriage.'

'An . . . an offer of . . . m . . . marriage!'

Melinda could hardly breathe the words. There was no mistaking her utter astonishment.

'That was something you were not expecting,' Sir Hector said with satisfaction. 'To tell the truth, neither was I.'

Melinda's mind was in a turmoil. Swiftly she considered the few men she had met in the last few weeks; for while she was in deep black her aunt had not permitted her to leave the house and grounds. The only man she could think of was Captain Parry; but she had not spoken to him more than to murmur, 'How do you do,' when Charlotte introduced them; and she prayed fervently that the man on whom Charlotte had fixed her affections should not have transferred his attentions to her.

'I can see you are confused,' Sir Hector said. 'That is indeed right and proper. Had I thought, Melinda, that you had so much as looked at a man with interest before he had approached me, I should have been extremely angry. There is a great deal of talk today of girls encouraging a man before he has received paternal approval. That is something I would not tolerate in my house.'

'No, no, of course not!' Melinda assured him hastily. 'In fact, I have no idea, Uncle Hector, of whom you are speaking.'

'Then let me inform you once again what a very lucky young woman you are,' Sir Hector told her. 'And now I will keep you no longer in suspense. The gentleman who has given you the great honour of asking you to become his wife is Colonel Randolph Gillingham.'

Melinda gave a little cry.

'Oh no!' she said. 'No! I could not possibly marry Colonel Gillingham.'

'You could not! And why not?' Sir Hector enquired.

'Because . . . b . . . because he is . . . so . . . so o . . . old,' Melinda stammered.

There was a little pause.

'It may interest you to know,' Sir Hector said icily, 'that Colonel Gillingham and I are the same age, and I do not consider myself old.'

'No . . . no, I . . . I did not mean . . . that,' Melinda forced the words out. 'It is . . . just that it . . . it would be . . . old for . . . me. After all, you . . . are m . . . my uncle.'

'I have already told you, Melinda,' Sir Hector said heavily, 'that you need curbing. You need more than that—you need a strong hand. You need a man to whom you can look up, who will discipline you and correct you. You are, in fact, in great need of discipline, Melinda.'

'But . . . I . . . I do not want to . . . marry him!' Melinda cried. 'In fact, I cannot contemplate such a step.'

'You cannot contemplate such a step?' Sir Hector echoed sarcastically. 'And who are you, may I ask, to be so self-opinionated? Colonel Gillingham is a man of substance—in fact, I consider him very wealthy. I cannot understand why he should wish you to bear his name, but he assures me that he already cares for you deeply. You should go down on your knees, Melinda, and thank God that a noble and respected man is prepared to assume the responsibility of a flighty creature such as yourself.'

'It is kind, very kind,' Melinda said, 'but I . . . I cannot marry . . . him. Please, Uncle Hector, explain my . . . my . . . gratitude and say that . . . that while I am sensible of the honour he has done me I . . . I must decline his offer.'

'Do you really expect me to convey a message like that?' Sir Hector roared.

The loudness of his voice and the sudden expression of ferociousness which transformed his face would have frightened Melinda on any other occasion. But now she stood her ground.

'I am sorry, Uncle, but that is my answer and I shall not change my mind. Papa always said that he would never force me to marry a man I did not love.'

'Love!' Sir Hector ejaculated. 'Your father must have been demented. I have heard that the modern Miss of 1856 thinks she can flaunt convention and ignore parental authority! But not in my house! Do you hear me? Not in my house! Decent girls still marry where their parents bid them, and as you have no father and I have undertaken to be responsible for your welfare, I shall decide whom you shall marry; and I have, in fact, already made my decision.'

'It is no use, Uncle, I cannot marry Colonel Gillingham. I do not like him. There is something about him which frightens and disgusts me.'

'You impertinent little chit!' Sir Hector shouted. 'How dare you speak about one of my friends in such a manner? Here you are without a penny to your name, daring to refuse one of the wealthiest men in the County and a man who has honoured you far more than you deserve by offering to make you his wife! You will accept the Colonel, and your aunt, out of the goodness of her heart, will arrange the wedding reception here in this house. Go back to the schoolroom! The matter is decided.'

Melinda was very pale and her hands were clenched together until the knuckles showed white, but her voice was quite steady as she said:

'I am sorry if I anger you, Uncle Hector. But to tell Colonel Gillingham that I will marry him will put you in a false position. I will not marry him, and even if you drag me to the church I shall still refuse.'

Sir Hector gave a bellow of rage.

'Refuse, would you?' he roared. 'Refuse an offer which most girls would accept gratefully? You'll do as I say! Do you think you are going to make a fool of me in front of one of my greatest friends? What is more, the marriage will be announced in the

Gazette and the *Morning Post* the day after tomorrow.'

'I do not care if it is announced by the Town Crier,' Melinda retorted defiantly. 'I will not marry Colonel Gillingham! I hate him! I will not marry him whatever you do to me!'

'We'll see about that,' Sir Hector growled.

He was shaking now with one of his frightening rages which his wife and the household knew only too well. His face had become crimson, his beetling eyebrows seemed almost to meet across his nose, the words he spoke were spat between his lips.

'You'll obey me!' he shouted. 'I won't be defied by anyone, least of all you—a penniless chit to whom I have offered the protection of my house. You'll marry him!'

'I will not! I will not marry a man I do not love!' Melinda cried. Her voice too had risen, if only to make herself heard.

The fact that she was now shouting seemed to break the last vestige of control that Sir Hector had over his temper. He picked up the riding-whip which was lying on his desk and in one swift movement brought it down on Melinda's shoulders with a savagery which almost knocked her off her feet. Somehow she did not fall but went on crying:

'I will not marry him! No! No! No!' while she held out her hands to protect herself.

Now quite insane with rage, Sir Hector seized her by the arm and raining blows upon her threw her down across the end of the sofa. Again and again the whip seared her shoulders and her back, the pain biting into her, but still she cried:

'No! No! No!' over and over again.

'You'll marry him if I have to kill you,' Sir Hector threatened between gritted teeth, the whip seeming to cut the air, until finally, almost in surprise, he realised that Melinda was no longer speaking. She lay there across the end of the sofa, her hair falling forward over her face, one hand very limp and still. Just for a moment he was frightened. He threw the whip on to the floor.

'Get up,' he shouted. 'You asked for it and you've got what you deserved.'

Melinda did not move. Breathing heavily he picked her up in his arms and laid her down on to the sofa. She was astonishingly light. Her head lolled limply on to one shoulder and her eyes were closed.

'Melinda!' Sir Hector called. 'Melinda! Damn the little fool! She's got to learn her lesson. I wish Randolph joy of breaking her in.'

He walked across to the grog-tray which stood in the corner of the room. There amid an impressive array of cut-glass decanters was a silver-crested jug containing water. He poured some into a cut crystal tumbler and walking back to Melinda threw the water violently into her face.

For a moment she did not move; then her eyelids fluttered. If Sir Hector was relieved he did not show it.

'Get up,' he said roughly. 'Go to your bedroom and stay there until tomorrow. You will have no food, and if you do not agree to marry Colonel Gillingham when I send for you, I shall beat you again—and again—and again. Your spirit's got to be broken, girl, and I'll brook no disobedience in this house. Do you hear me? Now, go to your room; and don't go whining to your aunt. You will get no sympathy from her.'

He walked away from the sofa to stand at the grog-tray with his back towards her, pouring himself a large brandy with the air of a man who feels he has earned a drink.

Slowly, with her eyes half shut, Melinda struggled to her feet. Holding blindly first on to the corner of the sofa, then on to a chair and then on to the desk, she reached the door. Outside in the hall, she moved as if she was sleep-walking, almost as if her will had ceased to function and only her instinct told her where to go.

She climbed the stairs, one by one, like a child learning to walk, moving first one foot on to a step, then joining it with the other. Up, up, conscious all the time that at any moment darkness might encompass her and she would go no further.

But her will prevailed and although it took her a long time she at last reached her small, cheerless bedroom at the end of the long passage and opposite the schoolroom. She shut the door, turned the key in the lock and collapsed on to the floor.

How long she lay there she had no idea. She only knew that, half-fainting, she still suffered agonisingly, not only from the pain but from the humiliation of what had occurred. It was dark and she was bitterly cold.

At last, she rose from the floor and groped her way towards the bed. As she did so there came a knock at the door.

'Who . . . is . . . it?' Melinda asked, her voice sharp with fear.

'It's me, miss,' a voice replied, and she knew it was Lucy, the young housemaid, who had come to turn down her bed for the night.

'It is . . . all right . . . Lucy. I will . . . manage . . . thank you,' Melinda managed to stammer.

'Very good, miss.'

She heard Lucy's steps recede down the passage and now, at last, Melinda forced herself to light the candles on the dressing-table. She stared at her face in the mirror, feeling that in some way she had changed, that she would not see herself but someone else staring back at her in the mirror.

She saw a white, distraught face; eyes that were great pools of pain and darkness; her hair tangled and dishevelled around her cheeks. She turned sideways and now she could see how the blood from her back had soaked through her cotton dress leaving dark, wet patches.

Slowly she began to undress; every movement was agony. She had to tear her dress and her underclothes from her back where the blood had congealed and stuck to the material. More than once she nearly fainted, but she knew she must rid herself of her stained clothing.

Finally she was free, and wrapping herself in an old flannel dressing-gown she sat down at the dressing-table to stare, with sightless eyes, into the darkness of the room. She believed herself unconscious and yet she had heard her uncle's words: 'You will have no food and if you do not agree to marry

Colonel Gillingham I shall beat you again—and again—and again . . .'

She knew now that he had been on the verge of beating her many times since she had come to the house, as he beat his dogs and his horses and—it was whispered in the house—as he had beaten one of the stable-lads so the boy's parents had threatened to sue him.

He was a savage man with an uncontrollable temper but she knew that what really infuriated him more than anything was the fact that if she refused Colonel Gillingham he, and other people in the County, would know that Sir Hector was not really master in his own house. It was the despot in him that demanded obedience from everyone, whoever they might be, and Melinda, like everyone else, must obey his commands.

'I will not marry Colonel Gillingham! I will not!' Melinda whispered. Then her voice broke and the tears came. Tears that seemed to well up from the very depth of her being, shaking her frail, tortured body until she trembled all over.

'Oh, Papa! Mamma! How could you let this happen . . . t . . . to me?' she sobbed. 'We were so happy; life was s . . . so wonderful until . . . you . . . d . . . died. You could not have meant me to . . . en . . . endure this.'

The tears blinded her and choked her voice, and yet she found herself murmuring over again, like a child who is lost:

'Papa! . . . Mamma! I want . . . you. Where . . . are you?'

And almost as if they did, indeed, answer her from

wherever they might be, she suddenly knew the answer to her problem. It came to her like a flash, clearly, unmistakably, just as if someone had spoken to her and told her what to do. Not for a moment did she question the rights or the wrongs of it, or even consider within herself whether it was good or bad for her and her future. She just knew the answer to her question was there. Her father and mother had not failed her.

She wiped her tears, rose from the dressing-table and taking a small carpet-bag from the shelf on the top of the wardrobe started to pack it. She put in only very essential things; for she knew that she was not strong at the best of times and that to carry anything at the moment would be agony, however light the object might be.

Finally she dressed herself, putting on clean underwear, freshly washed petticoats and her Sunday dress of lavender-coloured lawn with white collars and cuffs. There was a bonnet to match, plain and austere, for Aunt Margaret had allowed no frivolities while she was in mourning, but trimmed with purple ribbons. There was a worn, paisley shawl which had belonged to her mother and this she put beside the carpet-bag, ready to be donned at the last moment.

She must have sat longer in front of the mirror than she had realised; for she heard the grandfather clock in the hall strike two. She opened her purse. It contained only a few shillings—all that she had saved from the meagre pocket-money that her uncle allowed her for the church collection and other very small expenses.

Still moving resolutely, as if every action had been

planned beforehand, she took from her dressing-table drawer a velvet-covered box. She opened it; inside was a small diamond crescent brooch—the only thing she had been allowed to keep when her home had been sold and every piece of property belonging to her parents had gone to defray her father's debts.

This little brooch had escaped because it was already hers, having been left to her by her grandmother, when she died. It was little more than a child's brooch, but the diamonds were brilliant and Melinda knew it had a certain value.

Holding the box in her hand, very, very cautiously she opened her bedroom door. She crept along the passage, frightened every time a board creaked, holding her breath and listening just in case someone should appear and ask what she was doing. But the house was silent and still, only the tick-tick of the hall clock disturbing the peace.

She reached her aunt's boudoir, which was only a short distance away from the large bedroom where her uncle and aunt slept. Melinda moved like a ghost, her small feet seeming to glide rather than walk over the carpet. She opened the door. All was in darkness but she knew her way.

She crossed the room and pulled back the curtain a little to let in the moonlight. Her aunt's *secretaire*, an elegant piece of French Louis XV furniture inset with Sèvres plaques, stood in the window. Melinda knew only too well where the housekeeping money was kept; for every week she helped her aunt with the housekeeping bills and she remembered that even when the servants had been paid there was always a surplus for small purchases.

She pulled open a drawer. There, as she expected, were ten golden guineas. She picked them up and put in their place the diamond brooch she had been given by her grandmother. She was quite aware that her uncle, when he learned of it, would acclaim her as a thief, but she was convinced that the brooch was worth more than ten guineas and that should Aunt Margaret wish to sell it she would certainly not be out of pocket.

Melinda readjusted the curtain and groped her way to the boudoir door. She closed the door and went back to her own room. She knew, as she walked, that her back was stiffening, but it was useless now to think of her own aches and pains. If she was to escape she must go at once.

Putting the guineas in her purse, she looked round the room and blew out the candles. In the darkness she closed her eyes.

'Oh, Papa and Mamma!' she whispered. 'Help me! Help me, for I am afraid to go away—but very much more afraid to stay! Help me, because I am doing the only thing I can do.'

She finished speaking and waited, almost as if she expected a reply, but all she could hear was the tick of a clock on the mantelshelf telling her that time was passing. She picked up the carpet-bag and very, very quietly crept down the back staircase towards the kitchen entrance.

2

There was a fitful moon showing between windswept clouds which lighted Melinda down the dark avenue of the drive to the wrought-iron gates which led on to the road. The big gates were closed but, fortunately, a small side-gate near one of the lodges was unlocked and Melinda slipped through, moving on tiptoe for fear the lodge-keeper should wonder who was abroad at such an early hour of the morning.

She set off down the twisting, dusty road at a sharp pace. She was soon aware that her back was hurting her excruciatingly and that the bag containing the few things she had brought with her seemed to grow heavier and heavier with each step she took. She changed it from one hand to another and wondered to herself if there was anything she could throw away as unnecessary; but she knew that it was not so much the weight of the bag as the fact that she was overwrought and physically exhausted from the beating she had received from her uncle.

Her pace grew slower and soon a very faint glimmer on the horizon told her that the dawn was breaking. It was with a sense of dismay that Melinda realised that she had not yet got very far from her uncle's house: should anyone come in search of her they would not have to seek long.

The thought of being captured after having run

away was too unbearable to contemplate. She could almost see her uncle's furious, red face, hear his bellows of rage as he reached once again for his riding-whip. He would never forgive her, she knew, for trying to escape from his clutches.

She remembered him thrashing a dog which had 'run-in' at shooting! 'Oh God!' she whispered, 'I cannot endure another whipping.'

She knew all too clearly what would happen to her if she returned. From sheer physical weakness she would eventually have to accede to her uncle's wishes and agree to marry Colonel Gillingham. The mere thought of it made her shiver.

She did not know why she hated him so; she only knew that the idea of his touching her filled her with a repulsion that was almost like a nausea. She thought now that she might have guessed that his interest in her was not entirely casual. She had been aware that he had deliberately engaged her in conversation on one or two occasions when he had come to luncheon. They had merely exchanged a few commonplace words, but she had felt shy and embarrassed because of the expression on his face and the look in his eyes.

She had not, at the time, admitted even to herself why she had made an excuse to withdraw from his company, pretending that her aunt needed her assistance or that she had forgotten something in another room. She had only known that she had the same feeling for the Colonel as she had for snakes and that the idea of marriage to him was too horrible even to contemplate.

Her thoughts spurred her forward. For some minutes she walked so quickly she was almost running; but now, because the effort made her feel faint, she slowed down. It was almost light; the thin, yellow fingers of the sun were clearing away the sable of the night. The road was deserted. Soon, she knew, the first cottages of a little hamlet would come into sight; it was there she hoped she would be able to find a coach or a vehicle of some sort which would convey her to Leminster.

Leminster was five miles away and from there she could take a train to London. She had it all planned in her mind. The stage-coaches still ran regularly and were cheaper, but they were far too easily intercepted by a fast-travelling carriage or a man on horseback.

Melinda had the idea that her uncle would expect her to travel by stage-coach. He did not hold with trains himself.

'Newfangled rubbish!' he often said. 'Those puffing billies will never replace horseflesh.'

He would grow quite vehement on the subject, asserting that he would never spend his money in such a ridiculous manner, and that he and his family would continue to travel like ladies and gentlemen behind their own horses, tooled by their own coachmen.

He had, however, conceded that it might be interesting to see a train and, when the station at Leminster was opened, as Lord Lieutenant of the County he had agreed to perform the ceremony. As a great concession Melinda had been included in the party.

She and Charlotte had inspected the train carriages with their soft-cushioned seats and glass windows. They had however looked with dismay at the hard, wooden coaches in which the poorer passengers travelled, open to the elements, and from which they must inevitably emerge covered with smuts and coal-dust. Even so, the price for such discomfort was high. But the trains went far faster than horses and that, Melinda decided, was the one thing that mattered at this particular moment.

Her difficulty was how to get to Leminster. She almost regretted now having rejected her first idea, which had been to ride there on Flash. But she knew that had she gone to the stables the grooms would have been far too frightened of her uncle not to report her absence if she did not return within a few hours. They would also have thought it strange if she rode alone, for her uncle was most insistent that a groom always should accompany her.

But now she began to wonder if she would have the strength even to reach the little hamlet of Oakle, let alone arrive in Leminster in a fit state to board a train. She felt so faint that she knew she must rest for a moment. She sat down on the side of the road on a little hummock of grass, stretching out her legs and noting, with dismay, that her shoes were thick with dust. The hem of her skirts had fared no better, and she thought that should she have to walk much further she would look like a tramp by the time she reached London.

She wiped her face with the tiny square of white lawn that she had stitched herself and on which she had embroidered her initial, although nothing so elegant fitted her present needs. Both her aunt and Charlotte had insisted that she embroider dozens of handkerchiefs for their use, incorporating their initials in a most elaborate design. She had liked embroidering handkerchiefs, but there were so many other things to do as well and when her work was not finished they always tried to prevent her from riding Flash or even from going to see him.

Perhaps because she was thinking of her horse she did not at first hear the approaching clop-clop of horse's hooves, but when she did she started to her feet in a sudden panic. A quick glance showed her that she need not have been afraid of the village cart coming down the road—in fact at a second glance she recognised it. It belonged to Farmer Jenkins, the tenant on one of her uncle's farms. As it drew nearer she saw it was not the farmer himself who held the reins but his son, Jim, a red-headed lad with a cheeky smile whom she had frequently encountered when out riding.

Instinctively Melinda put up her hand and he drew the big farm horse to a standstill beside her.

' 'Mornin', Miss Melinda!' he said in his broad accent. 'Ye be up early.'

'Good morning, Jim! Where are you going?' Melinda asked a little breathlessly.

'It be Tuesday, miss, and Oi be goin' to th' market in Leminster.'

Melinda gave a sigh of relief.

'Please, Jim, take me with you! What a fool I was not to think of that before!'

'Think o' wot, miss? Ye be welcome t' travel with Oi, but 'tis no place for a lady.'

Melinda wasted no time in arguing with him. She handed up her luggage with a sense of relief and putting her foot on the wheel climbed up on to the high box beside Jim. The bare board seat was certainly not comfortable, but anything was better than walking.

'Thank you, Jim,' she said with so much gratitude in her tone that he looked at her in surprise.

' 'Tis naught to do with Oi, miss, but wot'll Squire say if 'e ears ye've been adrivin' loike this?'

'I hope he will never know,' Melinda replied. 'Oh, Jim, I cannot explain, but let us hurry to Leminster. I never thought that anyone would be on the roads as early as this.'

'Oi've t' be there when market opens,' Jim explained. 'Us gets the best prices if Oi be there early.'

Melinda looked back and saw that the cart was filled with hens in wooden crates, baskets of eggs and big pats of home-made butter covered with linen cloths.

'What is the time?' she asked. 'And will many people be awake in Oakle?'

'Naw, not many,' Jim answered. 'They be lazybones in Oakle.'

'I do not want to be seen, Jim,' Melinda said, 'and I should not like to get you into trouble for giving me a lift.'

'Ye mean Squire don't know that ye be agoin' to Leminster?' Jim enquired.

Melinda hesitated for a moment, then she told him the truth.

'No, Jim, he does not know.'

'Ye think Squire'll be angry when 'e foinds out?' Jim persisted.

'I am afraid so,' Melinda answered. 'But I do not want him to be angry with you.'

'Oi shan't tell 'e,' Jim said stoutly. 'Oi reckon there

b'aint many folk round 'ere which wants t' tell Squire things which makes 'e angry.'

'Yes, there is that about it,' Melinda agreed. 'Perhaps no one will see me with you, and if they do they will not say what they have seen.'

It was somehow a forlorn hope but she clung to it. Besides, she told herself, if anyone did see a woman sitting beside Jim Jenkins on the farm cart, they were not likely to suspect it was one of the young ladies from The Hall.

She kept her head lowered as they passed through Oakle and hoped that the sides of her bonnet would conceal her face. When they were through to the other side of the village she gave a sigh of relief.

' 'Tis all right!' Jim said. 'Oi told ye they be lazybones in Oakle.'

It was not quite five o'clock when they reached Leminster. Jim was willing to take her to the station, but Melinda refused, knowing it was not far from the market-place and fancying she would be less noticeable if she walked the last part of the journey alone.

'Thank you, Jim!' she said, holding out her hand. 'I am very, very grateful for your help. I only hope no one connects you with my disappearance.'

'They be unloikely t' do that, miss,' Jim replied. 'Good luck!' He shook her hand heartily, gave her a somewhat cheeky grin and went to fetch the nose-bag for his horse from the back of the cart.

Melinda moved away slowly, feeling that she was leaving her last friend behind. It was typical of the countryman's decency, she thought, that Jim had not questioned her in any way and had just accepted the situation. They had driven mostly in silence, which had given her time to fortify herself for what lay ahead.

She reached the station and discovered that the night express coming from the north would stop at Leminster at six o'clock. She went to the ticket-office and asked the price of the fare to London. She was appalled at the difference between the price of travelling in the open coaches and in the comfortable carriages. For a moment she hesitated and then decided that it would be a false economy to arrive in London blackened and dirty, her only decent dress soiled perhaps beyond repair. If she was to find herself employment she must look respectable and so, reluctantly, she passed over four of her precious golden sovereigns to receive only a few shillings change with her hand-written ticket.

Having nearly an hour to spare she went first to the ladies' waiting-room to clean herself up. Then, feeling hungry, she went in search of food. She had noticed near the station a baker's shop from which had come the delicious smell of fresh-baked bread.

She bought herself two buns, large, newly baked and covered with sugared currants, at one penny each; and taking them into the ladies' waiting-room devoured them hungrily. Not a very sustaining meal, Melinda thought to herself, and wondered where her next one would be eaten.

She was conscious all the time of her own nervousness: perhaps the train would not arrive, having broken down en route, perhaps someone who knew her uncle would recognise her and prevent her from travelling. She was well aware that the ticket clerk had looked at her in surprise when she had asked for only one ticket. Her cultured voice and her clothes, shabby though they were, proclaimed her to be a lady, and ladies did not travel by train alone.

Every time the door of the waiting-room opened Melinda looked at the newcomer apprehensively, but no one appeared more formidable than two hefty, young country girls who, she gathered from their conversation, were journeying to the next station down the line, more as a lark than because there was any particular reason for them to travel.

However, when finally, with much noisy blowing of whistles, hissing steam and puffing and belching smoke, the train came slowly into the station, a large number of people appeared apparently from nowhere. There were porters, passengers and station officials, and quite a number of men, women and children who, even at that early hour of the morning, had come just to stare at the phenomenon of the new age—the railway train.

As the train came to a stop everyone seemed galvanised with a kind of hysterical agitation. Porters shouted; passengers jostled against each other although there was no hurry. Almost against her will Melinda found herself being pushed forward and helped into a carriage. Five other people clambered in and the door was slammed to.

Melinda found herself sitting beside a window at the far end of the carriage. Opposite her was an elderly gentleman enveloped in a thick, tweed cape, apparently fearful of the cold even though it was summer. His wife was swathed in veils and wore a cape plenteously trimmed with jet beads and a bonnet which jingled with them.

The rest of the passengers were men. Melinda judged them to be business types, although she had little knowledge of such people. Her suspicions were confirmed, however, when they began to talk between themselves of deals and customers. One even produced samples of woollen materials which, as he said proudly, would make shopkeepers' eyes pop out of their heads when he got to London.

Outside on the platform the commotion seemed to increase until, with great clouds of smoke blowing past the window, the shrilling of whistles, voices shouting, hands waving, the train slowly started on its way. Melinda held her breath. She had done it! She had got away! The train, which could go faster than any of her uncle's horses, was taking her towards London. She had escaped and Colonel Gillingham was left behind!

For a moment she wanted to cry from sheer relief. But pride made her force the tears from her eyes although, as she looked out of the window, everything went misty for quite a long time. It was a strange sensation. The swaying of the coach, the noise of the wheels on the iron track, the clouds of smoke drifting past the window were all sensations she had never known before; it was all as unusual, she felt, as her life would be from now on.

Shutting her eyes she tried to concentrate on what she must do when she reached London. She reckoned they should arrive there about one o'clock. That would give her the afternoon in which to find somewhere respectable to stay and to enquire the way to the agency called Mrs. Brewer's Bureau where she had thought she might start her search for a post.

She would not have known the name had not she written various letters for her aunt to Mrs. Brewer when Lady Stanyon had required a new housekeeper. Mrs. Brewer's writing-paper had informed those who read it that her Bureau catered for every type of household staff required by the nobility and gentry and also could, on request, provide governesses and companions at reasonable salaries.

Melinda regretted that in her haste to leave The Hall she had not had time to look for Mrs. Brewer's address in London, but she was sure that someone would be able to tell her where it was. She was well aware that, even if she got to the Bureau, she would find it difficult to get a position without references. She thought that the best thing would be to say, frankly, that she was a relation of Lady Stanyon and hope that Mrs. Brewer would not insist on writing to her aunt for further particulars.

She began to see there were many more difficulties ahead than she had at first anticipated. She had run away blindly because she had been frightened, but somehow she believed, perhaps over-optimistically, that she would be able to find employment and not be forced by the sheer threat of starvation to return to her uncle's house.

'I have got to be practical; I have got to be sensible,' Melinda thought to herself. 'I have got to realise that it is not going to be easy.'

She began to regret now that she had not taken an outside seat and left herself more money. The six guineas she still had left seemed an enormous fortune to someone who had never previously had more than a few shillings in her purse; but she knew it would not last for ever.

'I must be careful of pickpockets,' she thought . . . 'and sneak-thieves!'

There seemed to be so many things she must remember and for a moment she felt something like terror sweep over her. Then she told herself that everything would be all right; that God would protect her. She tried to pray and must have dozed off for a few minutes; for when she opened her eyes she saw that the other passengers were all getting out their luncheon.

The gentleman in the cape and his wife had a huge picnic-basket, and the business-gentlemen—if that was what they were—had packets of sandwiches. Melinda, conscious of being very hungry, wished now that she had bought more of the penny buns from the baker's shop. It seemed a very long time since she had last eaten.

The old gentleman opposite her gnawed a wing of chicken. Afterwards he and his wife ate strawberries, having covered them with sugar from a silver-topped shaker and added cream from a small, silver jug. Melinda watched them almost with fascination. She remembered that she had eaten no supper the night before and had not felt hungry at luncheon. Her back was hurting her and she wondered if it hurt worse because she was hungry.

She shut her eyes for a moment so as not to watch the people opposite eating and eating.

'I am not really hungry,' the lady with the veil said testily. 'All this swaying of the carriage makes me feel sick.'

'Would you like a little brandy, my dear?' her husband asked.

'No, not brandy!' The lady spoke as if it was arsenic. 'But perhaps a glass of champagne.'

'Yes, yes, of course,' the old gentleman said. He produced a half-bottle of champagne from the picnic-basket which he had put down on the floor at Melinda's feet. She could smell the chicken and the strawberries and felt her hunger gnawing at her like a pain.

The old gentleman poured out the champagne and then said to his wife in what, to Melinda, was a quite audible whisper:

'As we have so much left over, my dear, do you think we should offer something to the little lady opposite? She apparently has no food with her.'

'No, no, of course not!' his wife replied. 'A woman travelling alone! One cannot imagine who she could be! Most certainly do not speak to her!'

Melinda shut her eyes. So this was what she was going to encounter in the future. A woman alone was open to suspicion, and must therefore be ignored or avoided. She was thankful when the picnic-basket was put away under the seat.

'We shall be in in another hour,' she heard one of the businessmen say, and she determined that before she did anything else she would get herself something to eat.

The train was slowing down, and she looked eagerly out of the window. Suddenly it came to an abrupt halt.

'Why are we stopping here?' one of the men asked.

His friend opened the window and put out his head.

'I cannot see anything,' he said. Then in another tone of voice: 'Oh, guard! I say, guard! What's happened?'

'I don't know, sir,' the answer was quite clear. 'I fancy there must be something on the line.'

There was indeed something on the line and it took five hours to clear it. The passengers climbed down with some difficulty from the high coaches and walked along to look at the landslide which had brought a great pile of stones and sand on to the tracks. Men were being fetched to clear it, they were told. They should be on their way in an hour . . . in two hours . . . in three hours!

Finally, in just under five hours from the hour at which they had stopped, the train got under way again. There had been nothing to do but to wander in the fields and the woods on either side of the track. Melinda had got hungrier and hungrier. Finally she spoke to the guard.

'I wonder if there is anywhere I could get something to eat?' she said. 'Unfortunately, I came away in a hurry and did not bring anything with me.'

'All sensible passengers bring some food with them,' he said. 'You never know when this sort of thing will happen, miss.'

'I realise that,' Melinda said with a smile, 'but it is too late to be wise and I am very hungry.'

He looked at her and his expression of puffing importance seemed to soften.

'I'll see what I can do for you,' he said. 'I've got a daughter of your age myself.'

He disappeared up the train and came back with a

big slab of home-made pork pie and a slice of bread on which reposed a hunk of cheese.

'There's a farmer's wife in one of the carriages,' he explained. 'Says she was taking the pork pie to one of her sisters as a present, but as it is they've about eaten the whole of it.'

'How very kind of her,' Melinda said. 'Could I pay her for it?'

'I think she would be offended if you offered,' the guard said. 'I told her there was a young lady in distress and she was only too willing to help.'

'Will you thank her very, very much?' Melinda asked.

It was so different, she thought, from the elderly couple in her carriage, and never in her life did she enjoy a meal more.

The train got under way again but it moved very slowly. The sun sank and the day was drawing to a close when finally they drew in to Euston Station.

'Well, thank goodness we have arrived at last!' the lady in the veil said. 'A more unpleasant journey I never experienced. Next time I go by carriage.'

'I knew you would prefer it, my dear,' her husband said mildly. 'Rail travel is not for ladies.'

'It certainly is not,' his wife said. 'Do not worry about the picnic-basket. We will tell the footman to collect it as soon as we find the carriage.'

'Oh, the porter will see to it,' her husband said. 'Do not agitate yourself, Gertrude. You know you always get yourself agitated on railway stations.'

'It is the very last time I ever travel by train,' the lady said firmly.

'You said that last time,' her husband reminded

her. 'But I agree with you. We will go back to the old-fashioned coach or, better still, travel with our own carriage by easy stages.'

'If you ask me, railway trains will soon cease to exist,' his wife said sweepingly. 'The public will just refuse to put up with this discomfort.'

Melinda hardly heeded their conversation. She was intent on looking out of the window. There seemed to be crowds and crowds of people on the station. For the first time she began to feel really afraid. It was getting late. It would be no use going to Mrs. Brewer's Bureau at this hour.

She wondered if she should ask the couple opposite if they knew of a decent lodging-house. She tried to summon up her courage and, just as the door was opened and the businessmen started to get out of the carriage, she said in a little, frightened voice:

'I . . . I wonder . . . if you could . . . t . . . tell me . . .'

The lady in the veils gave her a withering look.

'No!' she said hostilely. 'We can tell you nothing.' She swept out of the carriage followed by her husband.

Melinda was the last to alight. There was a pervading smell of smoke, the noise of the engine, the shouts of the porters. It all seemed very deafening.

'Porter? Porter? Porter, miss?'

'N . . . no, thank you,' Melinda said, clutching her bag and following the wake of the other passengers.

They all seemed to be going very fast. She moved more slowly up the platform.

'Ticket, miss?'

She had to put down her bag and open her purse for the ticket. She handed it over, finding she was almost the last person off the platform. Outside people were hurrying towards a long line of hackney carriages. Melinda stood looking about her. Surely there would be someone she could ask for information—perhaps a clergyman.

It was then that a quiet, very ladylike voice beside her said:

'You are looking a little lost. Can I help you?'

She turned round. A lady, tastefully but quietly dressed, was looking at her with a kindly face. She was a woman of about fifty.

'I . . . I am afraid I am . . . new to London,' Melinda said almost apologetically. 'I was just . . . wondering if I could find . . . someone who would advise me . . . where I could find lodgings for the night.'

'Have you no friends or relations?' the woman asked in a soft, sympathetic voice which to Melinda was somehow comforting.

'I am afraid not,' she said. 'I . . . I have come to London to . . . to find employment. The train was delayed and I cannot go to the employment bureau this evening.'

'No, of course you cannot,' the older woman said. 'And so you want a lodging?'

Melinda nodded.

'Just for a night or perhaps two,' she explained, 'until I can find something to do.'

There was a pause and then, as the lady did not speak, Melinda asked desperately:

'I suppose . . . you do not know of . . . anywhere?'

'I was just thinking that I must help you,' the lady replied. 'It must be very worrying for you, arriving like this and not knowing where to go. I have my brougham outside. If you will come with me I will take you somewhere where you can stay tonight.'

'It is very kind of you,' Melinda said thankfully. 'But will it not be a trouble? I mean . . . You must be meeting someone.'

'I will tell you about that as we drive along,' the lady said. 'Have you any luggage?'

'Only this,' Melinda said.

'Then come along, my dear. We have only a little way to walk.'

The brougham was very smart with a cockaded coachman and a horse which Melinda saw at a glance was well bred and well groomed. The lady gestured to Melinda to get into the carriage and climbed in beside her.

'Are you quite sure you are not meeting anyone?' Melinda asked.

The lady gave a little sigh.

'I come here very often,' she said. 'You see, my daughter, who is about your age, was coming to London from the north. I came to the station to meet her but she never arrived—in fact, she was never heard of again.'

'But how terrible!' Melinda exclaimed.

'I never knew what happened to her,' the lady continued in a sad voice. 'That is why I go to the station, hoping, always hoping, that one day she will come back and I shall find her there.'

'I am so sorry,' Melinda said. All her sympathies were with the bereaved mother, but she thought secretly to herself that the lady was, perhaps, a little deranged by her sorrow.

'Sometimes I am able to help young girls like yourself,' the lady went on. 'And in helping them I feel a little happier. Do you understand?'

'Yes, of course I do,' Melinda replied. 'And thank you very much. I wish, though, that I had been your daughter.'

'That is a very sweet thing to say,' the lady said. 'But, now, enough about my troubles. Tell me about yourself. Do your parents live in the country?'

'I have no parents,' Melinda answered. 'My father and mother were killed in a carriage accident.'

'Is that why you have come to London?' the lady asked.

For a moment Melinda hesitated, but she thought it would be dangerous, even to her new-found friend, to mention her uncle.

'Yes, that is why,' she said. 'I have no money so I must work. Perhaps you could tell me the address of Mrs. Brewer's Bureau.'

'We can think about that tomorrow,' the lady answered. 'How old are you?'

'I am eighteen,' Melinda told her, 'and I am sure I could teach children. Besides ordinary subjects, I can paint, play the pianoforte and, if they were country children, I could teach them to ride.'

'Then I am sure we can find you something,' the lady said. 'Perhaps, now, we should tell each other our names.'

'Yes, of course,' Melinda smiled. 'I am Melinda Stanyon!'

'What a pretty name!' the lady exclaimed. 'And I am Mrs. Ella Harcourt. Is it not lucky that we met?'

'Yes, very lucky,' Melinda agreed.

They were driving all the time through brilliantly

lit streets. Melinda longed to look out of the window and stare, but she thought that would be rude and, therefore, only managed a few sidelong glances.

Mrs. Harcourt seemed to be asking a lot of questions. Melinda suddenly felt very tired. It had been a long day and she had not slept at all the night before. She found herself answering the questions almost automatically. The brougham came to a standstill.

'We have arrived,' Mrs. Harcourt said. 'Now, I can see you are tired. I am going to take you straight upstairs to bed and tomorrow we can talk about all sorts of things.'

'Yes, of course,' Melinda said. 'And thank you for being so kind. I am sorry if I appear stupid. It is just that I have begun to feel very sleepy.'

'Poor child!' Mrs. Harcourt said gently. 'Now, come along.'

She stepped out on to the pavement. Melinda followed her. They appeared to be in a quiet street lined by expensive houses with porticoed doors. They went up the steps and, just as they reached the door, it opened. A footman in uniform was showing out a gentleman. He wore a top-hat on the side of his head and evening clothes with a very tall, white collar. There was a yellow carnation in his buttonhole. He let the monocle in his right eye drop as he lifted Mrs. Harcourt's hand to his lips.

'I thought I had missed you, dear lady,' he said suavely.

'I have been out, as your lordship sees,' Mrs. Harcourt replied.

'As I see!' the gentleman repeated slowly and with meaning.

He looked at Melinda. Still sleepily she looked up into his eyes. She thought she had never seen a man who looked more like a satyr, a man with a more debauched face. It might have been quite incorrect but that was the impression he gave her.

'Introduce me!'

The words appeared almost a command but Mrs. Harcourt said quickly:

'The young lady I have just met at the railway station, my lord, is very tired. This is her first visit to London and all she wants is to sleep. I hope your lordship will excuse us.'

'Introduce me!'

The words were slow, deliberate and authoritative, and it seemed to Melinda that Mrs. Harcourt was a little flustered as she said:

'Melinda, this is Lord Wrotham, an old . . . friend of mine. Miss Melinda Stanyon.'

Lord Wrotham took both Melinda's hands in his.

'Your first visit to London, my dear! Then we must make it a very enjoyable one. I think that you and I must see a great deal of each other.'

He held her hands tightly, staring down into her face. By the light shining from the hall Melinda could see the dark lines under his eyes, the thickness of his lips. She tried to pull her hands away from his.

'Thank you,' she murmured, 'but . . .'

'As I have already said, Melinda is tired, my lord,' Mrs. Harcourt said, and there was a sharpness in her voice.

'I heard you, dear lady, I heard you!' Lord Wrotham replied. 'A very sweet face. Very young, unspoilt—untouched!'

Melinda felt his eyes flicker over her and with an effort she tried to move away.

'Tomorrow, my dear Melinda!' Lord Wrotham said, and he kissed her hands. She had taken off her gloves in the carriage and she felt his lips, warm and somehow possessive, on her skin. It made her feel quite inexplicably afraid. She dragged her hands away, and, passing Mrs. Harcourt, pushed her way into the hall.

'You have no right, my lord,' she heard Mrs. Harcourt say angrily.

Then Melinda thought she heard Lord Wrotham reply: 'I will call tomorrow. Tell Kate she's mine!' But, of course, she told herself, she must have been mistaken.

3

A hansom-cab drew up at a brilliantly lit building in Prince's Street. An elegant young gentleman with a gardenia in the buttonhole of his tail coat stepped out, threw the driver half-a-guinea, which the recipient caught deftly, and walked up to the entrance which was flanked by two ostentatiously liveried commissionaires. They were strong, muscular men with a somewhat pugnacious air about them, which told an observer, all too clearly, that their duties did not only entail opening carriage doors or calling hackney carriages for the departing guests.

Captain Gervase Vestey nodded to the men, who saluted, before one of them hurried to knock on the closed door. A small panel slid aside and two eyes scrutinised Captain Vestey. The eye-hole was closed and the door was opened immediately.

'Good evening, Captain! It is very nice to see you,' a suave official enthused.

The Captain did not trouble to answer him. He walked down a long, tunnel-like passage and up a short flight of carpeted stairs into a large and brilliantly lit Salon. There was a chatter of voices and occasionally a shrill, uninhibited laugh which gave a kind of spontaneous gaiety to the place.

At the end of the room at which the Captain had entered there was an American bar dispensing mixed drinks under such names as 'Gum Ticklers', 'Eye Openers' and 'Corpse Revivers'. But the Captain had eyes only for the dais at the other end of the room on which there was a velvet-canopied throne. Seated on it, surrounded by a number of attractive young women, was the acknowledged queen of London night life—Kate Hamilton.

She was an enormous, hideous woman, and while the gas-lit lustres which surrounded the Salon sparkled on her jewels, the mirrors multiplied and re-multiplied her tremendous bulk. Everyone in London knew Kate: she was one of the sights for visitors from overseas.

As Captain Gervase Vestey moved down the room he nodded to a number of titled friends including the

Marquis of Hartington, waved his hand to several Members of Parliament and saw that the usual collection of officers from both services were enjoying themselves with the exceedingly attractive young women for which Kate Hamilton's Salon was noted.

As Captain Vestey reached the dais Kate, who had been talking in a booming voice to a rather effete young aristocrat who was obviously paying for her champagne, turned to the Captain with genuine pleasure.

'I was just saying to his Lordship here,' she remarked, 'that I had not seen you or your friend, the Marquis, for over a week. Where have you been hiding yourselves? The place has seemed quite dull without you.'

'I have missed you, too, Kate,' the Captain smiled. 'You are in excellent looks, one can see that. Are you going to give us a treat tonight by letting us see you in one of your poses?'

This was a very old joke which invariably convulsed Kate with laughter so that she shook like a blancmange. She had originally started her meteoric career by standing naked in the *poses plastiques* which had been one of the most popular sights in London some twenty years earlier.

'Get along with you,' she said almost coyly. 'You know I'm too old for that sort of thing. But I have got two girls just arrived from Paris who'll be the *dernier cri* by next week. I'll give you and your friend a private showing if you're interested.'

'Of course we're interested,' Captain Vestey exclaimed, 'but just now I want to talk to you, Kate, in private. It is very urgent.'

Kate Hamilton looked up at him. She seemed about to refuse, then putting down her champagne glass she turned to one of her young ladies who was standing near her almost in the attitude of a lady-in-waiting.

'Here, Rosie, you look after things until I get back,' she said. 'Stand no nonsense, and if there's any trouble come and fetch me.'

'Everything will be all right, ma'am,' Rosie promised, seating herself with an air of relish on the velvet throne that Kate had just vacated.

Waddling across the polished floor to the door which led to her private apartments took some time. Everybody wanted a word with Kate, from Lord Mohun, who was a well-known bully and a duellist, to the good-tempered but incredibly stupid Mr. Bobby Shafto, whose only claim to fame was that he had assisted the Marquis of Hastings to let loose two hundred rats one night on the dance floor of Mott's.

At last Kate reached the door which separated the Salon from the passages leading up to the private supper rooms and to her own sitting-room. Only the most privileged amongst Kate's acquaintances, distinguished visitors from overseas or some young man to whom he had taken a personal fancy, were invited into the luxurious boudoir decorated with velvet hangings and furnished with three huge, satin sofas—one sky blue, one coal black, one red.

'Sit down, Captain,' Kate invited. 'Make yourself at home. What'll you have to drink?'

'I will have a drink later, thank you,' Captain Vestey replied. 'I want your help, Kate, but I am frightened that someone will burst in and interrupt us.'

'Not much fear of that!' Kate assured him. 'I only admit the best class people into my Salon. Not like those other dirty places that are springing up all over the place and trying to rival me. As I says to anyone who mentions 'em to me, they'll have their work cut out.'

'You need not worry, they won't succeed,' Captain Vestey said. 'There is only one Kate and only one place any of us really enjoy visiting, except for a laugh or a brawl.'

'That's right,' Kate said, almost with relief. 'And I don't allow no brawling in my place, you know that.'

She seated herself on the black sofa which groaned under her weight.

'Now, what's troubling you?' she asked.

'It is not my problem,' Captain Vestey said. 'It is Chard who is in trouble and I really believe that you are the only person who can help him.'

'Money or a woman?' Kate asked sharply.

'Neither,' Captain Vestey replied. 'It is his stepmother.'

'The Dowager?' Kate asked, raising her eyebrows. 'I heard she was ill.'

'You know everything, don't you?' Captain Vestey said. 'Yes, Kate, she is ill; in fact she is dying!'

'Poor lady,' Kate said almost sympathetically. 'But there was never much love lost between her and her stepson, from all I have heard.'

'You are right there,' Captain Vestey agreed, 'and with reason. You see, the old man—the last Marquis—left all his money to his wife for her life-time. He was not fond of his son; in fact, if the truth was known, I think he disliked the idea of anyone ever succeeding him. Anyway, when he died, my friend, Drogo, got the title but nothing else.'

'Well, now her Ladyship's on the way out the money should come to him,' Kate said. 'She had no children, did she?'

'No, but the point is that she can leave the bulk of the money where she wishes,' Captain Vestey said.

'I see, and the old feud has not been buried?'

'Not exactly,' Captain Vestey said. 'And this, Kate, is where we need your help. The Dowager Marchioness has said that she will leave her stepson every penny of his father's inheritance on condition that he is married.'

Kate chuckled.

'Tying him up, is she? Well, he's one that will bite at the bridle. Marriage should tame him if nothing else will.'

'That is the whole point,' Captain Vestey said. 'The Marquis has said that he will be damned if he'll be forced into marriage.'

Kate was silent for a moment and then with a shrewd look on her face she said:

'Still hankering after Lady Alice St. Helier, is he?'

Captain Vestey looked startled for a moment; then he laughed.

'Damn you, Kate! There's not a secret in the length and breadth of England that you have not ferreted out some time or another.'

'My dear boy,' Kate replied, 'men who drink, talk!

And the men who come to my Salon drink or they don't come. It's as simple as that!'

'I see,' Captain Vestey said with a smile that he could not suppress. 'Oh, well, as you know so much, you might as well know the whole of it. The Marquis has sworn that as he cannot have Lady Alice St. Helier, he will marry no one else. But here is the Marchioness, on the point of death, according to her doctors, and refusing to sign the will unless her stepson produces for her inspection a wife. Not a fiancée, mind you! That would be easy enough to wriggle out of after the funeral. No, a wife! And she even suggests, once the girl has been found, that they should be married in her bedroom.'

'Taking no chances, is she?' Kate remarked. 'She must have the idea that her stepson is a slippery customer who can extricate himself from most uncomfortable situations.'

'He has certainly done that in the past,' Captain Vestey agreed. 'But you know that, for all his wildness, my friend is decent at heart. It would be easy enough for him, with his looks and his title, to get any milk-faced little chit being trailed around Mayfair by an ambitious Mamma to be his wife. But he will not sink to that sort of thing. In fact, at one moment he wanted to tell the Dowager to take the money to hell with her.'

'That would have been a very stupid thing to do, I should have thought,' Kate remarked. 'Money's money, wherever it comes from!'

'That is more or less what I said to him,' Captain Vestey told her. 'But I think that is what he would have done if it had not been for Chard.'

'His house?' Kate queried.

'His house and the great estates in Hertfordshire,' Captain Vestey said. 'He loves that house. It is the one stable thing in his life. He had a miserable childhood: his mother died, his father bullied him and his stepmother disliked him. But, despite that, Chard was father, mother and family to him. He could not see that thrown down the drain.'

'Then what can he do?' Kate asked. 'And what can I do, if it comes to that?'

'That is the point,' Captain Vestey said, leaning forward. 'We have an idea and we can only carry it out with your help.'

'What is it?' Kate asked.

'The Marquis shall be married in the Dowager's bedroom as she has demanded,' Captain Vestey said. 'But the parson will not be a real one and you will provide the bride.'

For a moment Kate's large mouth opened wide, accentuating the double chins resting on the great, vulgar, diamond necklace which encircled her fat neck. Then she threw back her head and laughed.

'Bust me! If that man hasn't always an ace up his sleeve!' she exclaimed. 'And I swear that the Dowager has brought it on herself! But won't she be suspicious?'

'Why should she be?' Captain Vestey said. 'We have exactly the right man in mind to be the parson. He was in the Regiment with us and used to keep us in fits in Mess with his impersonations. As it happens, his father was a vicar of some obscure hamlet in Northumberland, so he knows the ropes or, rather, the marriage service! What is much more difficult is the bride!'

'Yes, she is a very important part of the ceremony,' Kate said.

'She has to be a girl who will look the part; that was something the Marquis is insistent upon,' Captain Vestey said. 'He says the Dowager will smell a rat for a certainty if the girl looks common or in any way tarty. She has got to look a lady, Kate, and be dressed like one, too.'

'You're asking rather a lot, you know,' Kate said.

'If you fail us then I do not know where to turn,' Captain Vestey said. 'After all, Kate, you have the best-looking females in London in your Salon. One of them must be able to impersonate a Society miss cleverly enough for it not to be detected.'

'Now, look here, Captain,' she said. 'You and your friend have always been straight with me and I'll be straight with you. This isn't going to be easy. To begin with, Rosie, Gertie, Gwen and that lot out there —you know them all—look attractive and seductive under the gaslight, but they don't look pure virgins by day; and why should they? Certainly, after a few glasses of champagne, their voices seem melodious, but you listen to them at breakfast when you're stone sober and they jar like a corn-crake.'

'But, Kate, one of them must be able to play the part,' Captain Vestey said almost despairingly. 'You can dress her, make her look right, and she can keep her mouth closed, can't she? She does not have to enter into conversation with a dying woman.'

'But, what about afterwards?' Kate enquired. 'I choose my girls for their looks not their brains, but there's not one of them so stupid as not to realise when they are on to a good thing. A tale like this put about the town wouldn't do the young Marquis any good and he might have to pay through the nose to keep his bogus bride silent!'

'You mean blackmail?' Captain Vestey asked.

'It's a nasty word,' Kate said, 'and one that is never uttered in my presence in my Salon. But I know that such things happen in other places.'

'Then what are we to do?' Captain Vestey said. 'It sounded such a good idea and the Marquis felt you were the only person who could make it a success. He suggested, although, of course, you might not agree, that the fee should be five hundred guineas to the bride and five hundred to you, Kate. And, of course, he would pay for all the clothes and any other expenses on top of it.'

Kate said nothing although her eyes sparkled a little.

'Try and think of someone who could do it,' Captain Vestey pleaded.

'I am thinking,' Kate said.

She crossed the room and tugged at the velvet embroidered bell-pull, with its brass handle, which hung beside the mantelpiece. A waiter appeared almost immediately.

'Fetch me Mrs. Harcourt,' Kate commanded. 'And bring me a bottle of champagne. I need a drink.'

'Do you think Mrs. Harcourt might be able to help us?' Captain Vestey asked.

Everyone in Kate's knew Ella Harcourt. She was in charge of another part of the establishment which Kate ran, with great success, in a quiet street backing on to her Salon and which was connected with the Prince's Street entrance by a long, underground tunnel. Only the most important and distinguished of Kate's clients were entitled to enter 'The House', as it was called, from the Salon. To all intents and purposes, to the police records and to the casual visitor to the Salon, the two places were entirely separate.

While they waited for Mrs. Harcourt, Kate and Captain Vestey said little to each other. He knew that Kate was thinking and he was well aware that it would be foolish to disturb the train of her thoughts. The Captain began to feel, despondently, that perhaps the scheme was not as easy as it had seemed when he and Drogo had planned it out in the drawing-room in Grosvenor Square. Then, as they talked in hushed voices, more from respect for the Dowager dying upstairs than because anyone could overhear them, it had seemed the obvious solution to the Marquis's predicament. Now, all sorts of difficulties seemed to stand in the way of the Dowager signing that all-important document.

Finally Kate's silence got on Captain Vestey's nerves.

'You have got to do something, Kate,' he said almost roughly. 'Otherwise the Dowager threatens to leave the whole lot to some cats' home she's interested in.'

'How much is involved?' Kate asked.

'Something like a couple of million,' Captain Vestey replied.

'To cats!' Kate exclaimed. 'Why not to children?

There are enough of them walking about the streets half-starved.'

'Why not to its rightful heir?' Captain Vestey asked. 'I believe that when the Marquis comes into Chard he will be a different person.'

'It would be a pity if he settled down and became respectable,' Kate said with a smile. 'London would be a far duller place. Why, the wild Lord Chard is one of the attractions of the West End. Half the strangers who come here from the country say to me, "Is Lord Chard here? I want to see what he's like." '

'We've had a lot of fun together,' Captain Vestey said. 'But there won't be much in the future if the Marquis is left without a bean.'

'It's wrong of her Ladyship, I grant you that,' Kate said. 'Well, here's Ella! We'll see what she can suggest.'

She smiled at Mrs. Harcourt who came into the room looking incredibly sedate and ladylike. Kate opened her mouth to speak then changed her mind.

'Here, young man,' she said to Captain Vestey. 'I want to talk to Ella alone. You wait for us in the room opposite. It's empty.'

'Very well,' Captain Vestey said, rising to his feet. 'Good evening, Mrs. Harcourt! Everything all right in the House?'

'One of the girls was asking after you only this morning,' Mrs. Harcourt replied. 'Let me see, which one was it? Oh, Lily! The one with the dark hair you rather fancied a month or so ago.'

'Give her my love,' Captain Vestey said, 'and tell her I will pop in as soon as the little business I have on hand is concluded. Kate will tell you all about it.'

He smiled at both the women and went into the other room.

'Such a nice young man,' Mrs. Harcourt said. 'Don't tell me he's in trouble. Or is it that naughty friend of his—the Marquis? I must say, they are both so handsome they make my heart throb even at my age.'

'A pity you're not twenty years younger,' Kate said almost bluntly, 'or you'd have done nicely for the part.'

'What part?' Mrs. Harcourt asked.

Kate told her the story that Captain Vestey had unfolded to her, quickly and concisely.

'Now, who have you got?' she said at the end. 'I thought of Lily, as it happens, but I never trusted that girl very far. She'll talk and that would be a mistake.'

'There's Grace,' Mrs. Harcourt said tentatively.

'I'm not putting good money that young woman's way,' Kate said positively. 'She's cheated me more than once, I've evidence of that, and next time she does it she's out. She's not fit to be mixed up with young Chard and his friend.'

'Then, really, there's no one,' Mrs. Harcourt said. Then she paused. 'Wait! I have got an idea! Come with me. I want you to see someone I brought in to-night.'

'I don't want to go all that way,' Kate protested.

'I know it is a bother for you, but you must come,' Mrs. Harcourt said insistently.

Grumbling, Kate obeyed her and walked down the long, narrow passage, passing through several closed doors and coming, at last, into the little hall of the house that Melinda had entered several hours earlier.

Mrs. Harcourt led the way up the stairs. The house was very quiet. All the girls were in the Salon. On the top landing Mrs. Harcourt opened a door. There was one candle alight by the bedside, otherwise the room was in darkness.

'Will she wake?' Kate asked apprehensively in a whisper.

Mrs. Harcourt shook her head.

'We gave her the usual in her milk,' she said. 'She'll sleep till morning. Besides, she was dead tired after her journey.'

The two women stood at the end of the bed. Melinda's fair hair was spread out over the white pillow. She looked very small, fragile and exceedingly lovely. Her dark eyelashes swept her cheeks and her arm, lying on top of the sheets, was white and blue-veined. There was something beautiful and, at the same time, almost spiritual about the sleeping girl.

For a moment in Kate's coarse, ugly gaze there was a look of envy. 'Once,' she told herself, 'I looked young and innocent. Once, many, many years ago.' And then, almost as if she was ashamed of her own sentiment, she said harshly:

'Who is she?'

'Her name is Stanyon,' Mrs. Harcourt replied. 'Melinda Stanyon. She is from the North of England. Her parents are dead. She has come to London in search of employment. She asked me if I would tell her tomorrow how she could get to Mrs. Brewer's Bureau. She wants a position as a governess.'

'How does she speak?' Kate asked.

'Like a lady,' Mrs. Harcourt answered. 'She must

have good blood in her although she is poorly dressed. I should think that she is the by-blow of some nobleman.'

'Sure to be,' Kate said. 'Will she play the game?'

'I should imagine she needs the money,' Mrs. Harcourt said. 'Five hundred guineas to a girl like that could mean freedom from worry for a number of years.'

'She'll have her worries all right,' Kate said, 'with a face like that. Well, it's the best chance we've got. You tell her about it in the morning—and keep the others out of sight. We don't want her to get frightened—not if she's as pure and holy as she looks.'

'My impression is that she's completely innocent,' Ella Harcourt said.

'Then keep her that way,' Kate said almost savagely. 'You'd better get her around to that Mercier woman for some clothes. She has the best and his Lordship will be paying.'

'How much am I to buy her?' Mrs. Harcourt asked.

'Oh, plenty,' Kate said. 'We might as well fit her out at his expense as ours. The wedding dress is important; keep that as ladylike as possible.'

She turned towards the door, moving sideways so that her great bulk in her full skirts could pass through the narrow aperture. She had reached the top of the stairs when Ella Harcourt came hurrying after her.

'There is one thing I forgot,' she said. 'Lord Wrotham saw her just as we arrived. He was delighted—you know what he is—and he said to me, "Tell Kate she's mine." '

Kate snorted.

'If there's one man that gives me the creeps it's that there Wrotham,' she said. 'Well, on this occasion he'll just have to wait. Do him good, the nasty blighter!'

She descended the stairs like a ship in full sail. As she reached the bottom, Mrs. Harcourt, who was watching her go, heard her mutter almost beneath her breath:

'Wrotham and that girl! Poor little devil!'

Kate went back to Captain Vestey. He was waiting for her in her sitting-room, a glass of champagne in his hand.

'Good lord, Kate! I thought you had deserted me,' he said. 'I heard you and Mrs. Harcourt going down the passage and you were so long that I had to come in here for a drink.'

'Quite right,' Kate exclaimed. 'And I need one too.'

'Well, what is the verdict?' Captain Vestey asked as he poured her out a glass.

'We've found someone,' Kate said.

'You have! Kate, you're a wonder, you are really! I told Drogo you wouldn't let us down.'

'She's young and it'll take a bit of explaining,' Kate said.

'We'll leave that to you,' Captain Vestey said. 'And, now, about the marriage. It has got to take place tomorrow afternoon, you realise that?'

'Tomorrow afternoon!' Kate ejaculated. 'But how can we be ready so quickly?'

'The Dowager is dying,' Captain Vestey said

simply. 'There is always the chance that she might die tonight; that is a risk we have got to take but it is no use stacking the cards too high. Drogo can get a special licence in the morning. We have already spoken to the "parson" and all you have got to do is produce the girl.'

'It's not giving us time to breathe,' Kate said sharply. 'We don't even know that the girl will agree.'

'If she is one of your brood you will handle her all right,' Captain Vestey said. 'And, now, I am going to tootle off and tell the Marquis that it is all fixed. If I am ever in a hole I know who I shall come to, and that will be you, Kate. Bless you—you old dear! You're a trump!'

He bent forward and kissed her on the cheek. Kate almost simpered.

'Get along with you,' she said. 'All that blarney is only because you've got your own way. Well, I only hope it works out. Tell young Chard I shan't come to the wedding. I don't think I should look quite the part as a bridesmaid. But, he's to send the girl back to me as soon as he's finished with her. I don't want her hanging about and getting ideas.'

'The moment the will is signed, she's yours,' Captain Vestey said, and then stopped and added: 'No, that is not quite correct. She will have to wait until the Dowager actually dies. Her Ladyship might want to see her and if she wasn't in the house she would smell a rat. It is, honestly, only a question of days.'

'Well, she'll want quite a lot of clothes then,' Kate said practically.

'Send the bill to the Marquis. He'll be able to afford it after this,' Captain Vestey laughed.

'I shall,' Kate promised. 'And tell him that the five hundred guineas will be very welcome, too. I don't like waiting for my money.'

'You won't have to,' Captain Vestey promised. 'And, now I am going to tell the bridegroom the great news.'

He picked up his top-hat from where he had laid it on the chair when he entered the room, set it jauntily on the side of his head, and walked back to the Salon. As he reached the American Bar at the end, having taken some time greeting his friends and waving to several pretty girls, he looked back to see that Kate had resumed her seat on the dais. Her big voice was booming through the room, calling up several young men-about-town to pay for her drinks and commanding the girls to look lively. It was almost as if a new gaiety had come back into the room with Kate's return.

Captain Vestey smiled to himself as he went down the long passage towards the front door.

'Wonderful woman!' he said to himself. 'Wonderful! I wonder what Drogo's bride will be like?'

4

Melinda awoke slowly, feeling as if she was coming back to consciousness through a heavy, dark cloud. Slowly she opened her eyes and for a moment could not remember where she was. Then, as she moved slightly, the pain from the weals on her shoulders and back recalled all too clearly Sir Hector's brutality.

She shut her eyes as if to blot out the misery of it; then opened them again and with an effort sat up in bed and looked about her. The sunlight was shimmering beneath the curtains and carefully, because it hurt to move quickly, Melinda climbed from the bed and on to the floor.

For a moment she felt dizzy at the movement. She put her hand to her forehead. It felt as if her whole head was stuffed with wool. She remembered feeling like this once before. It was after she had had an accident out riding and her nurse had given her hot milk to drink with a spoonful of laudanum in it. She could remember herself saying:

'I do feel ill, Nanna! My head feels too big and heavy for my body.'

'It will pass off, dearie,' her nurse had answered cheerfully. 'I'm a real believer in having a long, deep sleep after an accident; and the doctor will say I was right when he comes, you see if he doesn't.'

Melinda never heard whether old Dr. Harrison had approved or disapproved of Nanna's action, but she had always remembered that feeling of heaviness and of being somehow apart from the world.

She knew that was what she must have been given last night by Mrs. Harcourt—milk with a spoonful of laudanum in it. But, why? She had been tired enough to have slept naturally.

She pulled back the curtains and gave an audible gasp. There were heavy bars across the window. Just for a moment, dark against the sunshine, they frightened her. And then she gave a laugh at her own stupidity. It was the laudanum that was making her feel so foolish. Of course, people in London had bars in their windows to keep out the burglars.

Melinda crossed to the washing-stand and poured herself a glass of water. It tasted stale and a little musty but it did seem to alleviate her headache a little and the heaviness of her eyelids. On an impulse she poured cold water from the china ewer into the basin and washed her face. Now, at last, she could feel the heaviness lighten.

'What I want,' she told herself with practical good sense, 'is some breakfast. After I have eaten, this feeling will pass. I am sure Mrs. Harcourt meant well, but it was quite unnecessary!'

She looked round the room and for the first time noticed how very different it seemed from the night before. Then she had been struck by the soft, shaded lights, the pink hangings, the luxurious carpet and the ornate brass bedstead. Now, in the sunlight, it looked tawdry. She could not quite explain to herself why it offended her, but it did. There was something vulgar about the plush chairs, the white dressing-table surmounted by carved doves, the pelmets on the window which were draped and befringed with silver bobbles.

Melinda had a sudden impulse to leave. She walked across to the door. 'I'll let someone know I am awake,' she thought, and turned the handle. The door was locked! For a moment she could hardly believe it was true. She turned the handle the other way; tugged at it. Then she glanced over her shoulder towards the window. Bars and a locked door! What did it mean?

At that moment there was a key being turned in the lock; the door opened and, as if to answer her very question, Mrs. Harcourt came in. There was something about her sane, sensible face which allayed Melinda's fears and made her, although she had said nothing, feel foolish.

'Good morning, dear!' Mrs. Harcourt said in her calm, cultured voice. 'I hope you slept well.'

'Yes . . . yes, very well,' Melinda answered. 'I . . . I was just coming to find you but the door was locked.'

'Yes, it was,' Mrs. Harcourt replied. 'I locked it because there are quite a lot of people in the house at the moment and I did not want anyone to burst in by mistake and waken you. You were very tired last night.'

Melinda opened her lips to say something about the laudanum and then decided it was unnecessary. After all, there would not be any opportunity of her being given it again, so what was the point of making a fuss?

'You were very kind, ma'am,' she said to Mrs. Harcourt. 'I am deeply grateful to you for letting me sleep in your house last night. But, now, I must leave and I should be extremely obliged if you could give me the address of Mrs. Brewer's Bureau.'

'I have already looked it up for you,' Mrs. Harcourt replied. 'But, I have just heard of something which I think will interest you even more.'

'A position in which I might be employed?' Melinda asked.

'Exactly,' Mrs. Harcourt replied. 'But, first, you must have some breakfast. Get back into bed. I have told one of the maids to bring it up to you. She should be here at any moment.'

She opened the door as she spoke and looked out on to the landing, leaving the door ajar. As Melinda had no dressing-gown there was nothing she could do but get into bed as Mrs. Harcourt had suggested. She sat there, chiding herself for the slight feeling of uneasiness which still lay at the back of her mind.

A moment later a maid, wearing a crisply starched mob-cap and rustling apron, carried in the breakfast tray and placed it down on the bed. Melinda saw that the maid was middle-aged and there was an expression on her face which she did not understand. To herself she described it as disdainful and wondered why a strange maid in this lady's house should look at her like that.

'And now, hurry up and get the rooms done, Doris,' Mrs. Harcourt said.

'I can't do number seven,' the maid answered in a surly tone. 'They rang about an hour ago and said they wanted a bottle of champagne. John took it up to them.'

'That will be all, Doris,' Mrs. Harcourt said sharply and closed the door behind her.

There were poached eggs on Melinda's tray, in a covered dish, toast, butter, marmalade and a pot of coffee. She helped herself to the coffee, feeling somehow embarrassed because Mrs. Harcourt was watching her.

'You are to eat up both the eggs,' Mrs. Harcourt said, as if she sensed her thoughts. 'You will only feel tired otherwise. There is a great deal for you to do today.'

'Is there?' Melinda asked. 'You were going to tell me about this position.'

Mrs. Harcourt twiddled the ring on her finger and looked down at it as if she were choosing her words.

'Have you ever acted on a stage?' she asked.

Melinda shook her head.

'No, of course not. And I have not even been to the theatre. I did see one of Shakespeare's plays performed by the children in the orphanage in which my father was interested, but I am afraid that is about all.'

She thought Mrs. Harcourt looked disappointed and added quickly:

'Of course, we have played charades at home when we have had young people's parties and, once, my mother arranged tableaux in the Village Hall at Christmastime.'

'Then you have acted,' Mrs. Harcourt said, in a voice almost of delight. 'At any rate, you will not find it difficult to do what I am going to suggest to you.'

'What is it?' Melinda enquired.

'A distinguished nobleman wants a young girl to act the part of a bride at a pretence marriage ceremony. Only pretence, but he does require someone who can act the part well. I thought you would be just the person.'

'Act the part of a bride!' Melinda ejaculated, thinking for a moment this must be some ridiculous, obscure joke. Here she was, running away from being a bride, only to be asked to pretend to be one!

'Yes, it is not very difficult,' Mrs. Harcourt said.

'I do not think I could do that,' Melinda said quickly.

There was a little pause.

'That is a pity,' Mrs. Harcourt said, 'because the gentleman in question is prepared to pay the sum of five hundred guineas to any girl who plays the part to his satisfaction.'

'Pay five hundred guineas for that!' Melinda cried. 'Is he mad?'

'No, of course not,' Mrs. Harcourt answered. 'It is just that it is very, very important to him that this particular ceremony should take place and that the person who is going to watch it should believe it to be genuine. Of course, there is nothing wrong in the whole thing. It is just a little bit of play-acting, but he wanted someone to do it well and I thought of you.'

'But, why should he want such a thing?' Melinda asked. 'And to pay such an enormous sum of money for it?'

Mrs. Harcourt did not answer and Melinda said:

'I suppose it is a wager.'

'Yes, I think that is exactly what it is,' Mrs. Harcourt said. 'A wager! You know what these young men are. They will do anything when it concerns a bet.'

'It must be a very important one if he is prepared to spend that money,' Melinda said.

'It is, indeed,' Mrs. Harcourt agreed. 'In fact, the sum concerned runs into thousands and thousands of pounds.'

'How ridiculous!' Melinda said. 'My mother always used to say how wrong people were to gamble with money which could be well spent on helping the poor and needy.'

'I do not think we need concern ourselves with the rights and wrongs of this particular case,' Mrs. Harcourt said. 'All you have to do is to go through the ceremony of marriage beside this very charming and, if I may say so, very handsome nobleman. He will then hand you five hundred guineas; you can come back here and we can talk about finding you something else.'

'It sounds very easy,' Melinda said.

Her mind was working quickly. Five hundred guineas would mean that she would not have to seek for a post immediately but could go at once to her old nurse, who was living in Sussex with her sister.

After she had lost her father and mother in the accident, she had clung to Nanna, as she called her, in her misery, finding comfort only in the arms which had held her when she had been a baby. But when Sir Hector had appeared on the scene he had made it quite clear from the very beginning that, although he was prepared out of the generosity of his heart to take his orphaned niece into his house, he had no room for old retainers.

Nanna was sent away with such a minute pension that Melinda had felt bitterly ashamed, not only that so many faithful years of service should be so meagrely rewarded, but by the fact that her uncle should stoop to such petty economy. But there had been nothing she could do about it except weep bitter tears as Nanna had said goodbye.

She wrote to her frequently and always at the back of her mind had been the dream that one day, as soon as she had a home of her own, Nanna would come back to her. Now this would be possible! They would be able to find a tiny cottage somewhere and be together—at least until the five hundred pounds was spent; and by that time she might have found some other way of earning a living so that she and Nanna could still keep house together.

Almost as if she was afraid that this was just a dream, Melinda asked:

'You did say five hundred pounds, did you not?'

'Five hundred guineas, to be exact,' Mrs. Harcourt replied. 'And now, if you are agreeable, we must hurry. The ceremony in question is to take place this afternoon.'

'But, what have we to do?' Melinda enquired.

'We have to get you some very beautiful clothes,' Mrs. Harcourt said. 'A wedding gown and some other garments as well, just in case you have to stay in the house overnight.'

'Why should I do that?' Melinda enquired.

'It is part of the arrangement,' Mrs. Harcourt said, a note of finality in her voice as if she was tired of being questioned. 'I will explain it all to you. But at the moment you must get dressed. Hurry, and I will order the carriage to be round in a quarter of an hour.'

She rose and went to the door. Just as she reached it someone knocked and Melinda heard Doris's voice asking about something which was happening in room number four. 'What a lot of people Mrs. Harcourt seems to have staying at the same time,' Melinda thought to herself.

She got out of bed and went towards the basin. Just as she did so the door opened and a girl looked in. She was wearing a filmy, almost transparent, dressing-gown of chiffon and lace and her hair was falling over her shoulders. To Melinda's astonishment her face was rouged and powdered and her eyelashes mascara-ed.

'Hello!' the apparition said. 'When did you get here?'

'Last . . . last night,' Melinda said, still staring almost rudely at the blue-shadowed eyes, the artificially pink cheeks and crimson lips.

'Where'd she catch you?' the newcomer asked. 'On the railway station? That's 'er favourite beat. Did she give you the sob-stuff about losing 'er poor little daughter?'

'I . . . I do not know . . . what you are talking about,' Melinda faltered.

'You'll soon learn,' the girl said. 'If it wasn't too late I'd tell you to skip it. But, as it is, I might as well give you my advice, for what it's worth. Just agree to everything. She can be real nasty if you don't; and they dope you until you feel too ill to care.'

'What are you talking about? What do you mean?' Melinda asked sharply.

There was the sound of voices outside and her visitor was already moving back into the passage.

'Wait!' Melinda cried. 'Wait! Tell me . . .'

She was too late. She could hear Mrs. Harcourt's voice, now hard and disagreeable, say:

'What are you doing, April? Who said you could go into that room?'

'I was looking for you, ma'am.'

'I haven't time now,' Mrs. Harcourt said. 'Whatever you have got to say can wait until later.'

'Very good, ma'am. It wasn't very important anyway.'

April—if that was her name—had left the door ajar. Melinda heard every word and now she was frightened. She did not know quite what was happening. She only knew that she was frightened and she wanted to get away.

'Never mind about the five hundred guineas,' she told herself. 'I will tell Mrs. Harcourt I want to leave now.' And then April's words came back to her.

'Just agree to everything. She can be real nasty if you don't . . .'

For five hundred guineas she could be independent. Whatever happened she must get that first, and then she must get away; though why or from what she was not certain. . . .

Three hours later Melinda was standing in a shop in Bond Street feeling as if her legs would collapse under her. She had given up asking questions, given up asking why she should want so many clothes, or even worrying as to who was going to pay for them.

Mrs. Harcourt had driven her to the shop and Madame Mercier, who owned it, it seemed to Melinda, had taken in the situation at a glance.

'Ma'mselle will need a great deal, I can see that,'

she said to Mrs. Harcourt meaningly.

'But the wedding-gown, Madame, must be very discreet,' Mrs. Harcourt insisted. 'Exactly what would be worn by a lady of fashion, you understand?'

'Exactly!' Madame Mercier had said, nodding her head.

'And also the gowns for the next few days. Ladylike; attractive, of course, or they would be useless afterwards; but definitely ladylike.'

'Leave it to me, Mrs. Harcourt,' Madame Mercier said.

'I came to you, Madame,' Mrs. Harcourt continued, 'because you dress so many of the *élite*. I am told the Duchess of Melchester gets all her gowns here.'

'She does, indeed,' Madame Mercier answered. 'And so does Lady Carrington and Lady Alice St. Helier. Now, there's a beauty, if ever there was one.'

'Of course, I realise that with your usual orders this is a desperate rush,' Mrs. Harcourt said. 'The wedding-gown and the gowns to be worn in the next forty-eight hours have to be ready immediately.'

'That is impossible!' Madame Mercier cried, flinging up her hands in horror.

'I know, and that is why the price is of no object,' Mrs. Harcourt said.

The two women's eyes met.

'In that case,' Madame Mercier conceded, 'I do have a wedding-gown that has been ordered for the Countess of Lansdown's daughter, a sweetly pretty girl who is to be married in three weeks. They are coming for the final fitting next Friday. I suppose it would be possible for us to make another gown in that time.'

'Then let us try it on,' Mrs. Harcourt suggested.

Madame clapped her hands and a few minutes later Melinda looked at herself in the mirror with incredulity. She had never imagined that clothes would make such a difference or that she could appear so elegant and, at the same time, ethereal. The very full skirt of lace, looped with ribbons and bunches of orange blossom, accentuated the smallness of her waist, and there was lace and orange blossom along the low décolletage of the tight little bodice and on the tiny, puff sleeves.

'Pretty as a picture!' Madame Mercier exclaimed. 'I can tell you, young woman, that the real bride who was to wear this is not half as attractive as you.'

'Thank you,' Melinda said.

She was still feeling embarrassed because when she had taken off her gown there had been an exclamation of horror from Madame Mercier when she had seen her back.

'What has happened to you, my poor child . . .?' she began, and then checked the words on her lips.

She turned to Mrs. Harcourt and said something in such a voice, disgusted but so low, that Melinda could not hear what she said. Mrs. Harcourt had shaken her head.

'No, no, it is nothing like that,' she said. 'This young lady only arrived in London last night. I found her, lost and bewildered, on the railway station, looking for some cheap, respectable lodging. I was only too willing to invite her to stay with me.'

Madame Mercier's lips tightened in a wry smile.

'I am sure you were, Madame,' she said in a voice that somehow held undertones of sarcasm. 'Well, we shall certainly have to raise the back of the gown. Those scars cannot be shown.'

'Surely the veil will hide most of them,' Mrs. Harcourt suggested.

'Oh, yes, of course, I was forgetting the veil,' Madame agreed. 'But the evening gowns must be raised.'

'The weals will fade, they always do,' Mrs. Harcourt said. Then turning to Melinda she asked: 'What had you done, child, to receive such punishment?'

'My uncle was angry with me because I would not obey him,' Melinda answered, blushing.

Mrs. Harcourt did not pursue the subject and Melinda was relieved. She had no intention of disclosing to any stranger why she had felt she must run away from home. She realised, however, that Mrs. Harcourt was not really interested in her explanations.

In fact Melinda soon felt that she was of no consequence save as a dummy on which Madame Mercier might display her wares. The shop-keeper obviously had only one aim—to sell as many gowns as possible; and Mrs. Harcourt, equally, wished to buy as many as possible. Melinda did not understand it and after a time she gave up worrying. On only one thing she was insistent, that the gowns should not have too low a décolletage.

'But, ma'mselle, you are not fashionable!' Madame Mercier protested.

'I do not mind if I am fashionable or not,' Melinda

said. 'And, indeed, I have no reason to believe I shall wear half of these gowns. But in case I have to do so, I would not have them as low as this one.'

She turned to the gown as she spoke, pulling it higher over her small, curved breasts.

'A little more tulle and some ribbons will raise it two or three inches, if you wish,' Madame Mercier said and glanced at Mrs. Harcourt as if for confirmation.

'Youth and innocence are always charming and very desirable,' Mrs. Harcourt said, and once again there was that wry smile on Madame Mercier's lips as she gave the fitter the order to raise the gown as Melinda had requested.

At last, to Melinda's relief, there was no time to try on any more.

'All these must be delivered at Grosvenor Square this afternoon,' Mrs. Harcourt said.

'Grosvenor Square!'

There was no mistaking the curiosity in Madame Mercier's voice now.

'I can trust to your discretion, I know that,' Mrs. Harcourt said. 'Not a word of this must be related to anyone.'

'I have built up my present clientele by learning when to keep my lips shut,' Madame Mercier assured her.

'Then you understand that this is of the utmost secrecy,' Mrs. Harcourt replied. 'And the bills should accompany the clothes and should be made out to the Marquis of Chard.'

Madame Mercier's eyes sparkled.

'The Marquis, indeed! A very dashing young man, from all I hear.'

'Very dashing,' Mrs. Harcourt agreed. 'And you need not worry about the payment for everything we have chosen. I am leaving it to you, Madame, to supply petticoats and the other underclothes which should go with each gown.'

'And shoes?' Madame Mercier asked.

'Shoes, of course; gloves, reticules, and I think definitely that every young lady of fashion should have scarves and cloaks.'

'It shall all be ready in time,' Madame Mercier promised.

'The wedding-gown we will take with us,' Mrs. Harcourt said, 'if you will be so kind as to pack it up. And Miss Stanyon will wear that pale blue outfit—the one we chose first. That is extremely becoming and although it is your most expensive, I feel that the Marquis will not grudge the cost.'

'But should we not ask him first?' Melinda enquired.

Both women turned to look at her in astonishment. It was almost as if, because she had not spoken for so long, they had forgotten her very presence there.

'He might not want me to have such expensive things,' Melinda said.

'I assure you, he will be delighted,' Mrs. Harcourt said with a note of satisfaction in her voice.

Melinda was still doubtful when, wearing the blue outfit and a bonnet trimmed with tiny blue ostrich feathers to match, they got into the brougham.

'Are you tired?' Mrs. Harcourt asked.

'I never knew choosing clothes could be so exhausting,' Melinda answered. 'But I think, actually, it is because I am hungry.'

'Yes, I am sure you are,' Mrs. Harcourt said. 'But I am afraid you will have to ask Lord Chard to give you something to eat when you arrive. I do not wish you to come back to my house at the moment as I have some guests waiting for me, so I am going to suggest that I drive you straight to Grosvenor Square. You are a little early, but I daresay no one will mind that.'

'Oh, but will that not be embarrassing?' Melinda asked. 'What time did they invite me?'

'Do not worry,' Mrs. Harcourt said, patting her hand. 'Everything will go beautifully. All you have got to do is to wear these beautiful clothes and ask the maid to help you change into your wedding-gown when you arrive. Then Lord Chard, or Captain Vestey, his friend, will explain to you how soon you can return to me.'

'It is very kind of you . . .' Melinda began.

'There is one thing I want to say to you,' Mrs. Harcourt interrupted. 'When they offer you the five hundred guineas, will you suggest to Captain Vestey—I think he will be handling the finances of the arrangement—that he gives it to me to keep for you? It would not be at all wise for a young girl of your age, ignorant of London and its dangers, to be walking about with a large sum of money on your person. Just tell Captain Vestey that your remuneration for your services should be given to Mrs. Ella Harcourt. Will you remember that? I should not like there to be any mistake.'

'Yes, I will remember it,' Melinda said.

'Now, be a sensible girl,' Mrs. Harcourt went on, 'and do exactly what is required of you. Remember that your performance has got to be completely convincing for the people who are watching; otherwise, of course, Lord Chard will lose his wager and you will lose the five hundred guineas, and that would be a great pity, would it not?'

'I will be as convincing as I possibly can be,' Melinda promised.

'You will just have to go through the normal marriage service, but remember it will be just an act. The clergyman will not be a real one, even though he will look real enough.'

Melinda held her breath. She had a moment of panic. Why was she doing this? Was it right? Was it safe? She had been aware of a feeling of danger ever since she awoke that morning, and now, it seemed to her, she was running into even greater dangers. It sounded simple enough, and yet she felt there were deep, undercurrent things she did not understand. Something was wrong.

She wanted to cry out that she would go no further and yet she knew she was irrevocably committed. She could feel the soft silk of her new gown beneath her hands. She knew that opposite them, on the seat of the carriage, lay the wedding-gown she was to wear. All they had ordered this morning must have cost hundreds and hundreds of pounds. She could not back out now and yet she was afraid, terribly afraid!

The brougham came to a stop. She saw a big, porticoed front door and looked round at Mrs. Harcourt almost appealingly.

'Don't be frightened, dear,' Mrs. Harcourt said. 'I shall be waiting for you. When this is over you will come straight back to me. Yes, straight back; that is all arranged. Just do what is wanted of you for the moment.'

She patted Melinda's hand and as she did so the door of the brougham was opened by a footman with silver-crested buttons on his uniform which glinted in the afternoon sunshine. Melinda stepped out. There was a red carpet rolled across the pavement on which she set down her feet in their new blue satin slippers.

Two other footmen stood inside the door. The butler, grey-headed and looking rather like an archbishop, advanced towards her.

'You are expected, miss,' he said before Melinda could speak. 'Will you come this way?'

He led her down a long, marble hall. She had a quick impression of elegant pieces of furniture; of mirrors in carved, gilt frames; of crystal chandeliers hanging from the ceiling. Then he flung open a door at the far end.

'The young lady, m'lord,' he said in stentorian tones.

The room was long and the walls were covered in books. At the far end, standing beside the mantelpiece, Melinda saw two men. One advanced to meet her—an elegant, exquisitely dressed young man with a moustache and fair, waving hair. He put out his hand and took Melinda's.

'It is jolly decent of you to come,' he said. 'My name is Vestey, Gervase Vestey, and this is my friend, Lord Chard, whom you have promised to help.'

Melinda looked towards the other gentleman who was still standing at the mantelpiece and had not moved. For a moment she thought he was the most handsome man she had ever seen in her life, and then she thought that he looked dissipated and rather cynical. He was clean-shaven, and his dark hair was swept back from his square forehead which was echoed by the squareness of his chin. His eyes seemed to be inspecting her as if she were a horse, taking in her points, wandering over her until she felt embarrassed and her first impression changed to one of dislike.

Almost instinctively, her chin went up and instead of turning away from the boldness of those eyes she faced him almost defiantly.

'My name is Melinda Stanyon,' she said.

As if he suddenly remembered his manners, Lord Chard held out his hand.

'Thank you, Miss Stanyon, for coming to my rescue,' he said. 'I believe the circumstances which necessitated my request have been explained to you.'

Melinda just nodded her head.

'There is not much time for explanations now,' Captain Vestey said quickly. 'I expect Miss Stanyon would like to change. It will take her some time and you will have to get into your wedding clothes, too, Drogo.'

'I think it would be more polite if we offered Miss Stanyon a drink,' Lord Chard said. 'There is no reason why we should undertake this joyful ceremony in a gloomy state of mind, is there?'

'No, no, of course not,' Captain Vestey said. 'What will you have, Miss Stanyon? Champagne?'

'No, thank you,' Melinda said. 'I . . . I wonder if it would be possible for me to have something to eat? Just a sandwich, or something.'

'Good heavens! Have you not lunched?' Captain Vestey said. 'But, of course, we will get some sandwiches for you right away.'

'I would rather not have it here,' Melinda said, feeling that she could not eat with both the men's eyes upon her. 'But, if they could be sent to the . . . bedroom where I shall change . . .'

Melinda had the uncomfortable feeling that Lord Chard's eyes were watching her critically. There was a kind of twisted smile on his lips which annoyed her. Because she felt compelled to speak to him she said:

'I hope that I shall do everything to your satisfaction, my lord.'

'Indeed, you will be able to do that,' he said. 'Only to look at you is to realise that you will be perfect in the part.'

Captain Vestey crossed the room to speak to one of the servants who answered the bell.

'You seem rather young for this sort of thing,' Lord Chard said to Melinda.

'I hope I do not look too young,' she replied. 'But, after all, one can be a bride at sixteen.'

'Can one?' he asked vaguely. 'I gather you never have been married?'

'No, never,' Melinda replied.

'And you have never thought that would be preferable to what you are doing now?' Lord Chard asked.

'Anything is preferable to some marriages,' Melinda answered, thinking of Colonel Gillingham.

The positive note in her voice must have surprised him, for after a moment he said:

'You sound as if you were afraid of marriage.'

'I am, very afraid,' Melinda said.

He laughed out loud.

'Then that is two of us,' he said. 'Come, let us drink to it. Where's that champagne, Gervase?'

'It is just coming,' Captain Vestey said.

He walked across the room to where a grog-tray held decanters and a big, silver wine-cooler in which reposed an open bottle of champagne. He picked up the bottle and poured out three glasses of the sparkling wine.

'Come along,' he said. 'Let us drink a toast to a successful marriage that never in truth existed.'

He gave Melinda a glass as he spoke and although she disliked champagne, having tried it once or twice with her father and declared she much preferred lemonade, she thought it would be churlish to refuse.

Lord Chard lifted his glass.

'To my bride!' he said. 'Who else should I drink to at this moment?'

'To you both!' Captain Vestey said. 'And may you never be discovered.'

They looked at Melinda and waited.

'To happiness!' she said, and there was an unexpected note of sincerity in her voice.

She took a tiny sip of the champagne and then set it down.

'Perhaps I had better go and dress,' she said, speaking to Captain Vestey. 'It will take me some time.'

'I have arranged for a maid to help you,' Captain Vestey said. 'And do not forget that for the moment no one in the household knows anything.' He paused for a moment and looked at his friend. 'In fact, we were talking about what we would say when you arrived. We just told the butler that we were expecting a young lady. I think now it would be right, Drogo, for you to announce to the staff that you are about to be married. They will know about it, anyway, as soon as they unpack Miss Stanyon's wedding-gown.'

'I will leave it all to you,' Lord Chard said.

'Very well,' Captain Vestey replied. 'This is the plan, Miss Stanyon. We are going to tell everybody that because of the Dowager Marchioness's illness, the wedding must be kept a complete secret. The staff will understand this. That class is always more preoccupied with death than with life. We will put them on their honour and say it is absolutely essential that the press should not get to know of it. Then, as soon as the Dowager is dead, you will conveniently disappear and we will have to announce that you have been killed in a carriage accident, or something like that.'

'And who is the Dowager?' Melinda asked. 'And what has her death got to do with it?'

'I thought this had been all explained to you,' Lord Chard said in a voice of irritation.

'I was only told that you were doing this for a wager,' Melinda replied, 'and that I had to convince the people who were watching.'

Captain Vestey looked at the Marquis.

'Well, that is more or less the position. It is a wager, in a way. A lot of money is involved in it and you must indeed make those who are watching the ceremony this afternoon believe it is the real thing. That is all that matters.'

Melinda's face, which had looked anxious, cleared.

'That was what Mrs. Harcourt told me,' she said. 'I did not understand what you were saying just now.'

'Think nothing of it,' Captain Vestey said. 'I always do open my big mouth too much. You just concentrate on what you have got to do and leave Lord Chard and me to cope with all the rest.'

'I am quite happy to do that,' Melinda said.

She turned to walk towards the door. Before she reached it she stopped suddenly.

'There is just one thing I wanted to ask you,' she said. 'When you give me the money—the five hundred guineas that you have promised me for doing this—will you please give it to me and not to anyone else?'

'But, of course,' Captain Vestey said.

Melinda hesitated again.

'On second thoughts, would it be possible to put it in a bank in my name?'

'Nothing easier,' Captain Vestey said. 'Have you a bank?'

'No, no!' Melinda exclaimed. 'But my father used to bank at Coutts. Could it be left at Coutts in my name?'

'Yes, of course it could,' Captain Vestey said.

'You cannot walk about with all that money on you, can you?'

'Thank you very much indeed,' Melinda said, a smile suddenly illuminating her face.

She looked back at Lord Chard as she spoke, as if to include him in her gratitude. He raised his glass to her.

'You are a pretty little thing,' he said, 'and as mercenary as they are made. We shall get on well together. At least we know where we are.'

His words seemed to strike the smile from her lips. She looked at him for a moment and then turned quickly away. She felt that she would be sorry for any girl whom he was really marrying. He was unpleasant and there was something about him which made her feel that he was cruel, trying to hurt, trying to be destructive.

Once again she had a sudden longing to drop the whole thing, to forget about the five hundred guineas, to leave this grand house and go in search of a more humble and less highly paid employment. And then she remembered Nanna. How wonderful it would be to arrive at the cottage she shared with her sister in Sussex with the news that their separation was over; they could be together.

'I will be ready as quickly as I can,' she said to Captain Vestey, and her voice was hard and resolute.

5

'Oh, miss, you do look lovely!'

The little housemaid, with her starched cap and frilled apron, clasped her hands together in admiration.

'That's quite enough, Gladys,' her superior said sharply, but added: 'She's quite right. You do look a dream bride, miss, there's no denying it!'

Melinda stared at herself in the mirror. She could hardly believe that it was, in fact, a reflection of herself. The long, Brussels lace veil, falling over the wide skirts of the gown, framed her face and made her look somehow ethereal. She was so small, so fragile, that it appeared she might float away or just be a figment of someone's imagination.

She wondered what she would feel at this moment if she were, in fact, about to marry someone she loved and someone who loved her. At the back of her mind there had been always a secret desire to fall in love; to feel herself thrill to a man's touch; to know that she belonged to him and that he would give her his name.

What she was doing, she felt suddenly, was a mockery of all that was sacred, all that was holy. She longed to be independent enough to say that she would go no further with the farce. Then she thought of Nanna eating her heart out in Sussex with the sister she had never liked. They would have that little cottage together and if, indeed, the time came when she would marry, Nanna must go with her. She would never again feel lost and lonely as she had been in her uncle's house.

'Will you inform his lordship that I am ready?' she asked, knowing that her eyes were misting a little at the thought of what she had suffered since her parents died.

'I will tell his lordship right away, miss,' the head housemaid said. 'And, Gladys, start tidying the room.'

With this parting shot the elderly woman, who was obviously something of a martinet, went to find a footman who, in his turn, would find the butler to convey Melinda's message to Lord Chard.

Now that authority had gone, Gladys burst into speech.

'It's a real shame, miss, that you can't have a big wedding at St. George's, Hanover Square. I've often stood outside on my day off and watched the brides going in, and there's not one of 'em as could hold a candle to you.'

'Thank you, Gladys,' Melinda said with a little smile. 'But there is nothing I should dislike more than to have my wedding full of strangers staring at me. If I had my choice I should like to be married very quietly in the country, in a small church, with just the people there that I love best.'

'It sounds nice, miss,' Gladys said wistfully. 'It won't be the same, being married in a bedroom, will it?'

'Married in a bedroom?' Melinda questioned in surprise.

'Yes, miss, didn't you know? You're to be married in her ladyship's room. And she's so near to death that Miss Matthews—that's her ladyship's maid—says she doesn't think as how she'll last the night.'

Melinda felt herself shiver; and then with an effort at common sense she told herself it was nothing to do with her. She just had to play-act the whole thing. But, surely, the wager must be in extremely bad taste if it involved a dying woman.

She felt her first impressions of Lord Chard concentrate still further into an active dislike. She would be glad to take his money and leave the house. There was something in the way he looked at her. She could not explain it to herself, but it made her feel cheap and of no consequence.

'I will not let him worry me,' she said beneath her breath.

'What did you say, miss?' Gladys asked.

'Nothing,' Melinda said. 'But I shall be glad when this is over.'

'I expect you feels shy, miss,' Gladys said sympathetically. 'But his lordship ain't as bad as he's painted, I can promise you that. He's ever so kind to the staff and in the country they all love him. I know, 'cos I was born on the estate.'

Melinda said nothing. She was hardly listening to the young housemaid's reminiscences.

'Of course, they says as 'ow he's wild. "Dashing Drogo" is what they calls him, I believe. Oh, miss! I shouldn't be speaking about his lordship like this. You won't tell Miss Jones, will you? I'll be packed back to the country if you do.'

'No, Gladys, I shall not repeat what you have said

to me,' Melinda said. 'It is of very little importance anyway.'

'But if you loves him, then everything will be all right, won't it?' Gladys said.

'Of course,' Melinda agreed, not wishing to deny the trust and faith in the girl's shining eyes.

'I knew it!' Gladys said triumphantly. 'It's just what my mum says. "Wait until his lordship gets a wife!" she says. "Her ladyship'll soon silence the gossips. He'll settle down. It's 'cos he's had such an unhappy childhood that makes him as he is!" '

Melinda was not interested. She was finding the waiting for the Marquis's summons irksome and somehow agitating. Supposing she failed him? Supposing she revealed that this was not, in fact, a real marriage? He would then refuse to pay her and what would happen to all the gowns that Mrs. Harcourt had ordered? Supposing he refused to pay for them as well?

She clasped her hands together in sudden agitation, just as the door opened and the head housemaid reappeared.

'His lordship's waiting for you, miss, in the Blue Salon. One of the footmen will take you there.'

'Thank you,' Melinda said. 'And, thank you for helping me dress.'

'It's been a real pleasure, miss, and the best of luck. We all hope that you'll be very happy.'

'You will be! I know you will be!' Gladys said impulsively. 'You're so beautiful!'

'That's quite enough, Gladys,' the head housemaid said sharply.

Melinda moved slowly from the room. The footman was waiting for her at the top of the stairs. He was very tall. Melinda remembered hearing her mother say that in grand houses all the footmen had to be over six feet tall. He was young but he seemed to have great composure.

'This way, if you please, miss,' he said, and led the way slowly down the thickly carpeted staircase.

As they reached the door of the Blue Salon, Melinda suddenly felt shy and knew that her heart was beating loudly against the tight lace bodice of her gown.

'It is because I am afraid of making a fool of myself,' she thought, but she knew, in fact, it was because she was afraid to encounter the Marquis again.

He was standing just inside the room, exceedingly elegant in his frock-coat, high cravat and white buttonhole. He stared at her as she entered and she dropped her eyes, the dark lashes sweeping against her pale cheeks. There was a moment's silence caused, if she had known it, by her appearance. But she had no idea of the compliment that was being paid her; she waited, trembling a little, conscious only of the thumping of her heart.

'Wonderful! Magnificent!' the Marquis exclaimed, and his voice seemed harsh and almost unnaturally loud. 'You could not fit the part more perfectly. I congratulate you, my dear.'

'I will get you a glass of champagne,' Captain Vestey said.

Melinda shook her head.

'I would rather not,' she said. 'I am . . . I am not . . . used to it.'

The Marquis threw back his head and laughed.

'Not used to it!' he repeated. 'That is perfect! You are a magnificent actress. If I had any sense I should rent a theatre for you and make a fortune!'

Melinda glanced at him from under her eyelashes. He might be good-looking, she thought, but he was exceedingly unpleasant in every other way. She could not imagine why he should doubt her assertion that she was not used to champagne, but she supposed that in the type of society in which he moved, champagne flowed as if it were water.

'If you are ready, then,' Gervase Vestey said, 'I think we should go up. The . . . "parson" is already there.'

'He is? Then we had better not leave him too long with her ladyship. She might become suspicious,' Lord Chard said. 'Now, how do we enter? Melinda upon my arm?'

'I should think that would be best,' Gervase Vestey agreed. 'The doctor said her ladyship was to speak as little as possible. He has given her some stimulant and it would be best not to tire her before the ceremony.'

'Before she signs, eh?' the Marquis asked.

He put down his glass but as he did so Melinda glanced at him and realised he had had a great deal to drink. He was not drunk, but what her father used to call jokingly, 'a trifle boskey'.

'How thankful I am that I am not his real wife,' she thought to herself, as, taking the arm he offered her, they moved across the room. Captain Vestey opened the door. They crossed the wide landing to a pair of large, mahogany doors on the other side.

'Are you ready?' Captain Vestey asked in a whisper. 'Melinda, you look charming. Do not be frightened; just repeat the words of the marriage ceremony. There is nothing else for you to do.'

Melinda did not answer but merely nodded her head. Just the tips of her fingers rested on Lord Chard's arm, but she was close enough to realise that his whole body was tense. 'This means a lot to him,' she thought, and wondered what was the size of the wager that could affect a man of his quality.

The doors were opened. The room was in shadow; the sun-blinds were drawn low over the windows. But after a few steps forward, Melinda could see quite clearly. On the left side of the room was a huge bed surmounted by a canopy. In the bed, propped up against innumerable pillows, was a very old woman. Beside her were two men; Melinda guessed one was the doctor. At the foot of the bed, waiting for them, was a parson; his surplice gleamed white in the dimness of the room.

No one spoke as they advanced, step by step, until they stood directly in front of the parson, the old woman watching them from the bed. The parson began the service in a low voice. Melinda had the idea that he, too, was tense and frightened, but she thought that if he was playing a part he played it well.

The prayers beginning the marriage service were considerably shortened but now came the crucial moment.

'Will you, Alexander Drogo Frederick John, take this woman, Melinda, for your wedded wife? To have and to hold, for richer, for poorer, in sickness and in health, until death you do part?'

The Marquis repeated the words, slowly, clearly,

and in a tone of voice that was completely expressionless. Melinda felt herself begin to tremble. It was too real, too frightening. She did not look at her but she was conscious all the time of the old woman watching from the bed, of the silence and the tension of the two men. She felt her knees tremble; felt she could not say the words—those sacred words that she had always longed to speak to someone she loved.

Almost as if he sensed what she was feeling, the Marquis suddenly reached out and took her hand and she felt the strength of his fingers through the soft lace mittens with which her own hands were covered. His clasp was warm, sustaining and somehow comforting.

'He thinks I am about to betray him, to break down,' Melinda thought, and pride came to her rescue, as it had done so often before in her life.

'. . . for richer, for poorer, in sickness and health, until death us do part . . . I plight thee my troth . . .'

Her voice was low but quite clear. She shut her eyes as she spoke, shutting out the bedroom and thinking herself, for a moment, back in the little church at home, listening to her cousin being married when she had been a bridesmaid.

The parson blessed the ring and then she felt the Marquis place it on her finger. They knelt down and he blessed them.

'Oh, God, forgive me this deception,' Melinda said. 'I am sure it is wrong, but it seemed such a little thing to do for so much money. Forgive me!'

She was still praying as she felt the Marquis help her to her feet.

'Are you all right?' he asked.

'Yes, of course,' she replied.

He turned away from her towards the bed.

'Drogo, have you forgotten?' a sharp old voice asked from the shadows.

'Forgotten what, ma'am?' the Marquis enquired.

'To kiss the bride. Surely you know that is the custom.'

'Of course, I forgot.'

The Marquis turned back to Melinda. She felt him draw her to him. If he had intended to kiss her on the mouth she circumvented him, turning her head so that his lips rested on the softness of her cheek.

'Do you call that a kiss?' the old woman chuckled from the bed. 'Men were not so weak-kneed in my day.'

'You have had your pound of flesh,' the Marquis said. 'You would not embarrass my bride at such a moment?'

'No, of course not,' the old woman said. 'Come here, girl, and let me look at you.'

'This is surely too much for you,' the Marquis said with a glance at the doctor.

'Nothing can be too much for you when you are dying,' his stepmother answered. 'Come here, Melinda, if that is your name.'

Melinda obeyed her, moving to the bedside and seeing the pale face, raddled with age and illness but still holding some semblance of beauty. The old woman looked up at her and her thin, bony hand went out to take Melinda's.

'So, you have married my stepson,' she said. 'You are a brave girl.'

Melinda made no reply, conscious that the old woman's eyes were searching her face as if she looked for something special.

Suddenly, the man who was waiting on the other side of the bed bent forward and placing a large document in front of the old woman held out a quill pen.

' 'Tis best if you sign, my lady,' he said, 'before you get too tired.'

The old woman chuckled.

'Your pound of flesh, eh, Drogo? Well, you kept your bargain and I must keep mine.'

She signed her name on the parchment. Melinda heard the Marquis, standing beside her, give an audible sigh of relief. The signature was scrawly and rather weak, but legible. As she finished, the old woman handed the man, whom Melinda now guessed to be a lawyer, the quill pen.

'Take it away,' she said. 'I have finished with the goods and chattels of this world. Let us hope I do not find myself penniless in the next!'

'Your ladyship's wishes shall be attended to in every way,' the lawyer said. 'Perhaps now I may withdraw?'

'Yes, go, go!' the old woman said. 'This is a moment for family, is it not?' She looked again at Melinda. 'You are very young. Do you think you can handle my stepson? He is a high-stepper and not yet broken to the bridle.'

'You are embarrassing us, ma'am,' the Marquis said hastily. 'Melinda is shy, and who shall blame her?'

'She will not be shy for long if she has married you,' the old woman retorted, with a touch of sarcasm in her voice. Then suddenly her face seemed to soften. 'Come nearer, child,' she said. 'There is something I wish to say to you . . . to you alone.'

Melinda bent over her, her lace veil falling forward on to the sheets as if she screened the dying woman and herself from the gaze of other people. She realised, as she did so, that the stimulant, which had been keeping the old woman going until this moment, was wearing off. She was growing weaker, drooping lower on the pillows, but she had something to say and her will-power, not yet fully extinguished, drove her on to say it.

'Be kind . . . to him,' she whispered, in a voice she, Melinda, alone, could hear. 'I . . . treated him . . . badly all . . . his life . . . Perhaps because I . . . was jealous that . . . I had no . . . son of . . . my own. He has had . . . little chance to . . . to be . . . happy. You must . . . not . . . fail . . . him.'

'No, ma'am,' Melinda replied.

There was nothing else she could say.

'Promise . . . me . . . you will . . . try.'

The voice now was very weak and Melinda could hardly hear it.

'Pro . . . mise . . . me.'

'I promise.'

The words came from her lips almost without her conscious volition of saying them, but she knew that the old woman heard. There was a sudden smile on her pale lips and then her eyes closed.

Melinda moved back from the bed and the doctor took her place.

'Her ladyship is sleeping,' he said. 'The wedding

ceremony has been a big ordeal but she was determined to go through with it.'

'Will you let me know immediately if there is any change?' the Marquis asked.

'Of course, my lord,' the doctor replied.

The Marquis held out his arm to Melinda. She looked back for one moment to the frail, white face against the pillows, so small, so old, so wasted, and yet still retaining an unquenchable personality. She felt she would have liked to have known the Dowager Marchioness before she was so ill.

The Marquis led her from the room. They moved in silence down the staircase, Gervase Vestey following, and they went into the Library at the far end of the hall. The sunshine was coming through the windows and Melinda could see that outside there was a small paved garden where a fountain was playing. It was bright with flowers and she felt the sudden contrast from the darkness of the bedroom upstairs had a poignant meaning that she should never forget. She could not put it into words, she only knew it was there.

'For God's sake give me a drink!' she heard the Marquis say to Captain Vestey.

He had moved away from her to the end of the room and she stood with her back to them both, looking out into the garden.

'A drink, Melinda?' Captain Vestey said, inviting her. 'You will not refuse one now?'

'I should like a glass of water,' Melinda said.

'Oh, you need not go on play-acting when we are alone,' the Marquis said roughly. 'It was splendid! Magnificent! But the curtain is down! What, by the way, did my stepmother say to you that was so secret that I was not allowed to hear it?'

Melinda looked at him and her voice was contemptuous as she replied:

'It was something that would not interest you. Just the last wish of a woman who is dying.'

The Marquis was very still and their eyes met. They knew that each of them was locked in a battle of wills and there was some undercurrent of emotion of which they were both well aware. It was the Marquis who looked away first.

'You are being very high-handed, are you not?' he asked in a voice which strove to be light. 'There is no need for you to pry into my private affairs just because you have undertaken a certain job—and done it exceedingly well.'

'I am certainly not prying,' Melinda said proudly.

'Now, Drogo!' Captain Vestey interposed. 'You are both on edge, and who shall blame you? It was a pretty uncomfortable show, but it is over, and I had best go and rescue Freddie and get him out of the house. I shall not bring him in here. If we all got hobnobbing, there is no knowing what might be overheard.'

'No, you are wise,' the Marquis said. 'Do not forget to pay him.'

'I have done that already,' Captain Vestey said, moving towards the door.

'I will change,' Melinda said quickly, having no desire to be left alone with the Marquis. 'Then will I be able to go?'

'Oh, no, not yet!' Captain Vestey replied. 'Did Mrs. Harcourt not explain to you that it would be best for you to stay here until the Dowager actually dies? She might want to see you, or something, and it would be very strange if you were not in the house.'

'Yes, of course,' Melinda said. 'But, it is rather horrible, is it not, just waiting?'

'It need not be horrible for you,' the Marquis said. 'After all, she is only a stranger.'

'She is still a person,' Melinda replied, 'a human being, who has been young, who has loved life but who has now come to the end of it. Whoever it is who may be dying, it is always sad and perhaps a little frightening.'

She spoke very quietly, yet somehow, even in that great room, her words were inescapable. Neither of the men said anything and then, suddenly, Gervase Vestey opened the door, passed through it and closed it behind him.

The Marquis sat down in the armchair by the fireplace.

'You are a very strange girl,' he said, and now Melinda knew he was not sneering. 'Come here, I want to talk to you.'

'I think I should go and change,' she said hastily.

'There is no hurry,' he answered. 'You look very attractive in that gown. I suppose you are well aware of that.'

Melinda looked down at her huge, lace skirts with the little bunches of orange blossom catching the satin ribbons.

'It is a very beautiful gown,' she said. 'In fact, the most beautiful gown I have ever seen.'

'You are very young,' the Marquis said, almost in surprise. 'Why do you do this sort of thing?'

Melinda thought that he was referring to her pretence of being his bride.

'I need the money,' she said simply.

'But, of course!' His tone changed. 'Money! Money! That is all that matters, is it not? For a pretty girl like you it is essential.'

Melinda said nothing and after a moment he added:

'But, why should I complain? I am very grateful to you. Ella Harcourt could not have chosen anyone to play the part better.'

'Thank you,' Melinda said. 'And, now, if you do not mind, I should like to go and change.'

'You make it very clear that you are not particularly interested in my company,' the Marquis said.

'I would not wish to appear rude,' Melinda answered. 'But as we are likely never to see each other again after this, I have a feeling it would be best for us both to forget. I shall try, although it may be difficult.'

'Forget what?' the Marquis enquired.

'What has happened,' Melinda said. 'You see, I think, really, it was wrong to have done what we have; to deceive a woman who is dying. I was told when I came here that you wished me to pretend to be a bride for a wager. I cannot conceive how a wager could involve your stepmother. I have a feeling that I may be wrong; that it was something very different.'

'Having said so much,' the Marquis said sharply, 'you might as well tell me what you do suspect.'

'I think,' Melinda continued slowly, 'that the man who looked like a lawyer had your stepmother's will, and that after she thought you were married she signed it, giving you, I suppose, a lot of money.'

'That is very perceptive of you,' the Marquis said in an ugly voice. 'And, now, what do you propose to do? Blackmail me?'

'I do not know what you mean,' Melinda answered.

'Of course you do,' he said roughly. 'What you are saying is that unless I up what you have already been promised, you will go upstairs and tell my stepmother that the marriage was a mockery, giving her the chance to revoke her will. Am I right?'

He rose as he spoke and stood there, looking tall and very formidable; the words, as he spoke, were almost spat from his lips and his eyes were dark with anger. Melinda stood very still.

'You should not judge everyone by yourself, Lord Chard,' she said, and her voice was icy. 'I think you are utterly and completely despicable and I can only hope that I may leave this house as quickly as possible and never see you again.'

She stared straight at him as she spoke and then swung round, with a flurry of her skirts, and marched resolutely towards the door.

'What the devil . . .?' the Marquis began, but his only answer was a resounding slam and the sound of Melinda's footsteps running down the marble hall.

He stood for a long moment looking at the door and then he went to the grog-tray and poured himself out a large brandy. When Captain Vestey returned, a few minutes later, he found him glowering at the glass as if it held poison.

'Melinda gone to change?' he asked conversationally.

'Where the hell did you pick up that girl?' the Marquis enquired.

'At Kate's; I told you,' Captain Vestey replied. 'I must say she is fantastic! Looks like a regular aristocrat. I swear no one could tell the difference. In fact, I was thinking to myself that she must be a love-child. There's blue blood in her somewhere.'

'I just do not understand it,' the Marquis said. 'She started to tick me off good and proper. I thought she meant blackmail, but it seems I was an out-and-outer even to think of such a thing.'

'Well, I must say,' Captain Vestey said, 'that you have made yourself pretty unpleasant ever since she arrived. I know you have been on edge, but those sort of women like a bit of blarney and kiss-your-hand; no one should know that better than you.'

'She didn't seem the type for it somehow,' the Marquis replied.

'Oh, don't worry,' Captain Vestey said. 'She's a nice little thing, and if she tries any tricks Kate will deal with her.'

'Yes, I suppose she will,' the Marquis agreed, but his tone was uneasy.

'Don't look so miserable,' Captain Vestey replied. 'Cheer up! The whole thing's done and once again you have pulled off the impossible. You have a genius for it, Drogo!'

There was a moment's silence and then the Marquis said:

'You may not believe it but that chit of a girl has made me feel damned uncomfortable. Dammit! I feel like a cad. Something I have not felt since I was caught cheating at Eton.'

Captain Vestey stared at him.

'This is not like you, Drogo. If you are getting a fit of conscience over deceiving the Dowager, just remember how she has cracked the whip over you all your life. Cut your allowance; made you sell your horses to pay up your debts; put you in a bad light with the old man. I would not have believed half the tales you told me about her if I hadn't seen the things for myself. I used to hate the times you asked me down to Chard. She made me feel so uncomfortable; always flicking you on the raw.'

'I know,' the Marquis said. 'But now she is dying I suppose I ought not to have deceived her.'

'Just because people are dying it doesn't make them into saints,' Captain Vestey said. 'She is just as venomous as she has ever been, and I bet you that if she recovers she'll be round tomorrow, revoking that will and keeping you on the hop for another twenty years.'

The Marquis said nothing, sitting, still glowering at his glass of brandy which he had not touched.

'Oh, cheer up!' Captain Vestey said. 'I cannot think what that little wench could have said to you to upset you like this. Do not forget that your step-mother did exactly the same when your father was dying; got him to sign a will at the last moment, leaving all the money to her. He was gaga, or too weak to say no. It is fair retribution! And if you had not done it, Chard would have been up for sale and that would have been a fine help to all the old retainers, the tenants and all the people who have worked there for generations.'

'It would have meant that Chard would have to go,' the Marquis said quietly.

'Then what are you worrying about?' Captain Vestey asked. 'The method may be a bit questionable, but the motive was right. That is all that matters. Now, let us hope we do not have to sit about here for too long. Then we can pack the little pigeon back to the roost and go off abroad for a few months. Paris might be rather fun! What do you say? Do you remember Desirée? God, that was a party!'

'The sooner she is out of the house, the better,' the Marquis said.

'Who are you talking about?' Captain Vestey enquired.

'That girl,' the Marquis replied. 'Kate is welcome to her, the little spitfire! At the same time, she didn't want any more money. I don't understand it!'

6

Dinner was an uncomfortable meal. Melinda was conscious all the time of the Dowager Marchioness upstairs. Her thoughts kept going back to the dying woman and she found it was difficult to follow the conversation.

The Marquis was obviously in a bad mood and waved away the majority of the rich, exotic dishes served on crested silver plates. His crystal cut glass embossed with the Chard crest was filled and refilled frequently by one of the liveried servants.

Captain Vestey did his best to enthuse an air of gaiety. He talked to the Marquis but tried to include Melinda, even explaining to her who the people were of whom they spoke, and giving her a description of the places they had visited. Once or twice he made her laugh, but she was conscious all the time of the cynical expression on the face of her host, and the fact that he remained gloomy and unamused.

After a time Captain Vestey also fell silent as the flunkeys brought round the Sèvres china dishes filled with huge peaches, purple muscat grapes and green figs.

'Do these come from the gardens at Chard?' he asked finally, to break the embarrassing silence.

'Of course,' the Marquis replied sharply. 'You don't suppose I should eat the rubbish that is on sale in the shops, do you?'

There seemed to be no answer to this and again there was silence. Then Captain Vestey said:

'Look, Drogo, we can't sit about here sunk in gloom. Why don't we go to Sebastian's party? It's not a big affair, and the people there are not likely to know whether your stepmother is in good health or not.'

'It would be bad form,' the Marquis protested.

'I suppose so,' Captain Vestey agreed. 'But who is to know? Besides it will entertain Melinda. She must be bored to distraction at hearing us carp away at each other.'

The Marquis raised his eyebrows.

'You are thinking of taking Melinda?' he said, speaking almost as if she were not present.

'Why not?' Captain Vestey asked. 'I daresay she'll meet some of her friends.'

'I have no friends in London,' Melinda interposed quickly.

'Then it is about time you made some,' Captain Vestey replied, determined not to be repressed.

'Very well then,' the Marquis said, getting up from his chair. 'We will go at once.'

Melinda rose slowly to her feet. As she did so she heard the butler say in almost shocked tones:

'The port, m'lord! You will not be partaking of any port?'

'No, I require nothing more,' the Marquis said, as if he were making an important decision.

Melinda could not help smiling at the butler's face as she left the room followed by the two gentlemen. Protocol had been outraged. She had not withdrawn, as was the custom, to the Salon, and the gentlemen had not sat on in the dining-room imbibing their port.

As they reached the hall, Captain Vestey said to her:

'You will need a wrap.'

'Of course,' Melinda said. 'I will go upstairs and get one.'

She ran up to her bedroom, thinking how strange her life had suddenly become. She had expected that this evening she would be in some cheap lodging-house, eating a meagre meal with the other boarders and wondering how long the precious sovereigns she had taken from her aunt's *secretaire* would last her.

Instead, she had been dined in a style which made even Sir Hector's most formal parties seem second-rate and insignificant. The food had been superlative.

'The Marquis must be very rich,' Melinda thought, and the last nagging sense of guilt at having spent so much of his money seemed to fade away.

She wondered if it was his conscience or just disagreeableness which made him avoid meeting her eyes, and talk as if she were not there, and to have appeared quite unnecessarily reluctant that she should accompany them to the party. Perhaps, she told herself, he was thinking of her reputation, but she doubted it. And, after all, in this strange city where she knew no one, there was no reason for her, or anyone else, to be concerned if what she did was unconventional.

She gave a little grimace at herself in the mirror.

'Fine feathers make fine birds!' she said aloud. 'At the same time, as Nanna always said—there is "a rub". Nothing is quite perfect.'

The rub, she knew, was the Marquis's behaviour. She could not quite explain it to herself. It was something she had never encountered before in any man she had met. It was as if he despised her and, at the same time, was almost antagonistic. She could not fathom the reason for such an attitude.

Anyway, she asked herself ferociously, what did it matter? She had five hundred pounds. For a year or two, at least, she and Nanna could live together without worrying. It was a wicked thought, she knew, to wish that the poor lady for whom she had gone through the pretence of marriage with the Marquis, would not linger long. At the same time, she had a longing to be free of this house; to disappear into the darkness outside and know that she never need see Lord Chard again.

She realised with a start that she had been quite a long time staring at herself in the mirror. She had not seen the grace and beauty of her new gown, which accentuated the outlines of her young figure, nor the elegant style in which one of the maids had done her hair, but only the worry in her eyes which, at the moment, were two dark pools of conflict in which one expression chased another.

'Free! I must be free!' she whispered aloud, and then wondered at her choice of words.

She had escaped from her uncle; he would certainly not expect to seek for her in Grosvenor Square. She had escaped from a repulsive marriage with Colonel Gillingham. Now, by sheer good fortune she had earned a large sum of money. In a few hours she would be on her way to Sussex and the comfort and security of Nanna's arms.

As she thought of it a smile came to her lips, and taking a wrap from the wardrobe she ran downstairs as gaily as any other young girl going to her first party. It was only when she reached the hall that she realised the wrap of pale blue velvet was lined with ermine. She guessed that it had been one of Mrs. Harcourt's more outrageous extravagances.

It was Captain Vestey who took the wrap from her and placed it around her shoulders.

'You look very lovely!' he said.

'I do?' Melinda's surprise was quite genuine and she blushed a little as Captain Vestey replied:

'Surely you have seen your reflection in your mirror. I am sure that in this house it has never framed a more exquisite image.'

'Thank you,' Melinda said gently. She looked down and her dark eyelashes swept her cheeks.

It was delightful to be paid compliments for the first time in her life. At the same time, she had the feeling that they were just a little too fulsome, a little too familiar. She was splitting straws, and yet the disquiet was there.

'The carriage is at the door, m'lord!'

The butler's stentorian voice relieved her of saying any more and she moved across the red carpet which was stretched across the pavement and into the soft, cushioned interior of the very elegant closed carriage. She saw it was drawn by two grey horses with black plumes nodding high from their foreheads. She only had a glimpse of them as the Marquis sat down beside her and Captain Vestey opposite, but she exclaimed impulsively:

'What beautiful horses you have! Could I visit your stables tomorrow? That is, if I haven't left!'

'Yes, of course,' the Marquis replied. 'Can you ride?'

'I have ridden since I was three years old,' Melinda answered.

'Then we'll have to take you in the Row,' the Marquis said. 'All the pretty little horse-breakers gather at the Achilles statue, as I expect you are well aware.'

Melinda looked puzzled. She did not know what he meant by 'horse-breakers'. She imagined it must be the slang term for someone who rode well.

'I should like, above all things, to ride one of your horses,' she said.

'Then that is agreed,' Captain Vestey interposed. 'We will take you riding, Melinda, and if you look as smart on a horse as you do in that dinner-gown you'll knock them all down like a bunch of skittles.'

He gave a side-glance at the Marquis as he spoke.

'Not very funny, Gervase,' his lordship said in a crushing tone.

'I thought it was rather neat myself,' Captain Vestey said. He turned to Melinda. 'I suppose you have heard of the famous "Skittles"?'

'You mean the game?' Melinda asked.

Captain Vestey laughed.

'No, I mean the lady. She's known as "Skittles" because she once told a number of Guards Officers that she would knock them all down like a lot of er . . . dashed skittles if they didn't do what she wanted.'

Melinda tried to look interested.

'And what is the lady's real name?' she asked.

'Now, really!' the Marquis interjected. 'You cannot expect us to believe that you have never heard of Caroline Walters or that she's known as "Skittles".'

'No, I have never heard of her,' Melinda answered.

In the light which flashed on their windows as they passed she could see a look of incredulity on the Marquis's face.

'You know,' he said disagreeably, 'I have come to the conclusion that you really are the most consummate lair!'

His tone, rather than his words, made Melinda stiffen and her chin go up.

'I cannot conceive, my lord,' she said formally,

'why you should speak to me in such a manner. But, I assure you that I am telling the truth. I have never heard of this Miss Caroline Walters, either by her real name or by the one by which, apparently, she is habitually referred to.'

She glared at the Marquis as she spoke. He was apparently quite unrepentant and leaned back against the cushions in the corner of the carriage, that detested smile on his lips.

'I say! Hold on, Drogo!' Captain Vestey interposed. 'You're being a bit bearish, aren't you? If Melinda says she doesn't know "Skittles", why on earth should she be lying?'

'All part of the act,' the Marquis said. 'I just dislike being taken for a greenhorn. I can't be expected to swallow everything, however ingenuously presented.'

'I cannot imagine why you should think I would stoop to lie,' Melinda said, 'and I very much dislike being called a liar.'

'Of course you do,' Captain Vestey said soothingly. 'Come on, Drogo! Apologise! You are in the wrong, and you know it.'

'If Melinda, indeed, is telling the truth,' the Marquis said, 'then all I can say is she must be phenomenal. For how on earth could she be here, in the position she is at this moment, and not have heard of "Skittles"?'

'Oh, do be quiet, Drogo,' Captain Vestey pleaded. 'What does it matter one way or the other? Melinda says she has not heard of "Skittles", but now she is unlikely to forget her. To even things up we'll introduce the ladies.'

'And then, perhaps,' the Marquis said, 'we shall find out whether "Skittles" has ever heard of Melinda!'

'Of course, she will not have heard of me,' Melinda said. 'Why should she? I wish I knew what all this was about. I think perhaps it would be better if I did not come to the party. Please let the carriage take me back to your house.'

'No! No!' the Marquis exclaimed. 'Now I suspect that you are frightened of being confronted with the lady of whom you disclaim all knowledge. How awkward for you if she greets you with open arms.'

'So you think I am running away?' Melinda asked.

'Aren't you?' he enquired.

She shook her head.

'Of course, we believe you,' Captain Vestey interjected soothingly.

'I do not understand what all this is about,' Melinda said.

'Neither do I,' the Marquis said, his voice almost too loud.

Melinda gave a little sigh. She could only hope that she would not have to be long in the Marquis's company. She was beginning to find him exceedingly exasperating.

Fortunately, the drive to where the party was taking place was not far. There was awning over a brightly lit doorway and then Melinda found herself in the hall of what was obviously a wealthy and luxurious mansion. She felt relieved. She had been afraid, somehow, that the Marquis and Captain Vestey were taking her to some night haunt of which she had heard very disreputable reports. It was inconceivable, of course, that they should have even thought of such a thing. But she had come to the conclusion that they were very strange young men, not at all like those she had met, either at home with her father and mother, or at her uncle's house, and she had begun to suspect that what she would consider outrageous, they would consider quite commonplace behaviour.

The house they were in now was obviously a gentleman's mansion and Melinda was led across the marble hall lit with silver sconces each holding a dozen candles. The butler opened the double mahogany doors and she walked first into what she immediately realised was the dining-room.

It was an enormous, long room stretching the whole length of the back of the house and round the table must have been seated at least thirty guests. It was brilliantly lit with silver candelabra on the table and huge chandeliers hanging from the ceiling. She saw that the guests had already finished dinner and only the dessert bowls were left on the table.

'Chard, it's good to see you!'

There was a big bellow from the end of the table. A young man, red-faced, whose collar had already crumpled a little in the heat, came running towards them with outstretched arms.

'It's fine that you could come. You've eaten, I suppose? Well, have some port. The little lady would like some champagne, I suspect.'

Without waiting for an introduction, which Melinda thought strange, he took her hand and led her to the top of the table.

'Move up, Arthur,' he said to one of the guests,

and signalled the servants to bring three chairs.

It was rather a crush but somehow they got round the table. Glasses were put in front of them and the wine was poured out.

Melinda looked about her curiously. The first thing she realised was that there was a tremendous noise—in fact she had never known such a noisy party. Voices almost completely silenced the music which was coming from a number of musicians playing in an alcove at the far end of the room.

Then Melinda looked at the women and had a shock. She had known that living as she had always done, in the country, she must be out-of-date, both with the fashion and with her knowledge of smart society. But she had not expected that ladies should look so *outré* or that they would use cosmetics so obviously. Their bright pink cheeks, mascara'd eye lashes, crimson mouths, had almost a grotesque appearance and she thought, too, with a slight sense of embarrassment, that never before had she seen such low décolletage.

There were shrieks of laughter and then, suddenly, amidst cheers of a small company of men, a lady and a gentleman rose from their seats. The other guests were betting on what they were about to do. Taking his dessert plate from the table, the gentleman balanced it on his head. There was suddenly a hush, then the lady, raising her skirts, kicked up her leg. She missed the plate and there was a roar of laughter and encouragement.

'Again! Try again! Three to one she misses!' But the second time she was successful. The tip of her slipper sent the china plate spinning across the room, where it hit a wall and broke.

'Hurrah! Do it again, Dora! I bet twenty guineas on her missing at the first attempt.'

Melinda felt herself blush. Never in her wildest dreams had she thought to see a lady make such a spectacle of herself—and at a dinner party. The gentlemen were shouting and standing up to see better. Dora was flushed, and the already low décolletage of her lace-trimmed bodice had slipped even lower. When she kicked she revealed not only her legs, but the frilly undergarments she wore beneath her petticoats.

Melinda shut her eyes. She felt the humiliation must be borne not only by the woman herself, but by every other woman at the table. And then, missing again, Dora collapsed on to a chair amid shouts of disappointment.

'I can't . . . get . . . me . . . breath,' she gasped. ' 'Ere . . . give me . . . a drink . . . someone.'

There was no doubting the commonness of her voice; and now, at last, Melinda realised with a sense of dismay that this was not the type of party at which she should be present.

She was wondering what she could do about it when their host, who had been cheering with the rest, shouted:

'Come on, let's dance! Dora can have another try later.'

Innumerable servants hurried forward to remove the table. The chairs were pushed back and, as everyone rose, so did Melinda. It was then that she heard the Marquis say:

'Skittles, I don't think you have met Melinda Stanyon! A newcomer, I understand, to the sister-fold.'

Melinda turned round. Facing her was a very lovely young woman. She was dressed with extreme elegance and there was nothing bold or vulgar about her appearance. Her fair hair was parted in the middle and arranged in curls on either side of her almost classically beautiful face. Melinda stretched out her hand but without even looking at her, Skittles smiled up at the Marquis.

'Where the hell have you been, my young buck?' she asked. 'It's been a bloody sight too long since I've seen you.'

Melinda felt herself recoil as if a snake had suddenly appeared at her feet. Never had she expected to hear such language from a lady. But Skittles had not finished. She chattered on, using an oath in every sentence that she spoke, and there was no mistaking the fact that she was determined to fascinate the Marquis. One of her hands, with its long, white fingers, was holding on to the satin lapel of his evening coat; her head was thrown back to reveal the long, white column of her neck and her blue eyes, seductive and beguiling, were looking up into his.

Melinda stared at them and then, as her presence was ignored, she moved away and managed to slip out through the door and into the hall. There was no one about. The servants were all busy, moving the dining-room table, and she opened a door to find herself in a charming little drawing-room with pale blue brocade curtains, an Aubusson carpet and some delicate French furniture. The whole room had an air of serenity and peace about it.

Melinda sat down in a chair and tried to think what had happened. She realised now that this was not the sort of party to which a lady would be invited. She could imagine her mother's horror at the woman who showed her legs and at the coarseness of Skittles' oaths.

This was a masculine party! Then why, oh why, had the Marquis and Captain Vestey brought her? With a little sigh, she thought it must be because she was of no consequence. Just as her Uncle Hector had treated her as the poor relation, as someone to be ordered about, who must have no opinions of her own; so, because they had hired her, the Marquis and Captain Vestey thought of her in the same way.

She could understand it. At the same time she felt utterly humiliated. She ought not to have agreed to play such a part, she told herself. She had shut her eyes to the fact that no decent lady would accept clothes from a man. But, then, no decent lady was, as a rule, whipped like a dog and forced to run away to seek her own living, with nothing between her and penury but a few stolen guineas.

She saw herself only too clearly, so obscure, so unimportant, that people could consider her as nothing but a servant commanded to obey.

The door opened and she started to her feet. A gentleman entered. He had a cigar in his hand. When he saw Melinda he looked surprised.

'Oh, I hope I am not disturbing you,' he asked. 'I came in here to get a light.'

She did not answer and he went on:

'Are you waiting for someone, or just bored with the party?'

'I . . . I have a . . . headache,' Melinda said quickly.

'Terribly tiresome thing to have,' the man said. 'Often have them myself. They always come on at the most inconvenient time. As Skittles said to me last week: "Your headaches are a damned nuisance! The sooner you get over them, the better." Made me feel as if I was back at school and being cursed by matron for having a temperature.'

'Yes, they are a nuisance,' Melinda said.

'Look, I don't want to disturb you,' the gentleman went on. 'You sit down. I'll tell you what. I won't light my cigar—might make you worse.'

'I would not like to put you to any inconvenience,' Melinda said.

'No inconvenience at all,' was the reply. 'Here, I'd better introduce myself. My name is Hartington.'

'The Marquis of Hartington?' Melinda asked. 'I seem to have heard of you.'

He grinned at her.

'Most people have! But only because the newspapers are always writing me up as being fond of a game of Skittles!'

He threw back his head and laughed.

'Do you see the joke? And they can get away with it. It's libel but I can't sue them.'

'You will find Miss Skittles in the dining-room,' Melinda said primly.

'Oh, she's here already, is she?' Lord Hartington asked. 'Told me she wouldn't be along until after eleven. Who's she with?'

'I did not see her with anyone, except that she was talking to Lord Chard when I left,' Melinda said.

Lord Hartington's good-humoured face seemed to darken.

'Chard! Perfect damned nuisance, that fellow! I begin to think Skittles rather fancies him. Do you think he's keen on her?'

'I . . . I do not know,' Melinda replied.

'Well, if he is, I'll slit his throat,' Lord Hartington said in a genial tone which seemed to belie his bloodthirsty words. Then he sighed. 'Have you ever been in love?'

Melinda shook her head.

'Then, don't be,' he said. 'Deuced uncomfortable thing to be in, I can tell you that. You like it and you hate it, if you know what I mean. You're happy and you're miserable. My advice is, leave it alone; that is if you can.'

'I shall certainly try,' Melinda said.

'You haven't got a chance,' Lord Hartington said, looking at her as if for the first time. 'You are too pretty. Men will fall in love with you and sooner or later you will fall in love with one of them. I am sorry for you, but there is no way out.'

'I shall try my best not to fall in love,' Melinda told him.

'And I shall do my best to fall out of it,' Lord Hartington laughed. 'Here, give me your hand. That is a bargain! Do you agree?'

'It is a bargain,' Melinda smiled.

He took her hand and raised it to his lips. He was awkward—almost ungainly—and yet there was a sincerity about him which she could not help liking.

As he kissed her hand Lord Chard came into the room.

'So, this is where you are hiding!' His voice was unpleasant. 'I am sorry the party was not to your liking.'

Melinda drew her hand away from Lord Hartington, feeling, for some unknown reason, almost guilty.

'I had a headache,' she said.

'So I see,' Lord Chard replied. 'Good evening, Hartington! Skittles is waiting for you inside; at least, that is what I understood.'

'Waiting for me!' Lord Hartington's face seemed to light up. 'I must go to her at once.'

He turned to Melinda.

'Goodbye, my dear! Don't forget our bargain.'

'I shall remember,' Melinda promised.

He went out of the room. The door shut with a little bang behind him. Melinda looked at Lord Chard. It seemed to her that he deliberately avoided her eyes. He walked across the room to the mantelpiece, to stand looking down into the fire.

'I wondered why you had left the dining-room,' he said.

She thought to tell him the truth, then changed her mind.

'It was rather hot and stifling in there,' she said instead.

'And you had the good fortune to find Lord Hartington,' Lord Chard said in a disagreeable tone. 'Was it a prearranged assignation?'

'No, of course not,' Melinda replied. 'I had never met him before tonight. He came into the room for a light for his cigar and found me sitting here.'

'And that,' the Marquis said in a particularly unpleasant voice, 'was when you made your little bargain, was it? Would it be indiscreet of me to ask the terms of your bargain or what it entails?'

Melinda felt her anger rise. How dare he speak to her in such a tone? And what did he suspect she had been about? Making an assignation, indeed! He might have bought her services but he had certainly not bought her body and soul!

'I think, my lord,' she said, trying to make her voice as cold and unpleasant as his, 'that my bargain, as you call it, with Lord Hartington, is none of your business.'

'I am glad to hear that,' the Marquis replied equally disagreeably. 'It would have been unfortunate, to say the least of it, if you had not terminated your commitments with me before entering into other arrangements with someone else.'

'I hope, my lord, that I know how to behave properly and decently,' Melinda said. 'And I am not in the habit of breaking my word to anyone, whoever they may be.'

There was no mistaking the anger in her voice now as she stared defiantly at the Marquis. Their eyes met, like duellists facing each other; both tense, waiting to strike. For a moment they sparred silently and, then, unexpectedly, the Marquis capitulated.

'What does it matter?' he asked. 'Tomorrow this ridiculous farce will be over and you will be free.'

'I am only hoping it will be tomorrow,' Melinda said, equally decisively, and wondered, once again, if it was wrong to wish for another person's death.

'And, now, until this moment of delicious freedom arrives, how shall I amuse you?' the Marquis asked. 'Shall I take you to the Cremorne, or Motts? Or would you prefer another escort? I daresay it could be arranged without much difficulty.'

'If you do not mind, my lord, I would very much like to go to bed,' Melinda answered. 'I am afraid I am not in the right mood for parties or places of pleasure.'

'Do you know, it is the most extraordinary thing,' the Marquis said in a very different voice, 'but when we were in the dining-room and that woman was kicking her legs about, I fancied that you looked shocked. Was it just another piece of superb acting?'

'Are you really interested?' Melinda asked. 'You have paid me to do a certain job. What my feelings might be in the matter of this, or anything else, is of no consequence.'

'I just want to know,' the Marquis persisted. 'Were you shocked?'

'Yes, I was,' Melinda replied positively.

'But, why . . .?' he began, only to be interrupted as Captain Vestey came into the room.

'Oh, there you are, Drogo!' he said. 'I wondered what on earth had happened to you both. It's getting pretty noisy in there. I think, honestly, it is a mistake for you to be seen in such company at this particular moment.'

'As a matter of fact,' the Marquis replied, 'I was not thinking so much of myself but of Melinda.'

'Yes, of course,' Captain Vestey said quickly, in a voice which showed all too clearly that he had not thought of Melinda until that moment. 'Then let us all go home, or do you want to go on somewhere? I do think, Drogo . . .'

'All right! All right! Spare me the sermonising,'

the Marquis said. 'I agree, we should not have come in the first place. We will go back and find out what the position is.'

They drove back in silence. In fact, it was a silence so oppressive that Melinda wondered whether it was her fault that the excitement and interest in the evening had been dispersed so rapidly. But when they reached Grosvenor Square she felt, in fact, it had been a premonition of what awaited them.

'The doctor was asking for your lordship,' the butler said. 'Her ladyship passed away some twenty minutes ago. I have sent for Mr. Smithers; I thought that was what your lordship would wish.'

'Yes, of course,' the Marquis said.

Without a glance at either Captain Vestey or Melinda he walked up the stairway, slowly and purposefully.

'I have put some drinks and sandwiches, my lady, in the small Salon,' the butler said.

Melinda started at hearing the way she was addressed. Then, with an effort, she managed to say: 'Thank you,' and followed the butler as he opened the door into the room.

There was a fire burning in the grate and, instinctively, Melinda went towards it. She felt suddenly cold and, although she could not explain it to herself, a little afraid. Now the moment had come! It was still startling, still frightening, although it had been expected. Death was so final, she thought, and wondered if, in fact, the Marquis was as elated as he had expected to be.

'Let me give you a drink,' Captain Vestey said.

Melinda shook her head.

'No, thank you!'

'A little champagne?' he insisted. 'You look pale. A pâté sandwich will make you feel better.'

'I want nothing to eat, thank you,' Melinda said. 'A glass of lemonade would be nice.'

'I am afraid it was a bit rough tonight,' Captain Vestey said as he poured out the lemonade. 'I always hate it when people break things, don't you? I suppose it is my Scottish blood. My mother came from a Scottish family, and I hate to see nice things smashed. Those china dishes were worth a fortune!'

Melinda realised that quite a lot of things must have happened after she left the dining-room. Instead of replying, she said:

'Why does Sebastian, or whatever our host's name was, give those sort of parties?'

'I suppose you have never met him before?' Captain Vestey said. 'Sebastian Hedley is in bad shape. His wife is in a lunatic asylum. He cannot be rid of her and he hasn't an heir or any chance of having one. So the only thing that amuses him is to give rough and rather noisy parties.'

'It sounds rather sad,' Melinda said.

'I suppose, in a way, it is,' Captain Vestey agreed. 'But sometimes the parties are fun. Tonight things went too far; at least, I thought so.'

They heard footsteps in the hall. Captain Vestey opened the door a crack and peeped through it.

'Old Smithers arriving,' he said.

'Who is he?' Melinda enquired.

'The lawyer,' Captain Vestey replied. 'Didn't you notice him at the ceremony?'

'Oh, yes, of course! The man who gave the Marchioness the will to sign.'

'That's the one,' Captain Vestey said. 'Well, I hope he has brought the will with him. Once Drogo knows that everything is all right, we can all relax.'

Melinda had a sudden thought.

'Will he want me to leave tonight?'

Captain Vestey smiled at her.

'No, of course not! Drogo's not inhuman. You have seen him at his very worst; all on edge. He has hated all this, you know. I mean, it's not the sort of thing anyone decent does. But we had to save the family fortunes somehow. You couldn't believe that the woman would be so insane as to want to leave it to a cats' home.'

'I . . . I did not know there were homes for cats,' Melinda said.

'Neither did I,' Captain V stey agreed, 'but I suppose she would have founded one, or something. Dammit all! With two or three million pounds you could found a whole colony for them.'

'Well, now it is all right,' Melinda said with relief.

'Thanks to you,' Captain Vestey answered. 'You have been absolutely magnificent. I cannot think of any other woman who could have done it so well.'

'Thank you,' Melinda replied. 'But it was not so difficult. I was only frightened I should let you both down.'

'Well, you didn't,' Captain Vestey said. 'And I think Drogo ought to be jolly grateful to you. In fact, I know he is, even if he doesn't say so.'

'I do not want his gratitude,' Melinda said. 'I just want to get away. I shall stay tonight and leave very early in the morning. Will you arrange that?'

'Yes, of course,' Captain Vestey said. 'Don't worry! You'll be going back to Kate, of course?'

Melinda was just going to ask him who Kate was, when the door opened. The Marquis stood there. As she looked at his face, almost instinctively she rose to her feet. Something was wrong! Very, very wrong!

The Marquis shut the door behind him, unnaturally quietly. Then he advanced into the centre of the room.

'Drogo! What has happened?'

Captain Vestey's question seemed to echo round the walls. For a moment the Marquis did not reply, and then he said:

'She has not finished with me yet! She has even reached out from beyond the grave to strangle me; to keep me subservient; as she has kept me all these years!'

'Why? What has she done?' Captain Vestey asked. 'You have got the money, surely?'

'Yes, I have got the money,' the Marquis replied. 'But there is a condition attached!'

'Condition! What do you mean?' his friend enquired. 'Surely you were to receive it if you were married?'

'If I am married,' the Marquis echoed. 'And if my wife is still living with me six months from the wedding day!'

7

For a moment there was a stupefied silence. Then Captain Vestey exclaimed:

'It's unfair! It's unjust! One could not imagine that anyone could do such a thing.'

'The point is, what can I do about it?' the Marquis asked bitterly.

'That is obvious, I should have thought,' Captain Vestey answered. 'You must go on as you are. After all, six months is not a very long time.'

'And do you imagine we could keep the story of my marriage secret?' the Marquis asked.

'Who knows about it at the moment?' Captain Vestey enquired. 'Only the servants, and they would be too loyal to talk. There is Smithers, of course! But surely he will realise that it would not be to your advantage to have it known that you contracted a secret marriage on the very day of the Dowager's death? He will see, or he can be persuaded to see, that the best thing for the family honour would be for you to announce that your marriage had taken place quietly—when you are out of mourning.'

'In six months' time,' the Marquis said.

'Exactly!'

'It's an idea,' the Marquis agreed, 'although I can see there may be many snags.'

'I cannot really see why you need worry,' Captain Vestey assured him. 'No one will expect you to appear in Society for at least six months. You can go to

Chard. The servants there can either be sworn to secrecy or, better still, Melinda can go as herself. A lady staying in the house with you will not, I think, be an unfamiliar situation!'

'There is one thing you have forgotten,' Melinda interrupted in a quiet voice.

Because she had not spoken until now, both men turned to look at her in surprise.

'Forgotten?' the Marquis enquired.

'Yes,' Melinda replied. 'I am not prepared to go on with this farce.'

'You are not prepared!' the Marquis almost spluttered. Then he stared at her, his eyes dark with anger. 'I see!' he said slowly, after a little pause. 'The delicacy of the situation has not been lost on you, Miss Stanyon. You have realised that you are in a key position and that, quite obviously, I cannot do without you. Very well! What is your price?'

'My . . . price?' Melinda asked.

'Yes, yes, do not let us pretend,' the Marquis replied sharply. 'You are a very fortunate young woman, are you not? You hold me in the hollow of your hand and you are not going to let me forget it. Let us cut all the pretences, the simperings and the girlish giggles, and get down to business. What do you want?'

'I . . . I do not . . . want . . . anything,' Melinda stammered. 'I just . . . want to . . . leave here.'

'Do you expect me to believe that?' the Marquis enquired, his eyes narrowing.

'I am trying to make myself very plain,' Melinda replied. 'I have done what was required of me. You promised me five hundred guineas. If it is not inconvenient, I should like the money as soon as possible tomorrow morning, and then I can leave.'

'And then you can leave!' the Marquis repeated. 'Was there ever a worse trap that a man might walk into unawares? You have got me completely in your power, haven't you? Well, as I have already said, name your price. What do you expect? A thousand? Two thousand? Five thousand? It does not really matter. You know, as I know, that I have to pay it.'

Melinda rose to her feet, her wide skirts billowing around her. Her face was very pale and her small fingers were twisting together.

'I must be very . . . foolish,' she said, 'because I cannot . . . make myself understood. It is nothing to do with money. I just wish to leave—to receive the money I have already earned and go away.'

'I heard you,' the Marquis said. 'But, surely, foolish though you may be, you must realise that is the one thing you cannot do; for at the end of six months I have to produce you as my wife.'

'Perhaps,' Melinda suggested, 'I could come back at the end of six months.'

'Do you suppose that someone would not have informed on me in the meantime?' the Marquis asked. His voice was harsh and it was obvious that he was making a tremendous effort to keep his temper in check.

'I am sorry,' Melinda said, 'but I cannot stay.'

She looked round the room wildly. She had a feeling that the walls were closing in on her, keeping her prisoner. She had a sudden vision of the party they had just left. If that was the sort of society she would have to endure for six months, then she could not bear it. She had not been aware that noblemen had such strange friends. She still did not quite understand what she had seen or what had been happening, but she knew that it was wrong and bad; and, exhausted from all she had been through in the last two days, she felt that she could bear no more.

'I am . . . sorry,' she repeated, 'but I . . . must go.'

'Listen, Melinda,' Captain Vestey interposed. 'You cannot do that to poor Drogo! Can you understand that it would cost him at least two million pounds? It sounds incredible, but that is the truth.'

'Why could you not have properly married some girl whom you knew and liked?' Melinda asked plaintively.

'Do you want the truth?' the Marquis asked sharply. 'It is because I loathe and detest all women. I have no desire to be married.'

'I can understand that, in a way,' Melinda said, thinking of Colonel Gillingham. 'But I cannot stay with you for six months, you must see that.'

'And why not?' the Marquis asked. 'What other arrangements have you made?'

'I . . . I had planned . . .' Melinda began, her thoughts on Nanna.

'It's Hartington, isn't it?' the Marquis interrupted. 'Well, what has he offered to give you? Whatever it is, I'll double it, treble it, if you like. A house? A carriage? Jewellery? Horses? Well, you'll have to make do with my horses for six months, but after that you will have the best pair that Tattersalls can provide for his lordship.'

'It is nothing to do with Lord Hartington,' Melinda protested in a tired voice. 'He is in love with the lady you call Skittles. He advised me not to fall in love, and I assured him that I had no intention of doing so.'

'That is obvious,' the Marquis said, 'for you have no heart. If you had the slightest touch of compassion in you, you would understand my plight and pity me.'

Melinda could not help smiling. There was something absurd in the idea of Melinda Stanyon, penniless and a nobody, pitying the powerful Lord Chard. Then, as she remembered how powerful he was, she felt afraid.

'Please, please, let me go,' she pleaded.

'But, you can't,' Captain Vestey exclaimed. 'You must see that, Melinda. Drogo will do anything you want—give you anything you ask of him. You will be a rich woman. Surely that means something.'

'I only wanted the five hundred guineas you promised me,' Melinda said. 'That was enough.'

The Marquis made a gesture of ill temper.

'You cannot expect me to believe that,' he snapped. 'What is five hundred guineas to a woman like you? Why, you would spend it on gowns in a month, if not sooner! How can you possibly prefer the life that you are leading now to what I can offer you? You will be your own mistress; you can bestow your favours where you wish; you will have no one to order you about. You can be comfortable, luxurious, even of importance in your own world. And you can entertain. Doesn't all that attract you?'

Melinda shook her head. She was thinking of the little cottage she planned to have in the country with Nanna. The party they had just left passed before her eyes with something like horror. People like that should never be entertained in her house.

'My God! What can I do?' the Marquis asked of Gervase Vestey in despair. 'Had it been any other woman but this one, she would have jumped at it. Rosie, Laura, Iolanthe, or even Skittles. What's she got at the back of her mind? Is she under someone else's protection?'

'Not that I know of,' Captain Vestey said. 'You must admit it was all done in rather a rush.'

He glanced at Melinda as he spoke and saw that, despite the drama of the situation, her eyes were dropped and she was half asleep. He looked at her for a moment and then said:

'I had best go, Drogo. You can see me to the door. Good night, Melinda!'

'Good night,' she answered.

'I shall be back in the morning,' Captain Vestey told her, 'to take you anywhere you wish to go, if by that time you have not changed your mind.'

'I shall not do that,' Melinda promised him.

Gervase Vestey walked towards the door and with a little jerk of his head beckoned the Marquis to follow. In the hall he said in a low voice:

'You've tried bullying her and it hasn't worked. Why not try your charms? They have never failed in the past to get you what you want. You're a good-looking fellow, Drogo.'

'I feel more like slapping the little idiot,' the Marquis said darkly.

'She's pretty enough,' Captain Vestey said. 'And we've always known that you are irresistible to the fair sex.'

'Oh, shut up!' the Marquis said crossly. 'But perhaps you're right. I'll try to appeal to her better nature. But I don't understand it! Why should one of Kate's "soiled doves" turn down a fortune?'

'It does seem incredible,' Captain Vestey agreed.

'I don't understand it,' the Marquis said again. 'But the point is, we can't make enquiries about her. If she does agree to this, we have got to keep her quiet.'

'I think the best thing would be to go down to Chard,' Captain Vestey said. 'After all, it's pleasant there in the summer. It won't be long before the shooting starts, and that will pass the time. Besides, you can give house-parties.'

'I do not really care for having the sort of house-parties to which you refer at Chard,' the Marquis said a little stiffly. 'But I suppose it doesn't matter; anything to make sure that I can go on living there for the rest of my life.'

Captain Vestey slapped him on the shoulder.

'Go and persuade her,' he urged. 'If you don't, I shall never again believe in your reputation as a lady-killer.'

He took his top-hat, which was handed to him by a footman, set it on the side of his head and was let out on to the street.

The Marquis gave a little sigh and returned to the Salon. Melinda was asleep. Her head had fallen back against the satin cushion and one hand hung limply over the side of the sofa. He stood looking down at her. She looked very young and very vulnerable. There was something curiously untouched and innocent about the little heart-shaped face with its pointed chin, long, dark lashes and pale cheeks. Her small mouth drooped a little at the corners as if she was unhappy.

Then, quite suddenly, the Marquis realised that he could not go on fighting her that night. He knew that, in his own interest, he should waken her and force her to agree to his plans, but somehow he could not. Instead he picked her up in his arms. She stirred but did not wake, and, as if instinctively she sought comfort, she nestled her face against his shoulder.

Bearing her carefully the Marquis mounted the broad, carpeted staircase to her bedroom. The maid who was waiting outside the door opened it for him, and he entered and set Melinda down on the bed. Again she stirred but did not wake. The Marquis took his arms away very carefully and went from the room without a word.

. . . . .

When next morning Melinda awoke and came to consciousness she wondered where she could be. The softness of the bed told her she was not in the austere little bedroom she had occupied in her uncle's house for nearly a year. Then the memory of how ill she had felt the previous morning came rushing back to her mind and she opened her eyes, frightened lest she should see again that tawdry, locked bedroom where she had slept in Mrs. Harcourt's house and which somehow now brought back a vivid impression of evil.

The sunshine was coming through at the sides of the heavy brocade curtains. She could see the outline of the large room and the end of the canopied bed in which she lay. Now she remembered it all. She was in Grosvenor Square and somewhere in the vast house the Dowager lay dead and the Marquis was waiting to argue with her.

She shrank down under the bedclothes, closing her eyes again as if she would shut out the world and all its worries.

'I must go,' she told herself, and at the same time she was conscious of the softness of the linen sheets, scented with lavender, and of the fragrance of the flowers which had been arranged in a glass bowl on top of the chest-of-drawers.

She had never been so comfortable; never before had there been a maid waiting to prepare her bath, to help her into her clothes, ready to arrange her hair, to put the satin slippers on her tiny feet.

'I must not think of such things,' Melinda warned herself; and yet, because she had been bullied and neglected as the poor relation for so long, to be waited on was a joy in itself. She thought of the elegant gowns hanging in the wardrobe. She could have those and more if she wished. All she had to do was to agree to what the Marquis asked of her.

She sat up in bed. She remembered now, vaguely, awakening while her maid undressed her. She could not remember coming upstairs; she only remembered feeling unaccountably sleepy when she was alone in the little Salon.

'No, I must go away,' she said aloud.

She did not know why, but she felt she was being hunted, like a fox being chased across the fields by the hounds and knowing it must run to earth before it could be safe.

She would be safe with Nanna. 'And when the five hundred guineas are spent?' a cold voice inside her brain asked her. 'But it won't be spent for ages and ages,' she told herself. 'But no money lasts for ever, and Nanna is old and may get ill. Why not make quite certain that you are safe for life? He has offered you thousands of pounds. Why should you be afraid to accept it? But it is wrong, I'm sure it is wrong,' Melinda argued with herself. 'Is playing the part of his wife any more difficult than being a governess or companion? Have you thought what that would entail, with perhaps a salary of only thirty pounds a year?'

'Thirty pounds a year,' Melinda whispered. 'And I can have three thousand for the asking!'

There was a knock on the door.

'Come in,' she said almost apprehensively, only to see Gladys, the little maid, who had helped her dress for the wedding.

'I did not know what time you would wish to be called, m'lady,' Gladys said, 'so I lets you sleep. But 'tis nigh on ten o'clock.'

'As late as that?' Melinda exclaimed. 'I must get up at once.'

Gladys threw back the curtains.

'His lordship said 'e would be pleased to see your ladyship as soon as you could come downstairs.'

'I am sure you ought not to call me "your ladyship",' Melinda objected. 'Have you forgotten that the marriage was a secret?'

'No, indeed, m'lady! As if any one of us would be likely to forget, and you making ever such a lovely bride. But we asked Mr. Newman—that's the butler—what would be the correct way to address your ladyship and 'e said as 'ow when you were alone we should say "your ladyship", and when there was company "Miss Stanyon".'

'I am sure Mr. Newman knows what is right,' Melinda said, 'but I would rather you called me Miss Stanyon.'

'Very good, miss, if that's your wish. But it does seem a pity. I always thinks "your ladyship" is such a pretty title.'

Melinda secretly agreed with her.

After she had eaten the breakfast that was brought to her on a tray, she had her bath and then stood looking at the array of gowns in her wardrobe.

'What can I wear?' she asked the maid, 'for I have nothing black.'

'Perhaps, your ladyship . . . I mean . . . miss, as you're not supposed to be in mourning t'would be best for you not to wear a black gown,' Gladys said with common sense.

'I never thought of that,' Melinda smiled. 'But, somehow I do not feel like wearing a coloured one. What about that grey one in the corner?'

It was what Madame Mercier had labelled a 'travelling gown'. It was very pale pigeon grey with a white muslin collar, and when she had it on Melinda looked like a very young schoolgirl. Her hair was arranged in long ringlets falling down the back of her head—a fashion she had noted on several of the women the night before—but she very much hoped she did not look like them.

'Is there anything else you want, miss?' Gladys asked as she went towards the door.

Melinda hesitated. She wanted to say: 'Yes, pack everything I possess!' But she thought it would be rude to Lord Chard to make preparation for her departure before he had a reasonable explanation to give to the household. 'He is certain to think of one,' she said to herself with a little twist of her lips as she went down the stairs.

'His lordship is in the Library,' the butler said, leading the way. 'I hope, m'lady, you passed a good night?'

'Yes, very good, thank you,' Melinda answered.

The doors were opened for her but, somehow, it was with an effort that she forced herself to go in. She felt nervous, a little afraid, but she revealed no sign of it as she moved across the floor to where the Marquis was sitting at a desk writing. The sunshine from the window was on him, and seeing his profile against the darkness of the bookcase beyond she realised, when he was not scowling at her, how handsome he was.

'Good morning!'

Her voice was a little unsteady, and with an exclamation the Marquis jumped to his feet.

'I am sorry, I did not hear you come in,' he said. 'Good morning, Melinda! I trust you slept well?'

'I . . . I am afraid I must have seemed rude last night,' Melinda answered. 'I was so tired, I do not remember getting upstairs to my bedroom.'

'I carried you up,' the Marquis explained.

'You . . . carried me?' She felt herself blushing.

'Yes, indeed! It was a very pleasant experience. You are so light, I might have been carrying a child, or perhaps a nymph who had strayed in by mistake from the woods.'

His voice was so genial that Melinda looked at him in surprise.

'I am sorry if I was rude,' she said.

'But you weren't,' he answered. 'And, now, what would you like to do today? I am at your service because I have already arranged with my attorney to cope with the funeral. It will take place tomorrow, and after that I suggest we leave for Chard.'

Melinda looked at him.

'I was not so sleepy last night,' she said, 'that I have forgotten our conversation. You will remember I said that I wanted to leave.'

'And I said you could not,' the Marquis answered. He saw the sudden expression on Melinda's face and said quickly: 'No, no, I don't mean that. I am not going to try to hold you by force or anything so theatrical. I am only going to beg of you to help me, simply because it means so much to me.'

'I quite see your difficulties,' Melinda said. 'It is a lot of money. But I am sure it would be all right if I came back for a few days, perhaps even a week, at the end of six months.'

'And if it was not, I should still lose the money,' the Marquis said. 'Can you remember what I offered you?'

'Yes, I have remembered it,' Melinda replied.

'Everything in the world a woman could possibly want,' the Marquis repeated. 'And if you were as rich as that, do you not see you could marry whom you wished?'

'I should not want a man who would marry me

for my money,' Melinda said. 'If I marry it will be because I love someone and he loves me.'

'You still have those ideals,' the Marquis exclaimed, 'after all you have been through! I think that is what is so charming about you.'

'What I have been through,' Melinda said, thinking of Colonel Gillingham, 'has made me realise that a marriage can be built only on love. That is where you were right not to marry just anyone to obtain the money. I think it was wrong of you to deceive your stepmother as you did and for me to play a part in it, but in a way it would have been more reprehensible for you to marry someone just because it was a matter of convenience.'

'I am glad you feel like that,' the Marquis said with a wry smile. 'I thought you were reproaching me.'

'It is all such a muddle,' Melinda explained. 'When I came here I did not really know what it was all about. It seemed such a little thing to do to earn five hundred guineas, and I didn't expect you to be as you are, nor indeed your stepmother to speak to me as she did.'

'What did she say?' the Marquis asked.

'She told me you needed love,' Melinda replied simply.

'She told you that!' the Marquis ejaculated. 'It is the last thing I should have thought she would say to anyone.'

'I think she was sorry for all she had done,' Melinda said.

'It was a little late, was it not?' the Marquis suggested with a sudden bitterness in his voice.

'Especially as at the last moment she must have inserted the clause about my remaining married for six months.'

'Do you think she was suspicious of me?' Melinda asked.

'No, of course not,' the Marquis replied, 'but of me. She always taunted me with being a will-o'-the-wisp and flitting from flower to flower, as she used to call it.'

'I suppose she thought that if she inserted that clause you would make an effort to make your marriage a success,' Melinda said.

'I do not care what she thought,' the Marquis retorted angrily. 'She ruined my life when I was a child. She incited my father against me, and now, even when she is dead, she tries to dictate what I shall and shall not do. If you ask me, I think she was determined that I should not have the money. But you will help me, won't you, Melinda, to prove her wrong?'

There was a sudden pleading in his voice that Melinda found difficult to withstand. She looked away from him, out through the windows on to the small flower-filled garden. She was wondering what her father and mother would have said. It was wrong and unconventional, but her whole life had been miserable and wrong ever since her parents had died. Would they have wanted her to go on suffering the brutalities of Sir Hector or being married to a man she loathed, because of the mere appearance of respectability? Would they not rather she did this strange, unconventional thing and, at least, achieve the satisfaction of knowing that she need no longer beg for her living in the future?

The Marquis was watching her face, noticing the straight, aristocratic little nose, the perfectly moulded features. There must be good blood in the child somewhere, he thought to himself.

'Come, I want to show you something,' he said.

He put out his hand and took hers. He felt her fingers, cold and rather frightened, in his grasp. He drew her across the room and through a door at the far end which led into an office piled high with deed-boxes. There was a large desk in the centre of the room and on the wall opposite where they had entered a picture was hanging. Melinda looked at it and gave a little gasp.

'This is my house,' she heard the Marquis say. 'Now, perhaps you will understand why it means so much to me.'

It was a big picture covering the whole wall and was of a great Elizabethan house built in the shape of an E, with the narrow, red brick of the period and the twisted chimney-pots silhouetted against the sky. It had been painted by a great artist and somehow he had given the impression of warmth and welcome in the latticed, shining windows, in an open front door at the top of a long flight of stone steps.

Melinda had gasped because, although it was immeasurably bigger, more impressive and more important, Chard was, in its way, the counterpart of her own home. Stanyon Manor, where she was born and where she had lived all her life before her parents died, was Elizabethan. It was only a small manor house, but because it was of the same period it had all the characteristics of Chard, and she knew, almost without going there, what Chard would be like inside. She could picture the rooms, with their diamond-paned windows, the uncovered beams, the oak staircase with its elegant newels, and an atmosphere of age, comfort, compassion and understanding. Elizabethan houses have a human warmth which no other period has ever introduced into its buildings.

'It is lovely, isn't it?' the Marquis asked almost eagerly, as if he really wanted her to admire it.

'It is like my home,' Melinda said almost beneath her breath, so that he did not hear her.

'It has not been touched since it was built by the first Lord Chard,' he was saying. 'Treasurer to the Court of Queen Elizabeth, he started the house when he was quite a young man and he retired there when he was still young enough to enjoy country life. He never cared for the Court. His picture hangs in the Great Hall; I should like to show it to you.'

'I did not expect your house to look like that,' Melinda said.

'What then did you expect?' the Marquis asked.

'Something big and imposing, with great pillars and huge windows. I do not know why, but that is how I imagined it when you talked about it.'

'And now that you see it?' he asked.

'It is lovely,' she answered, 'very lovely, and it is a house where one should make a home. Why do you not live in it?'

'Alone?' he asked. 'I think a home needs a wife and children, don't you?'

'But you love it?' she questioned.

'Because it is the only thing I have ever had to love,' he answered almost roughly.

It was then, for the first time, she thought of him as a little boy, without a mother, with nothing but a house to bring him comfort; and, impulsively, not really quite understanding why she capitulated, Melinda said:

'I will stay the six months!'

He had been looking at the picture, but now he turned round to face her.

'You will?' he asked eagerly. 'Why?'

'Because you love Chard,' she answered, 'and because you must have the money to look after it.'

'Thank you, Melinda.'

He spoke very quietly. Looking up into his face to smile at him she felt her eyes held by his. For a moment they were both very still as they stood beneath the picture just looking at each other. Then Melinda's eyelids fluttered and she turned away as if embarrassed.

'We shall have to be very careful that people do not find out the truth,' she said, and her voice was low and somehow caught in her throat.

'Yes, yes, of course,' the Marquis said a little absently.

Melinda led the way back into the Library. The picture of Chard seemed to have cast a spell upon her and somehow her tension had gone, she felt relaxed and at peace. She walked the length of the room and sat down on a sofa with her back to the window. The sunshine framed her fair hair like a halo and the Marquis stood for a moment looking at her before he said:

'I will never let you regret doing this for me, Melinda. Anything you want is yours.'

Melinda said nothing, and after a moment he went on:

'Perhaps we could be happy for those six months at Chard. There are many things I should like to show you, but I am afraid you might be bored. After all, it won't be very gay.'

'I have always lived in the country,' Melinda replied.

'I should like to show you the lake and the goldfish pool where I used to fish as a child,' the Marquis went on. 'There is a little chapel in the woods where the Jesuit priests used to celebrate Mass, with sentinels all round in case they should be discovered and sent to the Tower. And there is a ghost—a kind, gentle ghost—which walks the Long Gallery at night and which, if seen by one of the family, means good fortune and not bad.'

'Have you ever seen her?' Melinda asked.

He shook his head. 'I have had nothing but bad fortune up to now. Perhaps you have changed it for me.'

'Oh, I do hope so,' she replied.

She smiled up at him again and, impulsively, he sat down beside her and took her hand in his.

'I think, Melinda,' he said, 'that we might deal very well together, you and I. I want very much to give you a present. It is nothing to do with our business arrangement but something quite different. This is a present from me to you because you have been kind about Chard; and kindness has been rather rare in my life.'

For a moment Melinda let her hand rest in his and then she took it away.

'It is very kind of you,' she said, 'but whilst I am prepared to accept what you call our "business arrangement", I do not think I should accept presents. You have given me so much already. Mrs. Harcourt was very extravagant when she ordered my clothes; there is no need for you to give me anything else.'

The Marquis looked at her and laughed.

'Melinda, you are full of surprises!' he said. 'I have never, in the whole of my life, known anyone who refused a present. You must be teasing me! What are your favourite stones? Diamonds?'

'You called me foolish last night,' Melinda protested, 'but if anyone is foolish I think it must be you. I have just said I do not want presents. I do not think it would be right for me to take them.'

'You bewilder me,' the Marquis said, and then his expression changed. 'But I think I begin to understand what you mean,' he said in a different tone of voice. 'You feel that it would be wrong to take a present unless you were giving something in return. Is that right?'

'Not exactly . . .' Melinda began to say, but the Marquis interrupted her.

'But, my dear, it is all too simple. I am only too willing to accept your favours, and in return I may then give you all the presents you desire and deserve. Is that another bargain between us?'

'I do not think I know what you mean,' Melinda said.

He took her hand again in his.

'I think you do,' he insisted.

She was about to protest, when the expression on his face held her spellbound. Never before had a man looked at her in quite that manner. Never before had she been so close to a man and felt some strange response within herself, almost as if she trembled because of it.

'Melinda,' he said very softly, and his lips were very close to hers.

Unexpectedly the door was opened and Newman, the butler, entered the room.

'What is it?' the Marquis asked sharply.

'I am sorry to disturb your lordship,' the butler replied, 'but Lady Alice St. Helier is here. She insists on seeing your lordship and I could only say that I would inform you that she had called.'

'The devil take it!' the Marquis said, almost beneath his breath. 'Where is she?'

'Her ladyship insisted on waiting in the hall, m'lord. I tried to show her into the small Salon but she refused.'

The Marquis looked at Melinda.

'Would you wait in the office?' he asked. 'I am sorry, Melinda, but Lady Alice must not see you here.'

'No, no, of course,' Melinda answered.

She moved quickly across the room and had only just reached the door into the office when the door behind the butler burst open and a gay voice said:

'Drogo! Did you really think to keep me out?'

Melinda had a quick glimpse of an elegant figure in pink before she had slipped into the office, and could see no more. The door was ajar and she did not dare close it for fear it should make a noise, so she could not prevent herself from hearing Lady Alice say:

'Drogo! Dear Drogo! I am so glad that at last you are free of that monster. Now you have the money everything will be different.'

'In what way?' the Marquis asked.

'Drogo, do not be so obtuse.' Her voice was very beguiling. 'It has been so difficult while you have been poor and bedevilled by that terrible woman. Now you can entertain at Chard and here, as befits your position. Dearest Drogo, I know that you are very, very rich.'

'I still do not see how that affects our relationship, Alice,' the Marquis said stiffly. 'Unless, of course, St. Helier had died overnight, or committed suicide.'

'St. Helier is very much alive,' Lady Alice replied. 'But he is interested, as you well know, in only one thing—his racehorses! He stays at Newmarket week after week, and you and I, Drogo, are not interested in racehorses, are we?'

No one could mistake the soft but passionate tone which was almost a caress. Melinda reached out her hand and shut the door to with a little snap. So this was yet another example of how London Society behaved! She was disgusted; she was shocked. More than that, she suddenly felt as if something had hurt her personally, though why, she did not know.

8

Melinda ran upstairs to her bedroom, spurred by the desire to escape from something she did not understand but vaguely knew was wrong and, somehow, indecent. She could hardly credit that a married woman of the standing of Lady Alice St. Helier would say such things, and yet she had heard them with her own ears and had known that they both shocked and offended her. It was not her business and yet, despite herself, she was involved in it.

She went into her bedroom and shut the door. Everything, she thought, seemed confused and menacing. From the moment she had awoken in that tawdry bedroom at Mrs. Harcourt's she had been aware that an atmosphere she could not put a name to threatened her. It was evil! Or was she imagining things?

It required no effort of imagination to know that it was wrong to have accepted Mrs. Harcourt's suggestion that she should come to this house and make a mockery of the marriage ceremony. And then there had been that party last night—that shameful, indecent party where a woman had behaved immodestly and the company had included women who, Melinda knew, would have been an affront to her mother.

It seemed to her that she was getting deeper and deeper into a quicksand. Downstairs Lady Alice St. Helier, a woman of noble birth, was making suggestions to the Marquis which no lady with any self-respect would make. Melinda put her hands up to her face with a gesture of despair. Was she at fault, or had the whole world around her suddenly become crazed?

She walked to the window to look out on the trees in Grosvenor Square and the blue sky above them. They made her think of the countryside and she longed to be back in her own home, safe and secure, surrounded by love and ignorant of the beastliness of the world outside.

Then she looked downwards and saw a very elegant, open carriage waiting outside the front door. Melinda's eyes were immediately drawn to the horses—a pair of very fine greys, tossing the plumes on their foreheads and jingling their silver bits. As she admired them she saw a footman come from the house to open the door of the carriage and she watched Lady Alice—for she knew it must be she—walk across the pavement and step into it.

She was wearing a gown of strawberry pink and there were pink ostrich feathers on her bonnet and pink ribbons which tied beneath her chin. When Lady Alice had seated herself, she turned towards the doorway and gave a wave of her gloved hand to someone who was standing there. Melinda knew it must be the Marquis. As the coachman whipped up the horses and they drove away, almost as if she was aware of Melinda's curious eyes, Lady Alice looked up. Melinda had only a quick glimpse of her raised face but she knew it was lovely. With the big, liquid eyes, the small, straight nose and the pouting, rose-bud mouth, it was the face of a beauty, and Melinda could understand the Marquis's infatuation. At the same time, she told herself, beautiful or not, Lady Alice was married.

'He is utterly despicable,' she said aloud, and almost welcomed the fact that she would be able to tell him so.

She felt a sudden exhilaration in the thought that she had the courage to fight him. She was no longer afraid; for she was doing him a favour and staying on to save the fortune which he needed so badly. It was entirely within her power to deny him the money and she found herself smiling at the thought that he was not going to have it all his own way during the six months they were to be together. He might yearn for Lady Alice; he might want to enjoy himself with his disreputable cronies and the women with whom he was associating last night; but he must still live in the same house as her, they must still be together at meals, and he must still keep up the pretence that she was his wife.

'I won't be afraid of him. I will even try to reform him,' Melinda promised herself, and then knew that this was, in fact, but a fantasy of her over-active imagination. When she was face to face with the Marquis, with his cynicism and his disagreeableness, she would still find herself tongue-tied even though she might be brave enough to defy him when he was at his rudest.

She sat in her bedroom awaiting a summons to return to the Library, but to her chagrin, after she had waited for two hours, a message was brought to her by Gladys to the effect that relatives had arrived and would she be obliging enough to have dinner in the boudoir adjacent to her bedroom.

It was an anti-climax and Melinda found the meal, delicious though it was, depressing. There were all sorts of tempting dishes but she sent most of them away, refused the wine and found herself wondering exactly what was happening downstairs.

Gladys was only too eager to tell her when she came to prepare her for bed.

'There's been 'igh words in the dining-room tonight, m'lady.'

'With whom?' Melinda asked. She knew it was incorrect to discuss such matters with the maidservant and yet she could not resist it.

'Mr. Newman says that 'is lordship's uncle, Lord FitzBolton, 'as demanded to see the will and 'is lordship 'as refused. Lord FitzBolton was also very angry that the funeral should be taking place tomorrow morning. 'E wanted time for all the cousins and other relations to come up from the country, but 'is lordship insists on it being private; not even the house'old staff are to be there.'

'Who else was at dinner?' Melinda enquired.

'Lord FitzBolton's two sons,' Gladys replied. 'They've stayed 'ere sometimes and they ain't popular with the valets.'

'Why not?' Melinda enquired.

'They gives 'em nought but a few shillings,' Gladys explained and then put her hand to her lips. 'Oh, m'lady, I oughtn't to be telling you things like that, but, of course, they're discussed downstairs in the servants' 'all.'

'I am sure they are,' Melinda smiled. 'So Lord

FitzBolton's sons have a reputation for meanness, have they?'

'That's what we thinks they are,' Gladys answered, 'and forever ringing the bell. Why, James—that's one of the footmen—said 'e went upstairs more than a dozen times to 'em in one morning the last time they stayed 'ere.'

'Is there a Lady FitzBolton?' Melinda asked.

'I think her ladyship's dead,' Gladys answered, 'cos as I passed the dining-room door this evenin' I 'eard his lordship say, "My poor lamented wife would 'ave been 'orrified at such behaviour." '

'Gladys, you were listening at the keyhole!'

'Not really, m'lady,' Gladys asserted. 'Mr. Newman wouldn't stand for anything o' that sort; but I just 'appened to be passing.'

Melinda laughed.

'If you are not careful you will be sent back to the country.'

Her words made the expression on Gladys' face turn to one of terror.

'Oh, m'lady, you wouldn't tell on me, would you? It's just that you seem so young and understanding and they're all so stiff and starchy in this place. I never 'as anyone I can talk to natural like. If I says a word to that Miss Jones she snaps me 'ead orf.'

'It is all right, I shall not "tell on you",' Melinda smiled. 'In fact, I am glad to have someone to talk to myself.'

'It don't seem right that your ladyship 'as to keep your marriage so secret,' Gladys said. 'You ought t' be downstairs meeting 'is lordship's relations. It's proud 'e'd be to introduce you. There's never bin anyone in this 'ouse as lovely as you.'

'Oh, Gladys, you flatter me!' Melinda protested. 'And do not forget my marriage is a secret. Not a word of it must ever be breathed to anyone; you do realise that?'

'Yes, m'lady, we've all 'ad our instructions. Mr. Newman says that the first one as mentions it outside the four walls of this 'ouse'll find 'emselves straight in the gutter. Very fierce he was about it!'

'I am glad to hear it,' Melinda said. 'And now, Gladys, I think I shall go to bed.'

It was still early and she could not sleep. She lay awake trying to puzzle out some of the fantastic things that had happened to her since she had run away from her uncle's house. She found her thoughts continually returning to the Marquis. Why was he so antagonistic towards her? she wondered. Why did he look at her with that strange expression in his eyes which somehow seemed one of contempt? What had she ever done to him except to be obliging and do exactly as he wished?

In the morning Gladys came into her room with a sad look on her face and a trace of tears around her eyes.

'They're taking the coffin downstairs now, m'lady,' she said to Melinda with a gulp. 'There's something about death that always gets me upset. The poor old lady! She was kind to us in 'er way, and 'though I never spoke to 'er I used to watch 'er going down the stairs, slow like, but with a dignity.'

'I would like to have known her,' Melinda said, speaking more to herself than to Gladys.

'She 'ad a temper,' Gladys said frankly. 'I've 'eard

'er scream at 'is lordship before now. Then 'e'd storm out of the 'ouse with a black look on his face, slamming the door behind him. I used to wonder why they 'ated each other so much.'

Melinda thought how impossible it was to keep anything from household staff. She longed to ask more questions as to why and about what the Marquis had fought so often with his stepmother, but during the night she had felt ashamed that she had let Gladys talk in such a friendly manner. So now she busied herself with her breakfast and did not encourage the girl to chatter as she had done the previous evening.

The blinds in her room were to be kept lowered until the funeral party had left the house, and then the head housemaid entered to raise them a few inches to let in the light.

'I am sorry if the darkness is inconvenient, m'lady,' she said, 'but it was his lordship's orders that all the blinds were to remain drawn.'

'Yes, of course, they must be down,' Melinda said. 'Do not raise them too high.'

'A few inches won't be noticed,' Miss Jones said, 'and it's depressing for your ladyship. Do you mind if Gladys and I start your packing?'

'Packing?' Melinda asked in surprise.

'Hasn't your ladyship heard?' Miss Jones said curiously. 'I thought his lordship would have mentioned it. He is leaving immediately he returns from the funeral for Chard, and your ladyship is to go with him. The luggage, of course, will follow in the closed barouche.'

Melinda felt her spirits rise.

'How will we be travelling?' she asked.

'In his lordship's phaeton,' Miss Jones replied. 'I am sure your ladyship will be surprised at such a choice of vehicle, but then his lordship never was conventional.'

'No, of course not,' Melinda murmured.

She dressed quickly, choosing a travelling-gown of sea-blue sarsenet which had a small, tight-fitting coat for warmth. The bonnet which went with it was proportionately small. She hoped that the ribbons under her chin would prevent the wind from blowing it away.

It was a year since she had travelled in a phaeton. Her father's had not been up-to-date or particularly fast, but at least it was more exciting than trundling along in the closed carriages which her aunt and uncle had preferred.

When she was ready Melinda looked at herself in the mirror. There was no doubt that the sea-blue of her travelling outfit was exceedingly becoming to her fair hair and white skin, but it was the excitement in her eyes which gave her an air of gaiety completely out of keeping for someone who should be wearing deep mourning if she was indeed the Marquis's wife. She wondered if he would have expected her to wear black; but there was nothing of that colour in her wardrobe and she thought that the servants would accept her colourful attire as in keeping with the secrecy of the marriage.

The head housemaid and Gladys filled several large trunks with her clothes. With them taking the dresses to and from the wardrobe and kneeling on the floor, there seemed to be little room for Melinda;

so after a time she went from the bedroom on to the landing to listen for the Marquis's return. She did not dare to go downstairs in case she encountered one of his relations, and she was half afraid that when he did return he would bring some of them back with him; but to her relief she saw him come into the hall alone.

'I will change at once, Newman,' he said to the butler.

He turned towards the stairs. Melinda just had time to slip back into the boudoir adjoining her bedroom. She had had a quick glimpse of his face as he entered the hall, and seeing that he was scowling she had no desire to encounter him in that mood.

If he was cross, perhaps he would refuse to take her with him to the country. She might even have to travel with the luggage and the staff in the closed barouche. She waited anxiously and at last there was a knock on the door. She opened it to find one of the footmen outside.

'His lordship's compliments and is your ladyship ready to depart?'

'Yes, I am ready,' Melinda said eagerly.

She followed the footman down the stairs. The Marquis was standing in the hall, having changed from his dark funeral attire into long trousers of pigeon grey cloth with an elegantly cut coat of a deeper shade.

'Good morning, Melinda!' he said. 'I hope you slept well?'

His words were conventional enough, but she felt that his black mood had passed. Without saying any more he moved towards the front door. Melinda followed him. Outside was the smartest phaeton she had ever seen, with yellow and black wheels and drawn by a tandem of chestnut horses. A footman helped her up into the high seat and the Marquis sprang up beside her. He took the reins, the grooms sprang away from the horses' heads and they were off.

There was a small groom with a top-hat seated behind them. A 'tiger', Melinda had heard her father call the boy who filled that position. She wished she could show her father the horses in front of her: he would have approved of the way that the Marquis handled the reins.

The horses were fresh and needed some checking through the traffic-filled streets, but very soon they were out in the country and the Marquis let them have their heads. They were some miles out of London before he turned to her and said:

'You are very silent.'

'I have always been taught not to disturb a gentleman when he is tooling a pair of fresh horses,' Melinda replied.

The Marquis laughed.

'I can see you have had a good teacher. Do you, perhaps, drive yourself?'

'Yes, I can,' Melinda answered. 'But I have never had the opportunity of driving such horses as yours.'

'They are a good pair, aren't they?' the Marquis smiled. 'They cost me two thousand guineas at Tattersall's three months ago—so they ought to be!'

'It does not always follow,' Melinda said. 'The performance may not match the looks, but you cannot always discover that until you get your purchase home.'

'I can see you are quite an expert on horses,' the Marquis said pleasantly and without a sneer in his voice.

'I love them,' Melinda said quietly.

'What else do you love?' the Marquis asked. 'Or should I say whom?'

'I love the country,' Melinda said, ignoring the second part of his question. 'I do not think I would ever want to live for long in the town.'

'There are a lot of things that are very unexpected about you,' the Marquis observed.

Melinda did not reply. They had reached a straight stretch of the road and it was difficult to have a conversation with the wind blowing away the words from between one's lips. She forgot the Marquis and settled herself down to enjoy the drive; the feeling of the summer air on her cheeks; the sunshine glittering on the horses' bridles; the white, dusty road being eaten up as they sped over it, passing green fields, dark woods, rivers and streams banked with yellow irises and golden kingcups.

They must have driven for nearly an hour before the Marquis pulled up at an old black-and-white posting inn.

'We will have luncheon here,' he said. 'If you are not hungry, I am ravenous.'

Ostlers came running to hold the horses. The Marquis jumped down to the ground and held his arms out to Melinda. Just for a second she hesitated and then allowed him to lift her down. For a moment she was close against him. She found herself vividly conscious of the strength of his arms and his face so near to hers. Then she was free. But she felt almost as if something strange had happened because he had touched her.

She was escorted by the landlady to the best bedroom of the inn, where she washed her face and hands. Her hair was blown about her forehead; so she took off her bonnet, rearranged her ringlets as best she could and holding her bonnet in her hand went downstairs to the private room where the Marquis had ordered luncheon.

It was a small, oak-panelled room with low beams, so that the Marquis had to stoop his head. There was a bow-window overlooking a small garden and already the round table set for luncheon was groaning with a collection of cold dishes—boar's head, home-cured ham, stuffed turkey, roasted pigeons and a large leg of mutton.

'What do you fancy?' the Marquis asked. 'The landlord tells me he has a hot lark and oyster pie in the oven.'

Melinda shook her head.

'I never can bear to think of larks being used in a pie,' she said.

She ordered cold turkey with a slice of ham, while the Marquis enjoyed fresh salmon, two plump pigeons, large slices of under-done roast beef and several helpings of brawn.

'I needed food,' he said, looking across the table at her with a smile. 'I could not enjoy my breakfast this morning with my uncle carping at me and those two tiresome sons of his arguing about which shaped tie was correct wear at a funeral service.'

'I am afraid you do not like your relations,' Melinda said.

'I loathe them,' the Marquis answered firmly. 'Do you like yours?'

'No, like you, I find them singularly unpleasant,' Melinda said, thinking of Sir Hector.

They both began to laugh. For some reason it seemed very funny that they should have this, if nothing else, in common.

'Gervase says I have been unkind to you,' the Marquis said unexpectedly. 'Do you forgive me?'

'Yes, of course,' Melinda answered. 'I can understand that you have been under some strain.'

'Do not make excuses for me,' he said. 'No one should ever be unpleasant to anyone as pretty as you.'

There was something about the compliment which somehow jarred.

'Tell me,' Melinda said quickly, 'about your house. I am looking forward to seeing it.'

If she had meant to divert him from being personal she certainly succeeded. Immediately his face lit up.

'Do you know,' he said quietly, 'this is the first time I have been there knowing it is mine, all mine, and that I shall not have to lose it.'

The Marquis talked of Chard while they finished the meal, and when they drove off again Melinda had the feeling that at last he really was relaxed, no longer afraid, no longer on edge. She could not help thinking how much better it would have been if, in fact, he were really married, rather than facing the six months' subterfuge in a situation which, if things went wrong, might mean his utter destruction.

After driving for another hour they turned in

through some magnificent wrought-iron gates, set between stone pillars surmounted by huge eagles with outstretched wings. Then, just beyond a cluster of oak trees, the Marquis reined in the horses.

Chard lay in front of them. If it had looked lovely in the picture Melinda had seen in London, the reality was breath-taking. The beautiful red brick, mellowed to the colour of deep rose by age and weather, was framed by a wood of silver birch; in front were long, green lawns running down to a small, silver stream spanned by an ancient bridge. The house was spread out, shaped like an E in compliment to the Queen in whose reign it had been built, and its small, diamond-paned windows glittered in the sunshine as if they flashed a greeting to all who approached it. There was something warm, welcoming and happy about Chard. It was large and yet it gave the impression of being a home.

'It is beautiful!' Melinda exclaimed, and the Marquis turned to smile at her.

'The place I love best in the world!' he said. 'I feel sometimes as if Chard were a woman who has all of my heart.'

'The most beautiful woman in the world,' Melinda said softly, and longed to add to it, 'far more beautiful than Lady Alice.'

'Come and see it,' the Marquis said. 'There is so much I want to show you!'

When they reached Chard, he was like a schoolboy, taking her over the house from cellars to attic. They went round the gardens too: he showed her the goldfish pool which he had loved as a child; he took her into the vegetable garden and told her how he used to steal the peaches when the crotchety old head-gardener was not looking and how he had been beaten for putting a cricket ball through a pane of glass in the greenhouses.

They saw the swans, black and white, drifting down the stream, and then he took her to the stables and was amused by her delight in the horses. There was one which took Melinda's fancy above all the others.

'That is Thunderbolt,' the Marquis told her as they stared at the big, black stallion who tossed his head disdainfully at the carrots they offered him. 'I bought him a year ago. I wanted to ride him in London, for there is not a horse to touch him in the Row. But he was too excitable, so I brought him back here. I'll ride him tomorrow, Ned,' he said, turning to the old groom.

'Very good, m'lord, but you'll find him hard to handle. He doesn't get enough exercise and that's a fact. The boys are afraid to mount him. He gave young Jim a toss last week and he's refused to get up on him since.'

'I expect he wants someone to whom he can show off his paces,' Melinda said. 'Horses are like that. Take him out hunting: he will have some competition and feel the challenge of other animals nearly as good as himself.'

'Is that what you want, Thunderbolt?' the Marquis asked, patting the stallion's neck. 'Very well, we must see what we can do. Perhaps I will race him in a point-to-point.'

'It would be nice to see you doing that again,

m'lord,' the old groom said. 'We've missed you at the races these last two years.'

'I was, unfortunately, unable to come to Chard in the spring,' the Marquis said, and Melinda, feeling the repression in his voice, knew that it must have been his stepmother who had kept him away.

They went back to the house and realised it was nearly dinner-time. Standing in the big drawing-room which overlooked the rose-garden, Melinda thought there had never been a more lovely setting for two people if they had really been married and were in love. There were big bowls of pot-pourri to scent the room; there was the fragrance of carnations from the greenhouses; there was the lovely old walnut furniture which had belonged to the house for generations, and the ancient, gilt mirrors in which she saw herself reflected and re-reflected, a little, fair-haired figure in blue beside the tall, dark Marquis.

She had the sudden feeling that he was thinking the same thoughts as herself. She turned to find his eyes were looking at her enquiringly, and suddenly the gaiety which had made it so easy to talk to him all the afternoon turned into an embarrassment. For some unknown reason she felt herself tremble and dropped her eyes before his.

'We must go and change for dinner,' he said, but absently as if he were thinking of something else.

'Yes, of course.'

She was glad of the excuse to slip away from him, to go up to her room where her clothes had been unpacked and an elderly housemaid with pursed lips was waiting to attend to her.

'Which gown will you be wearing this evening,

miss?' she asked, and Melinda was quite startled by the note of disapproval in her voice.

'I do not know,' she answered and looked around her. 'What a lovely room!' she exclaimed.

The ceiling was low and yet there was room enough for a big four-poster bed hung with magnificent embroidery through which cupids, birds and flowers ran riot on white satin. The canopy of the bed was draped with a gold fringe and surmounted by two fat, golden angels holding aloft a heart.

'It is the bedroom to the bridal suite, miss,' the housemaid said and there was now no mistaking the disapproval in her tone.

Melinda understood that the servants at Chard had not been told of the 'secret marriage' and that the housemaid, quite rightly, thought she was presuming on a position which should be held only by the wife of the reigning owner.

'Who chose this room for me?' Melinda asked.

'His lordship's instructions,' the housemaid answered, her starched apron rustling at the affront.

'Then his lordship must have a very good reason,' Melinda said, wondering if it would not have been better to explain her presence to the servants at Chard.

'Yes, miss, that is obvious,' the housemaid said with such venom in her voice that Melinda almost recoiled.

'I will ring the bell,' she said quickly, 'when I am ready for you to help me into my gown. In the meantime I should like to be alone.'

'Very good, miss, if that is what you wish.'

The housemaid withdrew leaving an atmosphere of

dislike and suspicion behind her which made Melinda shiver. 'I suppose,' she thought to herself, 'it is very unconventional from the servants' point of view that I should be staying here without a chaperon.'

She felt so intimidated by the woman's attitude that she managed to fasten her gown herself and even arrange her own hair, so there was no need to ring the bell. It was only when she was dressed that she realised that quite unconsciously she had chosen a white gown, which made her look like a bride.

It was not as elaborate as her wedding gown had been; it was of white chiffon caught with ribbons and bunches of tiny roses and it was very lovely. The décolletage was a little lower than Melinda liked, and she found a lace handkerchief amongst her things which she arranged so that it was more modest.

Her hair, blown by the journey, framed her face in a tiny halo of curls, refusing to lie demurely on either side of the centre parting. She found her slippers where they had been placed in the wardrobe, and taking a last look at herself she slipped from the room without having to encounter the disapproving housemaid again.

She went down the wide oak staircase with its ancient, carved newels into the hall. The house was very quiet, but it had a kind of warmth about it which seemed to embrace her with loving arms. She opened the door of the drawing-room, to find the Marquis standing and looking out of the window. The evening sunshine was on his face and she saw that he wore a look of happiness which seemed almost to transform him. He turned his head as she approached and held out his hand.

'Come here,' he said.

He drew Melinda to the window, and looking out over the rose-garden she saw the sun sinking behind the high trees of a wood. The rooks were circling over the trees and the pigeons were coming in to roost.

'I used to envy those birds when I was a boy,' the Marquis said quietly, 'because they could always come home. The wood was theirs and when night came they returned to it instinctively, knowing it would give them sanctuary and rest until the morning.'

Melinda could feel underneath his words all that he had suffered in knowing, as a child, that he was not wanted, that his home was not really his because he was not loved; and she began to understand how much this coming back to Chard, as its owner, must mean to him.

'Were you very unhappy?' she asked in her soft voice.

'I think if it had not been for Chard,' he answered, 'I would have killed myself, not once but a dozen times. A child can live with harshness, even with cruelty, but not with hatred. It eats into the soul; it destroys everything, even the desire to live.'

There was such an agony in his tone that she looked at him with surprise, and then the dark bitterness in his eyes vanished.

'But now we can forget it,' he said gaily. 'I have won! It is mine! I did not altogether realise, until this very moment, how much it means to me. But now, it is mine and you have helped me get it. I shall always be grateful to you for that.'

His hand had rested on her shoulder whilst he had pointed out to her the wood in the distance, and now his fingers tightened a little. Instinctively she moved away from him. He smiled and would have spoken, but at that moment the butler announced dinner.

They sat at a table laden with shining silver engraved with the family crest; the long, oak-panelled room was lit with huge, gold candelabras. The food was delicious—vegetables and fruit from the gardens; meat and game killed on the estate; and trout from the stream where the Marquis had caught them as a boy.

He talked of the improvements he intended to make and how the gardens must be restored according to the plans that had been drawn up when the house was first built.

'We have them all,' he said. 'It is a pity that the herb-garden should have been allowed to wither away; that the fountain was moved to another place and the yew hedges cut down. I shall plant them all again and my farms shall be the best in the whole countryside. My stepmother grudged every penny that was spent on them. I shall see the farmers during the week and tell them there will be no more leaking barns and broken hedges, and that when they want to restock, I shall be there to help them.'

Melinda felt herself fired by his enthusiasm and after dinner they went into the Estate Office and the Marquis showed her the great plans of the estate. She found he knew the names of all the tenant farmers, and he pointed out to her where the land had been allowed to go waste because his stepmother and her agent charged the farmers so much rent that they could not make a profit, and where he himself would plough up, replant and put in new improvements.

They were so long in the Estate Office that it was dark when finally they went back to the drawing-room. The curtains had been drawn and a small fire was lit in the grate for fear they should find the evening chill. It seemed to accentuate the fragrance of the flowers and the smell of beeswax and pot-pourri which was prevalent all over the house.

Melinda sank down on the hearthrug, her gown billowing out around her, and said impulsively:

'This is just like home. The scent is the same.'

The Marquis sat down on the sofa. She could feel his eyes were on her, and after a moment he said almost in surprise:

'I am glad you are here. I had to talk to somebody; it has been bottled up inside me for so long and you seem to have understood.'

'I do understand,' Melinda said.

He bent over her and took her hand in his, drawing her towards him.

'Come and sit here, Melinda.'

She wanted to protest that she was quite happy where she was, but somehow she found herself obeying him, sitting beside him on the sofa. He said nothing for a moment, just looked at her, and then he said, almost as if he were talking to himself:

'Lovely! So lovely that it is a pity . . .'

He did not complete the sentence but put his arms around Melinda and drew her close to him. She was so astonished that for a moment she was powerless to resist him; then, almost before she knew it, his mouth was on hers.

She had never been kissed before, but his quickness and strength took her by surprise and she felt as if she could hardly breathe. His mouth was rough and his arms held her so closely that she could not move. She felt a fierceness and a passion in his kiss which frightened her; then his lips grew softer and she was able to struggle free.

'No . . .' she managed to protest, 'no . . .'

His fingers were beneath her chin, tilting her face up to his.

'Do not fight me, Melinda,' he begged. 'I need you! I need the softness and warmth of you; I need your understanding. We are here together. Can you not understand how I need you?'

She did not answer him, for his lips were on hers again, and he was holding her closer and yet closer. Somehow she found herself unable to struggle and she felt as if she was drifting nearer and nearer to him until they were almost one person . . . And now he was kissing her cheeks, her eyes, her neck, and then her mouth again until she felt something quiver and awaken within her, a little flame running through her body which she had never known before in the whole of her life. . . .

Suddenly he released her and looked down at her head against his shoulder. Her eyelashes fluttered against her cheeks; her lips were parted; a little pulse was throbbing in her neck where he had kissed it.

'You go to my head, Melinda,' he said and his voice was a caress. He pulled her gently to her feet and walked her towards the door, his arms round her shoulders.

'Hurry! I do not want to wait long. What shall I give you—fifteen minutes? Not longer, please, for I am very impatient, my sweet!'

His lips were against her cheek; then he opened the door and she found herself in the hall. Almost automatically she climbed the stairs. Only when she reached her own room did she try to understand what had happened and realised vaguely, with a kind of panic, what he had meant.

It could not be true!—what she thought, what she imagined he intended! She would hardly admit it even to herself, as the horror of it swept over her. And even as she recoiled from her own imaginings, she knew something else which seemed to strike her like a dagger running through her heart.

She loved him! She was quivering and the flame he had ignited in her body was rising high within her, leaping over her to consume her utterly with the warmth and passion of her own love.

She loved him! But what he wanted of her was something very different. She did not fully understand, but she knew that what he intended was wrong and a crime against her love for him. In that first kiss he had taken her heart, but it was not her heart he desired, but something which instinctively, innocent as she was, she knew was evil and wicked.

She leaned against the bedroom door and turned the key in the lock. Then, in a kind of terror, she knew that should he come and command her to open the door she would be unable to refuse him! She wanted to feel the touch of his lips again; she wanted his arms around her. She knew that once he came through the door she would be unable to resist him, whatever he asked of her.

In terror she ran across the room and flung back the curtains. Outside the moon was creeping up the sky, the stars were coming out. She opened the latticed window and looked down. Below was an ancient fig tree, its branches strong and sturdy, the growth of many years.

Melinda looked back. The door was locked, but she could almost hear his voice commanding her to open it.

'Melinda!'

She shut her eyes. She could still feel his lips on hers, on her eyes, her cheeks, her neck. She gave a little cry of despair and started to climb through the window.

She had climbed trees often enough at home when her mother had scolded her for being a tomboy, but she had never climbed a tree wearing a voluminous evening gown with half a dozen petticoats beneath it. She heard the soft chiffon of her gown tear; a bunch of rosebuds was left behind on the fig tree. But somehow she reached the ground and then, like a small, frightened animal fleeing from the lights, she ran across the lawns into the shadow of the trees.

9

Melinda awoke and wondered where she could be. A high, grey, stone pillar arose in front of her towards a curved roof. Then she remembered and sat up on the soft, red velvet cushion on which she had slept all night.

She had known when she entered the pew that it must be the one which belonged to the family. She had felt the carving on the door, known that the cushioned seat was soft and luxurious, as was the hassock on which she knelt to pray. The church, with its smell of must and age mingled with the fragrance of the flowers on the altar, had seemed a sanctuary, and in the faint light of the moon coming through the stained-glass windows she had groped her way up the aisle to enter the front pew and knelt there praying for protection, not only from the Marquis but from herself.

After a while her heart had stopped throbbing against her breast, and her breath had ceased to come in gasps from between her lips. She had run across the lawns because she was frightened, but she knew that in a way she had escaped nothing because there was still that deep emotion within herself which urged her to go back.

'Help me! Oh, help me!' she prayed, and wondered how she could have changed so quickly from someone who had had no interest in men to this new self who was quivering and trembling from the touch of a man's lips.

She knew now that she had been attracted to the Marquis from the first moment she had seen him. She had thought that she hated him, the cynical look on his face, the disdainful manner in which he spoke to her, the anger which he aroused in her. And yet, still there was something about him which had magnetised her into wanting to be with him.

She understood now the loneliness, the emptiness of the long day that she had had to spend alone in her bedroom. It had been long hours of frustration because she could not be with him. She gave a little moan and dropped her head in her hands. What was to become of her? How could she feel like this knowing it was hopeless and wrong, something she must fight with her pride and with everything that she held sacred?

In the darkness of the church she went over and over again what had happened and what he had said to her before she went upstairs. Even now, in her innocence, she did not quite understand. She only knew that what he had asked of her was wrong.

She chided herself for letting him kiss her. She should have resisted; it was not the behaviour of any decent girl. And yet she felt, once again, that strange, unaccountable excitement when his mouth touched hers; felt again that little flame leaping within herself. Something had awoken inside her; something which now would never sleep again.

How long she knelt trying to pray but finding her mind wandering away into thoughts of the Marquis, she had no idea. She only knew that the moon rose higher in the sky and the church grew brighter. Now she could see the cross gleaming on the altar, the stone figures on the tombs surrounding it and the carved choir-stalls with their unlighted candles attached to each choir-boy's place.

Gently the peace of it all seeped over her. She felt calmer, felt a new strength come to her, as if she were no longer alone.

'Oh, Papa and Mamma! Help me!' she prayed. and believed that they were beside her, sustaining her in this hour of fear.

She was not certain now when it was that she had felt too tired to kneel any longer. She only knew that she had found herself lying down on the pew and drifting instantly into a deep, exhausted slumber. And now, with her awakening, the troubles of the night seemed less intense and frightening.

She put her feet to the ground and gave a little shiver. It was cold in the church, though she could see the first rays of the sun glittering through the east window. 'I must go back,' she thought.

She let herself out through the little door of the pew. Now she could see it was more important-looking than any other in the church. Her footsteps made very little sound as she walked down the flagged aisle to the door through which she had entered. She pulled it open. Outside the world seemed golden and fresh, but for a moment she hesitated. She had the feeling that the church had protected her and that now she was going back to danger. Then she told herself that her family had never lacked courage and she had to face what lay ahead.

It was only a short distance to the garden and from there she could see the great house, rosy pink in the morning sun. Once again it seemed to give her a welcome, and for a moment she thought she must have dreamt her fear of the night before. But she knew, with a sinking of her heart, that she had to face the Marquis again. What would he say? And how could she answer him?

The blinds were still drawn in the windows and by the height of the sun Melinda guessed that it was not much more than five o'clock. She walked slowly back through the rose-garden and as she did so she saw an early housemaid open a side door and kneel down to start scrubbing the step. Melinda came up silently behind her, and as her shadow fell upon the kneeling girl she looked up in astonishment.

'Glory to goodness, ye did give me a start!' she exclaimed, and then, rising to her feet, added hastily: 'I beg pardon, ma'am, I didn't mean to speak like that.'

'It is all right,' Melinda smiled. 'I do not suppose you expected a guest in the house to be up so early.'

'No, indeed, ma'am,' the girl answered.

Melinda passed her, entering the house. It seemed quiet and dark after the sunshine outside. She found her way to the hall and climbed the staircase. She was conscious of a faint noise of blinds being drawn and curtains being pulled back but she saw no one and reached her own room.

It was then that she remembered she had locked the door the night before. For a moment she stood there nonplussed, wondering what she should do, and then she recalled that there was another door which led into the bathroom. It was, of course, unlocked and she reflected that had the Marquis really desired entry to her room he could have come to her through this door.

She entered her bedroom, unlocked the door and pulled close the curtains she had disturbed the previous night. It would be best, she decided, not to let the maid who attended her think anything unusual had occurred; so she undressed and putting on her nightgown got into bed.

She did not sleep but lay in the darkness wondering what she should do. Supposing the Marquis kissed her again? Would she be strong enough to refuse his kisses? Would she be able to fight him night after night? Would she be able to keep him from her room and refuse to acquiesce in anything that he might desire of her? She felt the questions hammering at her brain and, turning over, hid her face in the pillow.

Breakfast was brought to her and she arose slowly, dressing herself with care and taking more trouble than usual over her appearance. She knew, within herself, that she was playing for time; but when at last she could linger no longer it was resolutely, though with a weak feeling inside her, that she left her bedroom and went downstairs.

She had half expected to find the Marquis in the drawing-room, but he was not there and she sat down on a sofa wondering what she should do. She took a book from one of the shelves but found she was unable to read. She knew that every nerve in her body was tense and all the time she was listening, listening for one person.

Quite suddenly there came the murmur of voices; somewhere men and women were talking and laughing. She listened and then, because she was curious, she went to the door of the drawing-room and opened it. The Great Hall seemed full of people. For a moment Melinda thought she knew none of them and then she recognised one person, just as the Marquis came in through the front door.

He did not see her but her heart leapt at the sight of him. He was in riding breeches and his top-hat was at a jaunty angle at the side of his head. He carried a riding-whip in his hand and two of his dogs were bounding beside him.

'What an invasion!' he said slowly as he saw the assembled throng turn towards him expectantly. It was difficult to know whether he was pleased or angry at their arrival.

'Drogo! What the hell do you mean by going out of London without letting me know?'

There was no mistaking the outstretched hands or the parted lips on the lovely face that Melinda had recognised only too easily.

'I certainly was not expecting to see you this morning, Skittles,' the Marquis said.

'But you are glad to see me? Say you are glad to see me!'

Skittles' face was upturned towards his, her red lips pouting provocatively at him. Almost involuntarily Melinda clenched her hands together. It was then that Captain Vestey saw her and coming from the mantelpiece, where he had been standing, he exclaimed:

'Melinda, it's good to see you! Did you have a comfortable drive down yesterday?'

He raised her hand to his lips and she forced herself to answer him.

'Yes, a very nice drive, thank you. It is pleasant to be away from London.'

'That is what we all thought,' he said. 'And that is why Skittles insisted on setting off here at some ungodly hour before I'd even gouged my eyelids open.'

Gervase Vestey's eyes were on Melinda's face, and she felt as if he was giving her time to compose herself and deliberately keeping her from watching the way Skittles was exerting all her wiles to beguile the Marquis.

She was looking exquisite in a riding-habit of emerald green which made her waist seem fantastically small and her skin very white.

'You'll soon get bloody bored if you spend too much time in the country,' she was saying in her clear voice, but the Marquis had already detached himself from her clinging hands and was greeting his other friends.

They were all men, elegant, raffish, supremely at ease, and they greeted Melinda, as Captain Vestey introduced them, with a faint air of familiarity which she resented because she did not understand it.

'Well, I thought it would damn well cheer you up to see us,' Skittles said. 'Gervase told us of your bereavement and we thought it wasn't like you to sit moping when you should have your pals around you.'

'A kind thought, Skittles,' the Marquis said with a touch of sarcasm in his voice, 'but why such a large escort?'

'Had to bring a blasted chaperon with me, didn't I?' Skittles asked with a shriek of laughter. 'Not that little milk-face here seems to have wanted one!'

She looked at Melinda as she spoke, with unveiled hostility, and immediately the gentlemen looked uncomfortable, as men always do when women are antagonistic to each other.

'What about some refreshments, Drogo?' Captain Vestey asked quickly. 'Speaking for myself, I had no time for breakfast and I am extremely hungry.'

'And I'll tell you something else interesting,' Skittles said. 'As I was coming down your drive I thought to myself as we passed through the park, what a hell of a spot for a point-to-point.'

'By George! She's right!' one of the gentlemen exclaimed. 'The steps of the front door would make a first-class stand; you could see the riders the whole way round! Why did we never think of it?'

'Because you're bloody fools, that's why!' Skittles replied. 'Here, come on and have a look.'

She walked through the front door and the gentlemen followed her. Almost as if under some compulsion Melinda joined them. They stood grouped on the steps and below them lay the park with its great trees, and on either side fields with low hedges stretching away towards distant woods.

'You see!' Skittles said. 'A natural race-course.'

'She's right, you know,' Captain Vestey said. 'You must try it out some time, Drogo.'

'Why wait?' Skittles said. 'I'll take any one of you on. What shall we make the ruddy stakes? Five hundred guineas?'

'Too high, Skittles,' one of the gentlemen protested. 'You know you're bound to win.'

'Yellow-livered, are you?' Skittles said scornfully.

'Come on, you cheese-paring bastards! Five hundred guineas that Saracen and I will beat any one of you, with one hand tied behind my back if you like!'

The gentlemen looked rather sheepish. No one accepted the challenge. And then a small voice, coming, it seemed to Melinda, from some utter stranger, said:

'I will accept your wager.'

As she spoke there was a sudden silence. Then everyone's head turned and a dozen pairs of eyes stared at her in absolute astonishment.

'You?' Skittles asked scornfully. 'What do you ride? A cow?'

'I will accept your challenge,' Melinda said, looking her steadily in the eyes.

'Now, Melinda . . .' Captain Vestey started, only to be interrupted by the Marquis.

'It is impossible!' he said.

'Not at all,' Melinda replied. 'I should like to accept Miss Walters' challenge, with one proviso; which is, of course, that you let me choose whichever horse I desire from your stables.'

'Well, of course, he'll do that,' one of the gentlemen ejaculated. 'Drogo's got some jolly fine horseflesh. Have to look to your laurels, Skittles.'

'Laurels!' Skittles ejaculated. 'What the bloody hell do you think I'm made of? I'll lay you five to one that pullet falls off at the first fence!'

The colour rose in Melinda's cheeks at Skittles' rudeness, but her eyes flashed and her lips tightened as she heard the Marquis say:

'I will not allow it.'

'You cannot prevent me, my lord,' she said to him.

'No, indeed, he can do nothing of the sort,' one of his friends agreed. 'Don't be a spoilsport, Drogo. Let's give the girls their heads. After all, Miss Melinda's an unknown quantity.'

Captain Vestey caught Melinda by the hand.

'Don't! Don't!' he urged in a low voice that only she could hear. 'You are crazy! Skittles is a better rider than any woman in the land. Make some excuse; say you are too ill; obey Drogo.'

If Melinda hesitated she did not show it. She only looked across to where Skittles had once again laid her hand on the Marquis's arm and she heard her say:

'You haven't seen me ride for a long time. I would like to show you my paces.'

The *double entendre* in her tone was quite unmistakable and Melinda felt herself stiffen.

'At what time would Miss Walters like the race to take place?' she enquired.

'There's no hurry,' Skittles replied over her shoulder. 'It won't take me long to beat you, Miss Ambitious, and I only hope you'll be able to pay your losses. I don't care for welshers.'

'If you win you will be paid,' Melinda said quietly.

'Refreshments are served, m'lord!'

The butler's voice from the doorway came as a welcome break from the tension that seemed to vibrate between the two women.

'I can do with a drink, by Jove!' one of the gentlemen ejaculated as they stood aside to let Skittles sweep first through the doorway, not giving Melinda so much as a disdainful glance.

Melinda was forced to follow her. When she

reached the hall she turned to climb the stairs. She was only a short distance up when a voice behind her made her stop.

'Melinda!'

It was the Marquis and they were alone; for the rest of the party was already moving down the passage towards the dining-room. She turned round to face him.

'You little fool!' he said. 'You will break your neck!'

There was an almost savage note in his voice and somehow she could bear to hear no more. Without answering she turned and ran up the stairs, leaving him staring after her.

It was only when she reached her room that she realised she had no habit to wear. She could not ride without one. She rang for the housemaid.

'Is there, by any chance, a riding-habit in the house that would fit me?' she asked.

The housemaid looked even more supercilious than she had the night before.

'I have no idea, miss,' she said, 'but I will enquire from Mrs. Meadows the housekeeper.'

Mrs. Meadows was old, grey-haired and seemed to Melinda to look at her with searching eyes.

'A riding-habit! I have no idea, miss, if I could fit you up. You're so small.'

'Oh, please,' Melinda said, 'please see if you can find me something. It is very important.'

She felt now that to have to cry off the race would be an admission of defeat, not only to Skittles but to the Marquis. Just for a moment she thought that she was crazy to have risked all her money, all her hopes of the cottage shared with Nanna, on such an unequal race. And then she knew she hated Skittles, that she had to beat her—and not only at riding.

'Please, please, help me,' she implored the housekeeper.

Mrs. Meadows looked at her small, eager face and exclaimed almost involuntarily:

'I'm sure I don't know what a nice young lady like you is doing taking part in these wild pranks. You're too young for this sort of thing.'

'I just have to ride against her,' Melinda said almost to herself.

'I didn't mean the riding so much,' Mrs. Meadows said, and then checked herself. 'It's none of my business, of course. Come along, miss, and let me see if there's anything that will fit you in my store-room. It's a pity you're not a boy, for I have his lordship's clothes kept safe and in moth balls since he first was lifted on to a saddle. And then there's her late ladyship's; she always left some clothes here behind her but she was large and there's nothing of hers that would fit you.'

By this time they had reached the housekeeper's room, and beyond it was another room fitted entirely with wardrobes.

'Are these full of clothes that somebody once wore?' Melinda asked looking around her.

'They are, indeed, miss,' Mrs. Meadows answered, 'and some of them very lovely. There are his lordship's Peer's robes, which he wore at the Coronation of Her Majesty, and his father's before him and his grandfather's before that. And then there's her ladyship's coronet, and wedding-gowns for four generations. His lordship sometimes teases me and calls this my "museum". He's not far wrong, for it's part of the history of Chard.' Mrs. Meadows spoke with pride, and then there was a shadow on her face. 'But the house has never before seen ladies such as these,' she said and she made the term, 'lady', an expression of scorn.

'That is why I have got to beat her,' Melinda said. 'I think she is horrible. I did not know there were women like her in the world. At the same time, she is so beautiful!'

'There's no beauty in persons like that!' Mrs. Meadows snapped, and then she gave an exclamation. 'I have it! I have the very thing, miss! I had not thought of it before because it's with my fancy dresses. But 'tis a riding-habit worn by his lordship's grandmother when she visited France and hunted boar with King Louis the Fourteenth. Very small her ladyship was. I only knew her, of course, when she was a very old lady, but she had still kept her figure and there are many of her clothes preserved here for future generations to admire.'

All the time she was talking, Mrs. Meadows was pulling open doors and now she took from a shelf a riding-habit of deep blue velvet. It was trimmed with silver braid and had sparkling buttons of blue sapphires. There was a lace jabot for the neck and a tiny tricorn hat sporting a curling ostrich feather.

'It is lovely!' Melinda exclaimed. 'But the buttons! Are they real?'

'You don't suppose her ladyship would wear anything that wasn't of the best?' Mrs. Meadows asked. 'Now, try it on, miss. It's my belief that it will fit you exactly, and I've a good eye for measurements, I have. And, now, where are the boots?'

A quarter of an hour later Melinda walked slowly down the stairs. She was conscious that if she looked rather over-dressed, she was certainly looking her best. The blue velvet brought out the blue of her eyes; the feather curved against her cheek; the real lace jabot encircled her neck; and the sapphire and diamond buttons sparkled with every step she took.

She heard the noise of laughter coming from the dining-room but went out through the front door and down to the stables. The grooms were busy rubbing down the horses which had arrived with the guests. Skittles' horse, a fiery chestnut, was hard to hold and two grooms were having difficulty in getting him into a stall. The chief groom, an old man with whom Melinda had talked the day before, came forward.

'Are you wanting a horse, ma'am?'

'Yes,' Melinda replied. 'I will ride Thunderbolt.'

The groom looked thunderstruck.

'I'm sure 'is lordship wouldn't allow that, ma'am. I told you yesterday, 'e's 'ard to 'old for a gentleman, let alone a lady.'

'I will ride him,' Melinda said confidently. 'Let me go into his stall.'

'Be careful, miss. 'E kicked one of my boys last year and 'e was in 'ospital for nigh on three months.'

'I will be careful,' Melinda said.

She went to the stall. Thunderbolt lay back his ears at her approach and blew somewhat aggressively through his nostrils. She spoke to him, talking to him in the same voice that she used to her own horses. Very slowly, she laid her hand on his neck.

'Will you help me, boy?' she said softly. 'You have got to show them what you can do; I have got to prove something to myself.'

She went on talking and it seemed as if the horse was responding to her voice. Finally, she stroked him gently on the nose and turned to the old groom who was watching her.

'Saddle him now,' she said. 'I think he understands.'

'I've never seen anything like it in all me born days!' the old man ejaculated. 'I'll saddle 'im meself, ma'am. I don't trust any of them boys near 'im. But I'm sure I don't know what 'is lordship will say.'

'I will ride him round to the front door,' Melinda said, knowing it would be far easier to argue when she was mounted on the horse than if she were standing on the ground.

When the company came out of the dining-room, having eaten greedily of the cold collation that the chef had managed to serve at a moment's notice, and having imbibed a great deal of the Marquis's champagne, Melinda was walking Thunderbolt round slowly on the driveway in front of the house.

'Good lord!' she heard Captain Vestey exclaim. 'What horse is Melinda riding? I've never seen a more magnificent animal!'

'It is Thunderbolt,' the Marquis replied, and Gervase Vestey knew by the look on the Marquis's face that he was in an evil temper.

'She will be all right, won't she?' he asked.

The Marquis did not answer him. He was walking across to Melinda.

'I will not have it! Do you understand, Melinda?

I forbid you to ride that animal!'

'But, I am already riding him,' she replied.

'Then I will take him back to the stables and find you another,' he said. He put out his hand to take hold of Thunderbolt's bridle. Whether the stallion resented his interference or felt the prick of Melinda's spur it was hard to say, but he reared up, causing the Marquis to step back, and Melinda, holding Thunderbolt skilfully, took the horse a little way down the drive as if to calm him down.

'Gently, boy! Gently!' she said. 'If they get too nervous they may really prevent me from riding you and that would be a pity.'

Skittles' horse was being brought round from the stables. She came laughing and swearing down the steps and someone helped her into the saddle. She was screaming for her gloves, for her whip, and was cracking jests with the gentlemen before she looked round and saw Melinda standing a little apart on the great, black stallion. Just for a moment she did not speak and her eyes narrowed speculatively. Then she laughed.

'My God! I'd no idea this was such a dressy affair! My opponent's certainly got herself up to kill! And perhaps it will be a killing! Who knows?'

She waited for the laugh from the surrounding gentlemen. Then she bent down and put her hand on to the Marquis's shoulder.

'Tom's making a book, Drogo,' she said. 'Put your money on me. I'd like to win something for you.'

'Thank you, Skittles, but this is a race of which I disapprove,' the Marquis replied. 'I shall not place a bet on either of the competitors.'

'Then I will bring you my triumph just the same,' Skittles said softly. 'There's a little more at stake than five hundred guineas, you know that, don't you?'

'The bet is yours,' the Marquis said steadily. 'I had no hand in it.'

Melinda, watching them and being unable to hear what they said, felt a sudden pain in her heart. Foul-mouthed though this woman might be, she was very lovely. She wanted the Marquis and let the whole world see it. She wondered how he could resist her.

She turned Thunderbolt round because she could not bear to watch them, and trotted to the beginning of the drive which she knew was the starting point. There was a little altercation as to who was to start the race. The Marquis refused and finally Captain Vestey agreed to do it. He was given instructions of all kinds from the other gentlemen, before he mounted his horse and rode down to join Melinda, with Skittles beside him.

'You know the course,' he said to the two women. 'Over the first three fences which you can see from here, turn and come back on the other side of the park; over the other three in the far distance and here is the winning post.'

'Don't forget, I've got a side bet that my opponent falls at the first fence,' Skittles said.

She spoke aggressively and Melinda had the idea that she was not as sure of her superiority as she had been at first.

'Now, go to your places,' Captain Vestey said, 'and I will give you the start. I will call out, "one, two, three," and when I drop my handkerchief you will go.'

He went a short way ahead of them. The women turned their horses and brought them down slowly towards him.

'One, two, three . . .' Captain Vestey called out, and dropped his handkerchief.

As if Thunderbolt knew exactly what it was all about, he set off like an arrow from a bow. Melinda held him as tightly as she could, knowing that to go too fast at the beginning of the race would be a mistake. The first fence loomed ahead of them and she saw why Skittles had expected her to fall. It was a high fence with a broad ditch and a drop on the other side which would test both an inexperienced horse and an inexperienced rider.

'Steady, boy! Steady!' Melinda said, pulling Thunderbolt in so that he took the fence much more slowly than he had intended. He flew over it and landed without difficulty.

Melinda's precaution had given Skittles several lengths' lead. The next fence was quite near; the third was some distance. She took the next fence with the same caution and then let Thunderbolt have his head. She checked him just in time before the third fence and saw there was a small stream on the other side. He jumped clear, but only just, and had a slight scramble up the bank.

Again Skittles gained half a length. And now they were on the turn and heading for home. Melinda had a quick glance at her opponent and realised that Skittles was, indeed, a magnificent rider. She could understand how she had gained her reputation. She rode as if she were part of the horse. The going was soft;

the pieces of turf raised by the horses' hooves flew behind them.

Skittles was still ahead. She went over the fifth fence like a bird and, although Thunderbolt had gained a little on her now, she was still two lengths in the lead. They were over the sixth fence and now it was for home!

Melinda knew that this was the moment that Thunderbolt must make a supreme effort. She touched him with her whip but it was unnecessary. As if the stallion knew instinctively what she required of him, he began to gain, inch by inch, foot by foot, on the horse ahead, steadily closing the gap. Now she could see the crowd of gentlemen waiting at the winning-post.

'Please, Thunderbolt! Please! Come on, boy.'

She heard her own voice above the thunder of hooves and felt the words whipped away from between her teeth by the speed at which they were travelling. Then she felt Thunderbolt leap forward beneath her with a renewed strength which seemed to come almost from her own heart. She was urging him with her whole being and he was responding.

Now she heard the cries of the gentlemen waiting for them and it seemed as if the wind must tear the very skin from her face. Thunderbolt was level with Skittles . . . a nose ahead and now half a length as they thundered past the winning-post.

It was some moments before Melinda could rein him in, but finally she managed, with hands that were almost too tired to hold him and arms which seemed to have burst from their sockets, to bring him nearly to a standstill and to turn him round. They cantered back and now, for the first time, Melinda thought of herself and realised that she had lost her tricorn hat somewhere on the race and that her fair hair was falling around her face in dishevelled curls.

They crowded round her, applauding, cheering, telling her she was magnificent. But she had eyes only for one person. She looked over their heads towards the Marquis. She saw that he stared at her unsmiling, with an expression in his eyes that she could not fathom.

'Well done!'

'Bravo!'

'God! You were magnificent!'

The exclamations echoed around her but she hardly heard them. Someone was leading Thunderbolt towards the front door so that she could dismount. She was conscious of feeling very tired. Even the elation had gone. She only knew that the Marquis's expression had taken all her triumph from her.

She must have swayed in the saddle. Suddenly, strong arms reached up and lifted her to the ground. She did not need to look to know whose they were. He carried her up the stone steps and in through the front door. She thought he would put her down in the hall. Instead, he carried her up the stairs, her face hidden against his shoulder, her hair flowing over the blue velvet of her riding-habit.

He carried her into her bedroom and set her down on the bed. She wanted to cry out because he was taking his arms from her but she could say nothing, not even thank you, for her voice had died in her throat. And then, as she looked up at him with her head on the pillow, she heard him say harshly:

'You little idiot! You might have broken your neck!'

10

Melinda must have dozed for a time from sheer exhaustion, but when she awoke it seemed to her she could only hear the note of contempt—or was it anger?—in the Marquis's voice as he said, 'You little idiot! You might have broken your neck.' The words repeated themselves over and over again in her mind.

At the same time she felt as if the race had released something within herself. It was as if, in accepting the challenge, she had had as her opponent not only Skittles, but everyone else who had ever tyrannised over her, been rude, treated her with contempt or ignored her as a poor relation. All she had suffered in the last year seemed to have accumulated into one vast resentment within herself that had now burst its bounds and she was free of it.

But, most of all, she knew she had wanted somehow to gain the approval of the Marquis, to let him know she was not just a weak, stupid little pawn that he could move backwards and forwards according to his own machinations and who had no character or thoughts of her own. In this she felt she had failed—and yet she had won the race.

She could remember the astonishment in the eyes of the gentlemen as they cheered her as she passed the winning-post ahead of Skittles. They had not known that her father had brought her up to take the place of the son he had never had. He had taken her out with him as if she were, indeed, the heir he had longed for. He had taught her to ride; she had gone hunting with him; she had shot partridges at his side and swam in the lake, diving from a high bank. When her mother had remonstrated he had merely laughed.

'Give me a son,' he teased, 'and I will give you back your daughter.'

For Melinda it had been a joy beyond words to accompany her father at his sports. He had always treated her as if she were his equal, explaining to her what should be done, kind and understanding when she failed to jump her fence or to bring down her bird.

'You look frail enough,' he said to her once, 'but your hands on the bridle are like those of a man.'

It was the greatest compliment he could have paid her, and Melinda wondered whether he now knew of her race and approved of it. She had won and she had wiped that cocksure, arrogant look from Skittles' face; and, yet, what good had it done her? The Marquis still despised her.

For a moment she turned her face against the pillow; then, impatient with herself, she rose from the bed. She rang for the maid, washed and changed into an exceedingly becoming gown of white sarsenet trimmed with blue ribbons and innumerable tiny lace frills. The maid arranged her hair and Melinda suddenly realised she was no longer tired; instead, a strange excitement was rising within her—excitement at the thought of seeing the Marquis again, of going downstairs, not a crushed, ignored little nonentity, but someone who had beaten Skittles, a woman who had been acclaimed as the finest horse-woman in the country.

Just for a moment she could not help seeing the picture of Skittles' lovely face upturned towards the Marquis, of her white hand on his lapel, of her mouth, provocatively red, raised towards his. Then, impatiently, she brushed it aside. Skittles might hunt the Marquis and there was no denying that she was doing her best to capture him, but for the moment she, Melinda, was the woman in possession. For six months he could not be rid of her; for six months, however much Skittles might attract him, he was still obliged to keep Melinda at his side, to pretend, at least to the attorneys, that she was his wife.

Melinda looked at herself in the mirror. She knew it would be hard for anyone, least of all Sir Hector, to recognise her, in her fashionable clothes and skilfully arranged coiffure, as the quiet, mouselike, poor relation who had been stormed at and beaten and who was of less consequence than anyone in her uncle's household.

The thought made Melinda lift her chin high and she went downstairs, walking like a queen, knowing that her victory had given her a new confidence and a feeling of pride that had not been there before. To her surprise the house seemed very quiet. She opened the door of the drawing-room and found not the gay, laughing crowd she had expected, but only Captain Vestey who was standing looking out of the window, his back towards the door. He must have heard her enter, for he asked:

'Have they gone?' Then he turned and added: 'Oh, it's you. Melinda! I thought it was Drogo. He was speeding the departing guests.'

'So they have left,' Melinda said.

'They have left,' Captain Vestey said, walking towards her. 'Come and sit down, you must be tired.'

'I have been resting,' Melinda assured him, 'and I am no longer fatigued.'

'Then you should be,' he said. 'You were magnificent! I didn't know there was a woman born who could ride Thunderbolt and beat Skittles. Who taught you to ride like that?'

'My father,' Melinda said, 'and I have ridden since I was three years old.'

'There's riding and riding!' Captain Vestey exclaimed. 'And you were different! I never credited I would see anything so exciting as the way you handled Thunderbolt on that last half-mile.'

'And his lordship is angry with me,' Melinda murmured in a low voice.

'I am not surprised,' Captain Vestey replied. 'We all thought you would break your neck.'

'And . . . if I . . . had,' Melinda faltered, 'would that have . . . meant that . . . that he would . . . have lost his . . . inheritance?'

'I had not thought of that before. No, of course not,' Captain Vestey protested. 'He was concerned for you yourself—we all were. If you die in the interim period before the Dowager's conditions are realised, that will not be his fault; in fact, I should imagine he would receive the money immediately.'

'Then . . . then he was concerned for . . . me?' Melinda said as if to herself, and felt her heart leap at the thought.

'I think you have got the wrong conception of Drogo . . .' Captain Vestey began, but before he could finish the sentence the door opened and the Marquis came in.

'They have gone,' he said briefly and saw Melinda's little face turned towards him, a look of apprehension in her eyes.

He said nothing, merely advancing towards the end of the room where she was sitting. When he reached her side he stood looking down at her taking in, it seemed, her air of fragility, her small, white hands and the heart-shaped face with its big, anxious, blue eyes.

'I cannot believe it!' he said. 'I would not have trusted any woman on Thunderbolt.'

'Thank you for letting me ride him,' Melinda said.

Her words seemed to break what somehow had been a tense moment. The Marquis threw back his head and laughed.

'Let you!' he ejaculated. 'I had no choice in the matter. I think, now, I must have been besotted to acquiesce in anything so crazy. But, as it happened, it turned out well. You won!'

'Indeed, she won five hundred guineas,' Captain Vestey said. 'Do you think Skittles will pay up?'

'I am sure she will—or someone will pay for her!'

the Marquis said. 'Even in Skittles' world a gambling debt is one of honour.'

Melinda wondered what he meant by 'Skittles' world'. Was it a different world to the one in which the Marquis moved, she wondered. Then she remembered the other women who had been at that strange party the night the Dowager had died, and recalled the disgust, the distaste she had felt at their behaviour and at the flow of oaths that came continually from Skittles' mouth.

Quite suddenly all the elation she had felt at winning the race subsided, and she knew that by competing with Skittles she had, in some way, lowered herself to that woman's level.

'It was a fantastic race!' she heard Captain Vestey say and felt she could not bear to listen to them speaking of it any more. Impulsively she rose to her feet.

'May I ask you something?' she enquired of the Marquis.

'Of course,' he replied.

'Then do not let us talk again of this race,' she said. 'I think perhaps I was wrong in accepting Miss Walters' challenge. It was just that on Thunderbolt I knew that I could beat her. But I think, now, that it was wrong of me to exert myself in such a way. Would you please convey to her this message? I do not wish to accept the money. She may keep it.'

The Marquis said nothing, but his eyes were on Melinda's face.

'But, why should you do that?' Captain Vestey broke in. 'It was a bet! Of course you must accept the five hundred guineas so long as Skittles has the decency to pay it!'

'No, I would rather not,' Melinda asserted. 'If she insists I shall give it to a charity.'

There was a little pause, before the Marquis said:

'I thought that you were so interested in money. You told me once that it was the money which made you accept the proposition which was made to you on my behalf.'

'Yes, indeed, it was,' Melinda said. 'But I have enough. I do not require, nor do I wish, to take money from Miss Walters.'

'You have a dislike of her?' the Marquis enquired.

Melinda's lips tightened. For a moment she thought of telling him just exactly what she thought of Skittles and of those other women to whom he had introduced her. Then she thought that to speak of them in such a manner would merely be to show herself as being spiteful, and perhaps, she thought in a sudden panic, he would realise that she was, in fact, jealous of Caroline Walters.

'Please, can we discuss something else?' she said.

She would have turned away, but the Marquis reached out and caught her hand, holding her prisoner. She felt herself tremble at his touch and looked up at him, her eyes a little apprehensive.

'You are a strange creature, Melinda,' he said, speaking to her as if they were alone in the room and Captain Vestey was not there. 'I do not understand you. What goes on in that little head of yours, behind that incredible air of innocence? Tell me! Tell me what you are thinking!'

His fingers tightened on her wrist until they hurt,

and Melinda had a feeling that he was probing into her secret heart, drawing out feelings that she would not have him know.

'My thoughts are private, my lord,' she said, then looked up into his eyes and felt that it was not only by the hand that he held her prisoner but that he had captured her utterly beyond all escape.

For a moment they looked at each other and they were alone—a man and woman inescapably aware of each other. It was with a sense of shock that they heard Captain Vestey speak and break the spell.

'I think the whole thing is rather ridiculous,' he urged. 'Melinda should take the money and keep it for her old age. She won't always be as beautiful as she is now, and when she is no longer so attractive it will be a nice little nest-egg.'

'Exactly!' the Marquis said drily and released his hold on Melinda's hand.

'I will not take it,' she repeated, 'and that is all there is to be said on the subject. It is kind of you gentlemen to take so much interest on my behalf, but on this point I have made my decision and I shall not change.'

'Then, by all means, let us talk of something else,' the Marquis said with a note of irritation in his voice. 'Come, Gervase, I will play you a game of piquet and Melinda, if she wishes, can watch.'

'It is a game I detest,' Captain Vestey said somewhat petulantly.

'I will play with you if you like,' Melinda offered a little shyly.

The Marquis raised his eyebrows.

'Another of your accomplishments,' he said. 'There

appears to be no end to them!'

However, he went to the card-table at the far end of the room and they played together almost in silence. To the Marquis's surprise, Melinda was almost his equal as regards play, and she had a run of luck with the cards that was quite invincible.

They must have played for over an hour and Melinda was just thinking that it would soon be time for her to go up and change for dinner, when the door opened and the butler, in stentorian tones, announced:

'Lord Wrotham to see you, m'lord!'

Melinda had her back to the door. As the Marquis rose to his feet she put down her cards carefully in case the game should continue, and only after a few seconds turned round to see the new arrival. When she did so she gave a little gasp. There was no mistaking the man now shaking hands with the Marquis and turning to greet Captain Vestey. She had only seen him once, but she thought she would never forget him—that thin, evil face with the hooked nose, full mouth, the bags of dissipation under the eyes, and the long, bony fingers which had raised her hand to his lips.

She half turned again towards the card-table, hoping he would not notice her, and then she thought it was extremely unlikely that even if he did he would recognise her. He had only seen her once.

'Skittles sent me,' she heard Lord Wrotham say. 'I am here to pay her just debts and to meet this incomparable rider, this new star of whom, until now, we have been so ignorant.'

'You are almost poetical, Wrotham,' the Marquis

said, with a note of sarcasm in his voice. 'Let me present you! Melinda, this is Lord Wrotham who, as you hear, is here to pay your just dues. Lord Wrotham, Miss Melinda Stanyon!'

Melinda was forced to turn round. She dropped her eyes and then, as Lord Wrotham did not speak, raised them. What she saw in his face made her suddenly tense with fear.

'Miss Melinda Stanyon!' he said. 'I thought there could not be two of them. Melinda is an unusual name, don't you think? And, so, at last, my child, I have found you!'

He moved forward, took her hand which was lying limp against her gown, and raised it, as he had done once before, to his lips. She felt the touch of his mouth, warm, hard and possessive against her skin and with a little inarticulate murmur, she snatched her hand away.

'I have found you,' Lord Wrotham said, 'and now I suggest you pack and we leave at once. My carriage is outside.'

'What is all this about?' the Marquis asked almost angrily. 'You have met Melinda, I gather, before, but by what right do you suggest that she should leave? She is here as my guest.'

'I cannot understand in what circumstances she should have left Ella Harcourt's, except in my company,' Lord Wrotham said. 'I fear there has been some misunderstanding, but that can easily be rectified. Melinda will come with me now. As you well know, Chard, my house is but five miles away and I am entertaining Skittles for the week-end.'

'I think Melinda will thank you for your invitation,' the Marquis said icily, 'but she is already enjoying my hospitality and will have no wish to accept yours. Is that right, Melinda?'

Melinda moved a step towards the Marquis as if to seek his protection.

'Yes, yes . . . of course,' she said nervously. 'Thank you, Lord Wrotham, but I am . . . staying here and . . . have no desire to leave.'

'These are but words, Melinda, as well you know,' Lord Wrotham retorted. 'You belong to me, and now let us dispense with all this formality. Run upstairs like a good girl and pack your box. I am sorry, Chard; there are plenty of other little soiled doves for the taking, but you must not take mine.'

'I have no idea on what you base your assumption that you have a prior claim to Melinda,' the Marquis said, 'but she does not leave this house. As you are obviously determined to make things uncomfortable for her, I would bid you good-day, Wrotham.'

'It is not as easy as that,' Lord Wrotham objected. 'I do not relish being cheated out of what is mine. On a matter of principle I insist that Melinda comes with me.'

'And I insist that she stays,' the Marquis said.

'But, surely,' Captain Vestey interposed, 'Melinda has a choice in the matter. Let us ask her which she would rather do.'

He cast a desperate glance at Melinda as he spoke, almost as if he were afraid that she might refuse to stay when so much was at stake.

'Y . . . yes, of course,' Melinda said, her voice trembling. 'I . . . I wish to . . . stay. I have . . . promised that I would.'

'Exactly!' the Marquis said. 'There is your answer, Wrotham. Please bring this disagreeable scene to an end and return to your guests. I am sure Skittles will be waiting anxiously for you.'

'I have already told you,' Lord Wrotham said, and now his voice was smooth and calculating yet, somehow, his words seemed to cut like a knife, 'Melinda is mine. She comes with me.'

The Marquis put his hand to his forehead.

'You do not seem to understand plain English,' he said. 'You may have your reason for making these wild assertions, but Melinda is here of her own free will and, of her own free will, she has just informed you that she wishes to stay. In which case, there is no more to be said.'

'Very well, Chard, you force me to a most disagreeable decision,' Lord Wrotham said. 'If you will not permit Melinda to come with me, which I consider it her bounden duty to do, then, of course, I must fight you for her.'

'You mean a duel?' the Marquis said.

'I mean exactly that,' Lord Wrotham replied, a smile curving his lips. 'Tomorrow at dawn, which I think should be about half-past five; the usual place beside the Serpentine!'

'But this is ridiculous!' Captain Vestey interposed. 'Duelling is forbidden, as well you know, Wrotham. If Her Majesty got to hear of it . . .'

'Her Majesty will not hear of it until it is over,' Lord Wrotham said. 'And dead men tell no tales!' He turned to Melinda. 'I regret, my dear, that you will not be my guest until tomorrow night. I will fetch you from here about noon. Kindly be ready.'

Melinda tried to speak but the words were lost in her throat.

As if supremely in command of the situation, Lord Wrotham raised her hand once again to his lips, but this time perfunctorily. For a moment his eyes flickered over her and she felt herself shiver as if, mentally, he tore her gown from her breasts. And then, still with that horrible, confident smile upon his lips, he walked from the room.

For a moment they all three stood as if turned to stone. Then, without thinking what she was doing, Melinda flung herself against the Marquis, holding on to him with her hands, her face pressed against his shoulder.

'I won't go with him, I won't! Don't let him make me. I hate him and he . . . he frightens me!'

Slowly and deliberately the Marquis moved away from her. He walked across the room and without looking at her or Captain Vestey opened the door and went out.

Melinda stood where he had left her, the tears running down her cheeks.

'Stop him! Oh, stop him!' she cried to Gervase Vestey.

'No, let him go,' Captain Vestey replied. 'He has to be alone for the moment and face what lies ahead.'

'A duel! What did he mean by . . . a duel?' Melinda asked, half distraught. 'They . . . are . . . forbidden.'

'But they still take place,' Captain Vestey said quietly, 'and Wrotham is a crack shot.'

'What do you . . . mean?' Melinda's voice faltered.

'I mean,' Captain Vestey explained, 'that he has already killed three men. It is my belief that he has always hated Drogo and he has made this an excuse—beside the fact of wanting you for himself—to challenge him.'

'His lordship must refuse,' Melinda demanded.

'Don't be ridiculous!' Captain Vestey retorted. 'You know as well as I do, if he showed himself yellow-livered he would be laughed at by every friend he's got.'

'But why should he . . . fight Lord Wrotham? And over what?' Melinda asked.

'Over you, apparently,' Captain Vestey replied.

'But, why . . . why does his lordship not . . .' Her words tailed away and Captain Vestey, sitting down at the card-table as if his legs could no longer support him, finished the sentence:

'. . . Give you over to Lord Wrotham? Even if he wished to do so, you know he cannot. Refuse to fight and be ostracised by every decent man in the country. No, Melinda! A man must behave honourably, however dishonourable his opponent.'

'But, if . . . if Lord Wrotham . . . kills him?'

'As he said himself,' Captain Vestey said in a low tone, 'dead men tell no tales! It is whispered at the club, only whispered, mind you, that he fires before his opponents turn. But when his man is dead, there are few who will speak up for him and Wrotham has great influence in some circles.'

'Then, what . . . c . . . can we . . . do?' Melinda asked piteously, tears running down her cheeks.

'Nothing, except pray,' Captain Vestey answered. 'By Jove! I haven't thought of doing that since I was at Eton! But if ever there was a time when prayer was necessary, it's now. It's a woman's job and you'd best get on with it. Drogo will need some sort of strength if he's to beat Wrotham's bullet which, make no mistake, will be aimed straight at his heart.'

'Oh, why, why did I ever . . . meet him?' Melinda asked.

'Why, indeed?' Captain Vestey said, and the question was almost a cry of despair as he walked from the room.

Melinda put her head down on the card-table and cried. She cried bitterly and despairingly, feeling that she was like some animal caught in a trap from which there was no way out. The room was almost in twilight and she struggled to regain her composure; then realising she must look a fright she went upstairs to her bedroom to wash her face in cold water.

Her eyes were still swollen when, without her having rung the bell, the maid came into the room.

'It must be time to change for dinner,' Melinda said.

'I came to ask, miss, if you'd be dining downstairs or in your room?' the maid enquired.

'Why should I dine upstairs?' Melinda asked, wondering if the Marquis had given some order to that effect because he could not bear to see her.

'You will be alone, miss,' the maid said. 'You might prefer to have something brought upstairs.'

'Alone?' Melinda questioned.

'Yes, indeed, miss; didn't you know? His lordship and Captain Vestey left a short while ago for London. I imagined . . .' The maid looked at her curiously and Melinda knew that she was wondering if there had been a row and she had been left behind on purpose.

'Yes, of course, I knew,' she said. 'I had forgotten his lordship was going so early.' At the same time, she wondered despairingly what she was going to do. How could she sit here alone in this vast house, knowing that the Marquis was going to fight a duel, perhaps to die, on her behalf?

She wondered how he could have gone without saying good-bye; and then, with a sudden ache in her heart, she wondered if he hated her. She could almost imagine his feelings as he had driven away down the drive. Had he looked back and thought perhaps he would never see Chard again?—the house that had meant so much to him, the house that he had intrigued and fought to keep. It would be an ironic tragedy if now, after he had risked so much, he should die at the hand of a man who wanted only the woman who had been used in a plot to deceive the Dowager.

Melinda put her hands up to her face. 'Oh, Drogo! Drogo!' she sobbed in her heart. 'How could I have done this to you? How could I have brought so much upon you when I love you! I love you!'

'Is anything wrong, miss?' the maid asked.

'No, nothing,' Melinda answered. 'I . . . I have a headache. But, will you please pack my things and order a carriage for me. I shall be leaving for London in one hour's time.'

'A carriage, miss?'

There was a question in the maid's voice and Melinda knew that with an impertinence that hardly seemed possible she was querying the order.

'Yes, a carriage,' Melinda said. 'Ask for it to be round at nine o'clock—unless, of course, his lordship has ordered it for me. He may, however, have forgotten in the speed of his own departure.'

The maid accepted this.

'I will go and see to it at once, miss,' she said respectfully. 'But will you have something to eat before you leave?'

'Yes, of course,' Melinda said. 'Tell the chef to send up a small meal. I am not very hungry.'

'Very good, miss.'

The maid went from the room and Melinda jumped to her feet. She had got to do something; she had got to! She could not stay here waiting and wondering. And yet, if she arrived at the house in Grosvenor Square, what would be her reception? She could almost see the anger in the Marquis's face. Perhaps, she thought pitifully, her presence might do more harm than good. He must be calm before his duel; he should not be preoccupied or irritated. And yet she knew she must go to London.

It seemed to her as if she was beset by demons tormenting her. This was her own doing. If she had never accepted Mrs. Harcourt's invitation to stay the night at her house she would never have met Lord Wrotham. And yet, on the other hand, she would never have met the Marquis! It was all such a tangle in which she felt she was only a small, insignificant creature, caught in a monstrous cobweb of intrigue and treachery.

It was Skittles who had sent Lord Wrotham to pay her debt and Melinda knew that, knowingly or unknowingly, the woman had revenged herself very effectively. She must have spoken of her by name—in fact, they would all have done that—and then Lord Wrotham would have remembered. As he had said,

Melinda was an uncommon name. She had won a race but she had, perhaps, lost everything! She might have destroyed the man she loved!

She gave a little cry, like an animal in pain, and then, suddenly, she swept across the room. She opened the door, and lifting up her skirt ran down the stairs. She was not certain, but she thought that she had seen what she wanted in the Library.

She opened the door and went in. The dying sun made it possible for her to see her way across the room. She walked to where she thought she had seen what she sought—and she was not mistaken. They were lying on the table by one of the windows, in an elegant, polished box, engraved with the Chard crest—a pair of highly polished duelling pistols!

11

The mist was heavy over the Serpentine but the sky was lightening and the evening stars were fading away into the sable of the night.

Melinda shivered, whether from cold or fear she was not sure. She only knew that her hands were trembling as she held the duelling pistol hidden in the folds of her satin skirt. She was half-kneeling in the bushes which surrounded the small, open glade hidden from the roadway and out of sight of everyone who did not directly enter it.

In the darkness Melinda had groped her way from the high road across the grass, and then, as the morning light grew stronger, had found herself a hiding-place amongst the lilacs and flowering shrubs whose blossoms scented the air. It had not been hard to find the place to which Lord Wrotham had referred the previous evening.

When Melinda had commanded the carriage to come to a halt a few miles after they had left Chard, the coachman had climbed down from his box and given the reins to the footman. He had then peered through the carriage window with an expression on his face which told Melinda all too clearly that he did not approve of his passengers demanding that they should speak to him.

'What is your name?' Melinda asked.

'Travers, ma'am.'

He was a middle-aged man and she guessed that he had been in the service of the Chard family for many years. There was the look of an old and respectful servant about him. At the same time she had a feeling that he would speak his mind with an independence which she knew she would not find in one of the younger servants.

'I want your help, Travers,' Melinda said.

'I'm at your service, ma'am,' he said, and she fancied there was a suspicious look in his eyes as if he wondered what she was about to ask of him.

'Your master is in danger, Travers,' she said. 'In grave danger—and I believe I may be able to help him.'

'Indeed, ma'am!'

There was just the suspicion of disbelief in Travers' tone which told Melinda all too clearly that he thought any service she might be able to offer the Marquis could not be of much consequence. She felt as if she were up against a brick wall of imperturbability; that Travers trusted the Marquis to look after himself and found her assertion hard to credit. Her only hope lay in being frank.

'The position is this, Travers,' she said. 'His lordship has been challenged to a duel by Lord Wrotham.'

For the first time she knew she had made an impact. The coachman stiffened. She saw by the expression on his face that the truth had gone home.

'That be bad news, ma'am,' Travers said slowly. 'If what I've 'eard is to be believed, his lordship's a dangerous customer.'

'You have heard of him then?' Melinda asked.

'Indeed, I 'ave, ma'am! 'Is lordship's place isn't far from 'ere and I knows 'is coachman. 'Is lordship's a crack shot, and there's talk, too, that 'e often fights duels and always wins 'em.'

'That is what I have heard,' Melinda said. 'And that, Travers, is why I want your help.'

'Indeed, ma'am! But what can I do?'

'You can take me to the place where the gentlemen will fight,' Melinda said. 'They are to meet at dawn. It is somewhere by the Serpentine, I know that; but it would be hard for me to find it by myself.'

'And what will you do, ma'am, if I takes you there?' Travers enquired. 'If you'll pardon me for asking.'

'I have a plan which may save his lordship,' Melinda replied.

She saw that she had not won the coachman entirely to her side and added quickly:

'Tell me something, Travers. Do you believe that Lord Chard, good shot though he may be, is the equal of Lord Wrotham in a duel?'

There was a long pause before Travers answered and then, almost reluctantly, he replied:

'I may be maligning 'is lordship, but from what I've 'eard, ma'am, Lord Wrotham is always the winner.'

'By fair means or foul,' Melinda said softly.

She saw a glint in the coachman's eye and knew she had struck home.

'Indeed, ma'am, I've 'eard rumours to that effect, but it's not for the likes of I to speak scandal about the gentry.'

'No, of course not,' Melinda said softly. 'But our only concern must be that his lordship survives.'

'Yes, indeed, ma'am,' the coachman agreed.

'Then take me there,' Melinda said. 'I would not wish to arrive more than, perhaps, twenty minutes before dawn. Could we rest somewhere on the way? But at not too far a distance from London, just in case a horse might cast a shoe, or something else contrive to hinder us.'

'There'll be no shoes cast with my team, ma'am,' Travers said almost angrily.

'Then you will take me there at exactly the right time?' Melinda said. 'I promise you that you will, in fact, be helping his lordship more than you realise.'

'I'll obey your orders, ma'am,' Travers said,

' 'though what 'is lordship will say to me afterwards I've no idea.'

He touched the brim of his top-hat respectfully, then climbed back on to the box of the carriage and, taking the reins from the footman, whipped up the horses which had been champing restlessly whilst he had been away from them.

They started off towards London at a brisk pace and Melinda sank back against the cushions of the carriage with a sigh of relief. She had been afraid, desperately afraid, that she would not be able to find the exact spot where the duel would take place. She had guessed the servants would know it—what was ever hidden from servants?—but she had been apprehensive lest the coachmen from Chard, who had not been let into the secret of her supposed marriage, might consider it their duty to prevent a woman attending what was traditionally an entirely masculine occasion.

Now, as she waited in the bushes, she felt almost overwhelmed by her own inadequacy. However wild her schemes, how could she really help the Marquis? And if she did, would he thank her for her interference? She felt cramped and uncomfortable crouching amongst the shrubs. She shivered again and knew it was not the cold which caused it; for the morning was mild and airless with a promise of heat later on.

She had eaten at a small inn to which Travers had taken her on the outskirts of the city. The landlord, overcome by the arrival of so important a guest, had offered her all the hospitality of his inn. He had begged her to sample his fine ham, the salmon from the Thames and oysters which, though cheap, he assured her were very tasty to those who liked them.

To please him she had eaten a few mouthfuls, but she was too tense and apprehensive to have any appetite. Indeed, the food seemed to choke her, but she had sipped a glass of wine because she felt it would steady her nerves and keep out the cold.

Finally Travers had sent a message to say it was time they were moving. She had climbed back into the carriage, and now one of the duelling pistols she had brought with her from Chard was primed and ready in her hand, hidden by the short cloak she wore over her shoulders.

When they arrived in the Park and the horses came to a standstill she had had one moment of panic. Would it not be best for her to drive on and wait for the Marquis to come to Grosvenor Square? But suppose he never came! The mere thought of him lying motionless on the ground gave her back her courage. She got out of the carriage, thanked Travers and told him to drive away, but to return for her within the hour in case she wanted him.

'I will put the carriage round the corner, ma'am,' he said, 'so no one will see it. Fred, 'ere, will look after the 'orses. They be tired and won't give 'im too much trouble. I'll come back and be within call.'

He saw even in the darkness that Melinda made a movement of her hand as if she would have forbidden him, and he added quickly:

' 'Is lordship will not see me, ma'am, 'ave no fear o' that.'

'Then, thank you, Travers,' Melinda said in her

soft voice. 'It will be a comfort to know that you are here.'

She had slipped away from him and although it had been hard, in the semi-darkness, to find what she sought, she saw now, as the sun rose, that she was in a place of vantage. She was facing about the centre of the little glade so that the duellists would be on either side of her; and, now, as she listened, she heard voices.

Someone was coming! She pulled herself back a little further, just in case she should be seen. She thought she must have known instinctively who would come first. It was the Marquis accompanied by Captain Vestey and another man she had never seen before.

The Marquis was looking magnificent. A touch of flamboyance or disdain for his adversary had made him choose a coat of pale grey whipcord and a grey stock with a diamond pin which seemed to catch the light. How foolish to make himself an easy target, Melinda thought to herself, and yet, at the same time, she understood that his dislike of Lord Wrotham would not deny him any advantage in this game of life and death.

'Is this the place?' she heard Captain Vestey ask.

'It is, indeed,' the Marquis replied. 'The last time I was here it was as a second to Peregrine Cunningham.'

'What was he fighting about?' Captain Vestey enquired.

'His wife,' the Marquis said briefly. 'She had run off with a bounder. Peregrine forced a duel on him.'

'And who won?' the Marquis's other second asked.

'My friend,' the Marquis replied, 'to some cost. He lost an eye in the engagement.'

Melinda gave a little gasp of horror but the three gentlemen seemed quite unperturbed.

'I often wondered what had happened to Peregrine,' Captain Vestey said.

'Did his wife return to him, Drogo?' the other man enquired.

'No, Freddie! She patched up what remained of her lover. They went to live in Ireland.'

'A most unsatisfactory story,' Captain Vestey declared. 'For God's sake, Drogo, take no chances with Wrotham! He's known to be a tricky devil. I don't trust him!'

'If he turns too soon, denounce him,' the Marquis said.

'And what good will that do if you're dead?' the man he had called Freddie enquired. 'Anthony Merville told me that he acted as second to John Coombe and you remember what happened to him! But Coombe was dead and there seemed no point in Anthony making a fuss. Besides, it was only his word against Wrotham and his seconds. Who was going to believe him?'

'I can't think how he manages to get away with it,' Gervase Vestey said testily, and Melinda knew that his nerves were on edge.

'Merville told me that Wrotham brings a doctor with him who's in his pay,' Freddie said. 'The quack is prepared to swear that the victim died of a heart attack. They get him buried quickly and who's going to ask questions?'

'Oh, shut up, Freddie!' Captain Vestey said. 'You'll be making Drogo nervous.'

'You started it,' Freddie said resentfully.

'I know I did,' Captain Vestey replied. 'I only want Drogo to be on his toes.'

'If you are suggesting that I should fire before the correct moment,' the Marquis said, 'you are making a great mistake. I'll fight clean and if Wrotham cheats I'll come back and haunt him!'

Melinda felt the tears rise in her eyes. Somehow the Marquis's courage made her feel like crying. At the same time, she was frightened because she saw, all too clearly, that the two men with the Marquis were desperately apprehensive of what might occur.

Then, just as the first rays of the morning sun dispelled the last shadows of the night, Lord Wrotham came into the glade. He was looking more debauched and more dissipated than ever, Melinda thought. He was dressed in black from head to foot; his stock, which was also black, practically obscured the faint line of his white collar. He was dressed so as to be almost indiscernible in the half-light and she felt, although she could not see it, that when he looked at the Marquis there was an expression of cynical amusement in his eyes.

'Good morning, Chard!' he said. 'Good morning, Gervase! And Freddie—I wasn't expecting to see you here.'

'And I have no inclination to see you,' Freddie answered rudely.

Lord Wrotham ignored him.

'You know my seconds, I think,' he said, and the Marquis nodded to the two men coldly, as if he knew them and had no desire to further his acquaintance with them.

Lord Wrotham looked back the way he had come.

'Now, where is Dr. Chambers?' he enquired.

'He shouldn't be long,' one of his seconds replied, and at that moment a man carrying a small, black doctor's bag came hurrying into the glade.

One look at the doctor told Melinda why Lord Wrotham found it easy to employ him and why he was ready to acquiesce in any scheme, however nefarious. Dr. Chambers was dirty, threadbare and looked as if he had spent the night in debauchery. His face was red and swollen and he seemed a little unsteady in his gait.

'Sorry, m'lord! Sorry!' he said. 'I'm late only because I was kept on an important case.'

'I know what your cases amount to,' Lord Wrotham said disdainfully. 'Well, keep out of the way and don't come near me; you smell of spirits.'

'Sorry, m'lord! Sorry!' the doctor repeated and obediently moved away to the far corner of the glade.

'Will you choose your weapon?' Lord Wrotham enquired of the Marquis, and his second opened a box in which reposed two duelling pistols not unlike the one which Melinda held in her hand.

'I suppose ten paces will suit you?' Lord Wrotham said.

'Yes, *ten* paces,' the Marquis repeated, with an emphasis on the number.

'We count aloud,' Lord Wrotham said, 'and turn on ten.'

'Is there not some other way?' Captain Vestey interposed.

'This is the way I have always done it,' Lord Wrotham replied, 'and I imagine that Chard accepts it.'

'I accept ten paces counting aloud,' the Marquis said, 'and we both turn at ten.'

'Very well, then,' Lord Wrotham answered. 'I regret, Chard, it should have come to this; but the girl was mine, you know, and when Kate made excuses that she was ill—or some sort of nonsense—I suspicioned that she had been up to mischief.'

'I have no wish to discuss it,' the Marquis said icily. 'If you are ready, Wrotham, I am.'

The two men stood back to back in the centre of the glade. Melinda held her breath. The Marquis was on her right; Lord Wrotham was on her left. She moved a fraction nearer, pushing her pistol through the bushes. No one would be looking for her, she was well aware of that, and she tried to remember all her father had told her when he taught her to fire a pistol.

'It kicks,' he had said. 'You must either bring it down on the object on which you are firing or aim lower. The best way is to bring it down.'

Very slowly, so that the leaves would not rustle, Melinda raised her hand. The two duellists were already moving away from each other, taking a pace as they spoke aloud.

'One . . . two . . . three . . . four . . . five . . . six . . . seven . . . eight . . . nine . . .' They were speaking in unison and, now, as they reached the ten, Melinda, whose eyes were on Lord Wrotham, saw him swing round and bring his pistol down towards the Marquis who still had his back to him.

Hardly without thinking, almost instinctively, Melinda fired, and almost instantaneously she heard the report of Lord Wrotham's pistol. She hit him and he fell, but even as she saw him fall she saw the Marquis stagger and slowly collapse on to the ground at the other end of the glade.

She burst through the bushes and throwing down her pistol she lifted up her skirts and ran across the grass to reach the Marquis almost as quickly as Captain Vestey.

'The damned swine!' she heard Freddie say. 'He fired as he said "nine". You saw him, Gervase!'

Captain Vestey was kneeling on the ground and helping Melinda raise the Marquis. Blood was pouring down his face and Melinda gave a little cry.

'Is he . . . dead? Oh, is he dead?' she said, and did not recognise her own voice because of the agony in it. And then she heard Captain Vestey say:

'Thank God! It's only a scratch! Look, the bullet seared the side of his head. It's not even entered the skull. It's the blast that's knocked him over.'

'But, look at Wrotham!' Freddie said in bewilderment. 'There was a shot, but Drogo hadn't turned!'

Melinda was mopping with her handkerchief the blood streaming down the Marquis's face.

'Is he dead?' she asked. 'I hope so.'

'But, what happened?' Freddie asked in amazement. 'I was watching Drogo.'

'Melinda must have shot him,' Captain Vestey answered. 'You did, didn't you, Melinda?'

'Yes, I shot him as he turned,' Melinda admitted. 'But do not worry about him. Are you quite sure the Marquis is all right?'

'I expect he is concussed,' Captain Vestey said, 'but nothing worse than that. You can see for yourself: the bullet has seared its way through his hair but it isn't lodged in his skull, thank God!'

'I should have fired sooner,' Melinda said. 'I waited too long.'

'Go and see if Wrotham is dead, Freddie,' Captain Vestey suggested. 'And best send for a carriage. Drogo came in his phaeton, but we shan't be able to get him into that.'

'The carriage in which I came from Chard is just a little way round the corner,' Melinda said. 'Shout for Travers. He promised he would be within earshot.'

'Hurry up, dear fellow!' Captain Vestey urged. 'Then come back and help me carry Drogo; he's no light weight.'

Melinda threw her blood-soaked handkerchief down on the grass and took a clean, white linen one from Captain Vestey.

'Are . . . are you quite sure he's . . . all right?' she asked. She felt suddenly terrified at the Marquis's pallor; the blood running down his face; the way he lay inert on the ground. It seemed to her there was no breath coming from his parted lips.

'He is alive,' Captain Vestey said. 'I swear to you, Melinda, he is all right. I've seen too many men die in battle not to know a dead man when I see one. Just support him for a moment while I go and hurry up Freddie. I can see he's talking to Wrotham's seconds. The sooner we get Drogo to a decent doctor, the better. I wouldn't have him touched by that drunken old saw-bones that Wrotham brought with him.'

'No, no, of course not,' Melinda agreed. 'Let me put my arms round him.'

With Captain Vestey's assistance she found herself holding the Marquis, with his head against her breast. He was very heavy and yet somehow, she felt to herself, she had never been so happy in her life. She could touch him and, for the moment, he was all hers. They were alone in this little glade, with the scent of the flowers and the birds singing their morning song.

She did not look to where the men were standing round Lord Wrotham's body. She was conscious only of the Marquis. She did not even worry that she had probably killed a man or that there might be retribution. She only knew that the Marquis was in her arms; that he was not angry or cynical but, suddenly, very young—a child who needed her protection and help.

Nevertheless, her arms were aching when, finally, Captain Vestey returned and with him Jim, the footman, who had accompanied her from Chard. Freddie was not far behind.

'The carriage is there,' Captain Vestey said to Melinda. 'It was a good thing you brought Travers with you. Capital chap, Travers! He's got everything fixed up so that Drogo can lie across the two seats. It won't be long now before we get him into bed.'

The three men lifted the Marquis very gently from Melinda's arms. He left a trail of blood across her breast, but she did not notice it as she rose slowly to her feet. Then, as they started to move, Captain Vestey said:

'Oh, by the way! You didn't kill Wrotham.'

'I didn't?' Melinda exclaimed.

'A great pity, if you ask me,' Freddie said, supporting the Marquis on the other side. 'But you shattered his right arm. That doctor of his—if he's to be believed—says he'll live; but he thinks the arm will have to be amputated. Anyway, the double-crosser will never fight a duel again.'

'I am glad of that,' Melinda said almost fiercely. 'He deserved it.'

'He did, indeed!' Captain Vestey said. 'At the same time, Melinda, I see your pistol lying there on the ground. Bring it with you if it bears the Chard crest, which I think it does. It would be best not to leave it behind as incriminating evidence.'

'What can that swine, Wrotham, do even if he does live?' Freddie asked.

'Nothing, I should imagine,' Captain Vestey replied. 'At the same time, it is always wise to be careful with an outsider of that sort.'

They passed Lord Wrotham lying on the ground; his doctor trying to stem the flow of blood; his seconds standing by helplessly. Melinda did not look at them. She was glad when a few minutes later they were out of sight and the carriage, moving slowly so as not to shake the Marquis, had started on its way to Grosvenor Square.

Melinda tried to believe Captain Vestey when he said that the Marquis's wound was but a scratch; yet her fear that it might be something far worse did not lessen until after the surgeon, a man with the most reassuring presence, told her that, indeed, all was well.

'His lordship is badly concussed,' he said. 'It is inevitable when the blast hits the head at that particular angle. At the same time, he is a very lucky man. If the bullet had been even a tenth of an inch closer, it might have entered the skull and then there would have been nothing we could do.'

'How long will he be unconscious?' Melinda asked.

'He might come round at any time,' the surgeon replied. 'But I doubt if he will remember what happened until tomorrow. Do you want me to send you a nurse?'

'No, thank you,' Melinda answered. 'I will nurse him myself.'

'No nurse is better for a man than his own wife, eh?' the surgeon suggested.

Melinda flushed as she realised the servants must have spoken of her as 'her ladyship'.

'You do not want me to change the bandages?' she asked quickly.

'Not until I come tomorrow,' the surgeon told her. 'Just keep your husband quiet and give him some broth if he seems hungry. No spirits, of course, and don't have a lot of people around him asking stupid questions. Give him a chance to remember or not to remember—whichever may seem best.'

'I understand,' Melinda said, 'and thank you.'

'It is a great pleasure to meet you, Lady Chard,' the surgeon said. 'I knew your husband's father well. He was a fine man in his youth and a great sportsman.'

Melinda walked with him to the top of the stairs.

'There is just one thing I should like to ask you,' she said. 'Would you please not tell anyone that I am here.'

The surgeon's eyebrows went up.

'Our m . . . marriage is a secret,' Melinda explained. 'You will perhaps recall that the Dowager died only a few days ago.'

'Oh, yes, of course, I remember now,' the surgeon said. 'Your secret is safe with me, Lady Chard. But when your wedding is announced, I hope you will allow me to offer you both my most hearty congratulations.'

'Thank you! Thank you very much indeed!' Melinda said, and leaving the surgeon to descend the stairs alone she went back into the Marquis's bedroom.

The blinds had been lowered and the room was in semi-darkness and very quiet. The Marquis was lying still against the pillows; his head bandaged; his arms outside the sheet. Melinda stood looking down at him, then drawing up a chair to the bed she started her vigil. A little while later there came a very soft knock at the door. She opened it.

'Captain Vestey to speak with you, m'lady,' one of the footmen said.

'Ask him to come upstairs, please,' she replied. 'I do not want to leave his lordship.'

'Very good, m'lady.'

She waited until Gervase Vestey was outside the door and then went out to him, leaving the door ajar.

'Haven't you a nurse?' Captain Vestey enquired.

Melinda shook her head.

'I want to look after him myself, and the surgeon agreed it was best.'

'You are quite sure you know what you are taking on?' Captain Vestey enquired.

'Quite sure,' Melinda declared.

He looked at her, seeing her blood-stained gown and dishevelled hair. Her face was very pale, but her eyes were shining.

'Nevertheless, you have had a long night,' he said. 'Go and change your clothes. I will sit with Drogo if you do not trust anyone else.'

She smiled at him and understood that he was thinking only of her.

'Thank you,' she said, 'I shall not be long.'

'You must also eat something,' Captain Vestey urged. 'Did you know there is a sitting-room off this bedroom?'

'No, I didn't know,' Melinda said.

'Why should you?' he asked, again with a smile. 'I am going to order you some breakfast—and I need some, too. I will leave the door ajar. You will make a better nurse if you are well fed.'

'You think of everything, don't you?' Melinda said.

'I will tell you something else I have thought about,' Captain Vestey said. 'I thought of your clothes. I'll wager you didn't remember them!'

'No, I didn't,' Melinda admitted almost guiltily. 'I think I left one gown behind here, but the rest are at Chard.'

'I have sent for them,' Captain Vestey said. 'I thought you would want to nurse Drogo—and who else should have the right?'

Melinda flushed.

'You love him, don't you?' Captain Vestey asked in a low voice.

Melinda raised her face to his and he saw the sudden fear in her eyes.

'How . . . how did you guess?'

'You forget, I saw you run towards him when he fell,' Captain Vestey explained. 'And I saw your face when you thought he was dead. You are not a very good actress, Melinda.'

'I thought I was,' Melinda said, trying to speak lightly.

'Oh, my dear!' Gervase Vestey said. 'Are you wise? Do you realise what heartbreak lies ahead of you; Don't love him too much. Remember this marriage is only a pretence; a means to an end as far as Drogo is concerned. And then, good-bye!'

Melinda walked away from him to grip the top of the rail which ran along the landing. From here she could look down into the empty hall. She could almost see herself walking down the stairs; going out through the front door; leaving this house and all it contained behind her—leaving her heart!

'I know . . . I know,' she whispered. 'But what can I do?'

'I don't want to see you hurt,' Captain Vestey said. He, too, had moved to stand beside her, his eyes on her profile—her straight, aristocratic nose, her small chin, her sweetly moulded lips.

'You are too good for this sort of thing,' he said, and his words seemed to come straight from his heart.

Melinda gave a little sigh.

'Thank you for thinking of me,' she said. 'But don't you understand? I am happy—happier than I have been ever in my life. Happy, after a year of misery, humiliation and, at times, despair.'

'What will you do when he no longer needs you?' Captain Vestey asked.

'I do not know,' Melinda answered. 'Do not let us speak about it.'

'I had hoped that it would really mean nothing of importance to you,' Captain Vestey said. 'And yet, I suppose from the first moment I saw you I knew that you were a sensitive person, someone who, even in the way of life you had chosen, had feelings that were different from those of the other women with whom you associated.'

Melinda did not really take in what he was saying. She was thinking of the Marquis; thinking that for once he was no longer arrogant, commanding and powerful, but a man who had been wounded; a man, for the moment, lost to the very world in which he lived.

'I must go back to him,' she said. She did not realise that Captain Vestey had put out his hand to take hers and that something he was about to say was checked on his lips. 'Go and sit with him,' she commanded. 'I will be only a few minutes—and perhaps you were right about that breakfast.'

She gave him a fleeting smile and moved swiftly away down the passage to the room she had occupied when she had stayed at Grosvenor Square. There was something springlike and ethereal about her; something which made the man watching shake his head as he went towards the sick-room.

'Dammit, Drogo! She's too good for you!' he said beneath his breath, as obediently he took his seat beside the bed.

12

The footman crossed the road to open the gate to the private garden with a special key. Melinda thanked him and put out her hand to take the key from him.

'I will wait for you, m'lady,' he said, so she smiled and passed into the garden.

The afternoon sun, already sinking low behind the roofs, played on the water rising from a small, stone fountain. There was a profusion of flowers, their fragrance heavy on the air. There was purple and white lilac; pink cherry blossom; golden laburnum; and crimson tulips, standing like guardsmen, surrounded in their tidy beds by blue forget-me-nots.

There was no one else in the garden, although it served all the houses in Grosvenor Square. Melinda walked slowly across the well-cut lawn. The flowers and the peace reminded her of Chard and she had a sudden longing to be back there. Perhaps, when the Marquis was better, they would return, and then—she felt her heart leap at the thought—they would be alone again.

She had had him to herself since the duel and it was only now, on doctor's orders, that she had left the Marquis's bedside to walk in the fresh air and, as the physician had urged, 'Put the roses back into your cheeks'.

It had required hours of patience, hours which she had found tiring, and yet, at the same time, which had brought her a hidden elation. The Marquis had relied on her. He was no longer autocratic and demanding, withering her with his words or bewildering her with accusations she did not understand. He was just a man laid low and in pain and she had been able to bring him solace.

She had sat beside him through the long hours of the night, curled up in a big armchair which the valet had insisted on moving to beside the bed. Sometimes she had dozed a little, but mostly she had watched the Marquis in the dim light of the candles and knew that she loved him with all her heart, with every fibre of her being.

She had always wondered whether she would ever fall in love and had dreamed of it, as girls do. But she had not expected it to be a comsuming fire which seemed to give her a physical hurt and, at the same time, an ecstasy which swept her to the skies.

This was love, she told herself, and felt her heart throb and her fingers tremble as she touched the Marquis to straighten his pillows or cover him with a fresh blanket. But it was hopeless! There could be nothing in the future for her but heartbreak. And, yet, she could no more stop loving him than prevent the tide from coming in.

Her happiness in having him to herself was, she knew, doomed to be short lived. This morning the Marquis had been much better and, although he still seemed a little muzzy and still unaware of what had happened, he was more like himself. He had insisted on being washed and shaved and had risen from his bed to receive the doctor in his dressing-gown. When Melinda had remonstrated with him for wishing to exert himself, he had protested:

'You're making me soft! I have a feeling there is something I must do. I'm not certain what it is. My brain seems fuzzy and stupid; but it will come back to me, and lying here won't help.'

'You have been hurt,' Melinda said gently.

The Marquis put up his hand to the bandage round his head.

'What happened?' he asked. 'Was it an accident? Did Thunderbolt throw me? No, it was you he should have thrown! Oh . . . ! Of course, I remember! The duel!'

There was a sudden sharpening of his tone and Melinda said hastily:

'Do not talk about it now. You have to rest. The doctor will be here later and if he thinks you are talking too much he will give you one of his sedatives.'

'He'll do nothing of the sort!' the Marquis said abruptly. 'I'm not going to have anyone pumping laudanum into me, or any other poisons which take away my senses.'

Melinda gave a little sigh. She knew by the tone of his voice that it would be useless to argue with him, and when he rang for his valet she could only leave the room and wonder if ever again he would be dependent on her.

As she went downstairs to the hall she heard a footman at the front door speaking to another flunkey.

'Tell 'er ladyship 'is lordship is better this morning, but 'e's not yet receiving visitors.'

'I'll tell 'er ladyship,' the other man replied. 'And be so obliging as to give 'is lordship this note.'

There was a moment's pause before the footman

who was handing over the note added with a snigger:

'I'm always taking these 'ere billers-doos around t' town. If yer asks me, I'm nothing but a Cupid's messenger.'

'Well, I'll tell yer one thing,' the first footman replied. 'If yer were naked, yer'd look even worse than yer do now!'

There was a roar of laughter, quickly subdued in case they should be overheard; then the sound of the door closing and the footman, resplendent in his claret uniform with golden buttons, walked sedately across the hall, the note he had just received lying on a silver salver.

Melinda would have been amused at the exchange of pleasantries had she not guessed whom the note was from. Who but Lady Alice would be sending the Marquis a *billet-doux*? She felt a sudden surge of anger which she knew only too well was jealousy.

Now, in the beautiful, quiet garden she faced the hopelessness of her position. And yet even Lady Alice could not take the Marquis from her for six months! She walked twice round the little fountain and then, because she could not bear to be away from the house for so long, she retraced her steps.

The footman was waiting at the gate where she had left him. He opened it when she appeared and then locked it behind her while she waited on the pavement. Several carriages were passing and she looked at the horses with interest: a pair of chestnuts, nothing like so fine as those that were owned by the Marquis; a fat roan drawing a closed brougham; and an open tandem tooled by a young man with his top-hat at a jaunty angle, a big carnation in his buttonhole.

'You can cross now, m'lady,' the footman suggested respectfully and Melinda became aware that although the traffic had passed she was still standing on the pavement.

She walked across the road, having the feeling that she was returning home after a long absence. As she entered the hall clock struck six. She realised that the doctor must have gone and wondered if anyone had remembered to take the Marquis some tea.

She was just about to walk up the stairs to find out when the butler, coming into the hall, said in a quiet voice:

'His lordship has asked me to inform you, m'lady, that he is in the Library.'

'He is downstairs!' Melinda exclaimed.

'Yes, m'lady. The doctor said he was well enough. In fact, from what Sir Henry said to me, he is very pleased indeed with his lordship's progress.'

'That is good news,' Melinda said in her soft voice, forcing herself to walk slowly across the hall to the Library door.

For a moment she thought the room was empty, and then she saw that the Marquis was sitting in front of the fire at the far end of the room and that a servant had placed a small screen round his chair to keep out the draught. Abandoning all sense of dignity, Melinda ran down the room and reaching the Marquis's side said almost breathlessly:

'You are better! Oh, I am so glad!'

He put out his hands and took hers, smiling up at her and looking, she thought, very like his old self save that he seemed gentler and the expression on his face was kind.

'I have been hearing how well you nursed me,' he said in his deep voice.

She quivered at the touch of his hand and knelt down on the floor beside him, her skirts billowing out around her.

'It was not difficult,' she said, feeling her eyes drop before his. 'You were a very good patient.'

'Sir Henry tells me that I had concussion,' the Marquis said. 'I still feel a trifle bemused and cannot remember really what happened.'

'Do not let us talk of it,' Melinda said, feeling she could not face a disclosure of the part she had played in the duel.

'I must get Gervase to tell me all about it,' the Marquis exclaimed. 'Has he been to see me?'

'Yes, indeed, Captain Vestey has called three or four times today,' Melinda said. 'But Sir Henry forbade any visitors.'

'Except you, of course,' the Marquis said.

'I . . . I do not think I count as a visitor,' Melinda stammered.

'No, indeed! Sir Henry congratulated me on the ministrations of my wife. Where did you learn to nurse, amongst your other accomplishments?'

'I nursed my father when he broke his collar-bone out hunting,' Melinda explained. 'And my mother was ill at various times. But I wanted to nurse you; I would not have liked some starchy nurse to keep me away.'

'I am touched by your solicitude,' the Marquis said quietly.

She glanced at him quickly and realised he was not sneering or being cynical.

'I should have thought,' he went on, 'that you would have found it very dull sitting by the bedside of an unconscious man. Were you not bored?'

'No, of course not,' Melinda replied. 'I wanted to be with you.'

She spoke impulsively and the blood rose in her cheeks as she realised she had said something which might give away her true feelings.

'Why should you want to be with me?' the Marquis asked and his voice was somehow insistent.

Embarrassed, Melinda reached up, untied the ribbons from under her chin and took off her bonnet. Outside, the setting sun had left a glow in the sky and, combined with the firelight, it turned Melinda's hair to gold, making it frame her little face like a halo.

She knew the Marquis's eyes were on her and hastily, because she was nervous, she said:

'I was just going upstairs to see if you had had your tea. Did they bring it to you? I was so afraid they might have forgotten.'

'I had everything I wanted,' the Marquis assured her. 'But you haven't answered my question.'

'I . . . I think I . . . have forgotten what . . . it was,' Melinda said in a low voice.

'That is not true,' the Marquis replied. 'Tell me, Melinda, for I wish to know.'

There was something so compelling about him, something in the look in his eyes which made her heart feel as if it turned over beneath her breast. Melinda sprang to her feet.

'I . . . I am sure there is . . . something you want,' she said and looked down at the Marquis to see a smile on his lips. He held out his hand.

'Come here, Melinda,' he said, and as she did not move he added: 'At once!'

As she stood there irresolute, before she could move, the door opened and the butler's voice said:

'Sir Hector Stanyon to see you, ma'am.'

Melinda stood suddenly paralysed as into the room, large, red-faced and overpowering, strode Sir Hector. For a moment she could only stare at him, her eyes wide and frightened in her face, like an animal that has been trapped.

He looked at her and advanced slowly until he stood in the centre of the room.

'So this is where you have been hiding!' he said, and his voice was harsh and noisy. 'I thought I could not have been mistaken when I saw you cross the road just now; and yet I could hardly believe my eyes when you entered this house.'

'Uncle . . . Hector!' Melinda faltered.

'Yes, your uncle, indeed,' Sir Hector said. 'And your guardian, if it will please you to remember, who is entitled to an explanation.'

'I . . . I . . .' Melinda began, only to be silenced by a sudden roar from Sir Hector.

'There is no need for explanations, they speak for themselves! You dared to run away, to leave my house; but now you will return to it with me immediately. There will be time for explanations later, but let me make it quite plain to you, miss, that you have escaped me once but you will not escape me again. After I have given you the biggest thrashing that you have ever had in your life, you will marry Colonel Gillingham as speedily as it can be arranged. Fortunately he does not know of your escapade. Your aunt was clever enough to keep it from him. But I know about it and you shall be punished —make no mistake about that—punished as you have never been before, you ungrateful little wench!'

'Please . . . Uncle Hector, I . . . I cannot . . .'

'Don't argue with me,' her uncle bellowed. 'Go upstairs immediately and pack your things. I do not know what position you hold in this household, but if any explanations are necessary I will make them. Obey me! Do you hear me? If you don't, I will give you, now, some of the punishment that I have in store for you when I get you home!'

Sir Hector took a step towards Melinda and raised his hand. Instinctively she gave a little cry, feeling herself utterly oppressed and overpowered. Then, because for the moment she had forgotten everything but her terror of her uncle, she was as startled as Sir Hector was to hear a firm voice from behind her say:

'I cannot allow you, sir, to strike a lady in my presence.'

The Marquis had risen from his chair and, advancing a few paces, stood beside Melinda. She glanced up at him and felt her terror abate. He looked so strong and distinguished, and there was no mistaking Sir Hector's astonishment.

'May I ask who you are?' Sir Hector enquired.

'My name is Chard—the Marquis of Chard,' was the reply.

'Chard!' Sir Hector ejaculated. 'Then what is my niece doing here?'

There was a pause and he added unpleasantly:

'Or is that an indiscreet question to ask? I expected little of the girl, for she always has been a problem to me, but I did not anticipate she would so quickly become a strumpet!'

'Your niece,' the Marquis replied, and his voice was icy, 'if that is the relationship between you—and, if it is a fact, she has my deepest condolences—has done me the honour of going through the ceremony of marriage with me and, under the circumstances, I must ask you to apologise.'

'Marriage! My God! You've married her!' Sir Hector choked and in a moment his bluster evaporated. 'I did not know. The Marquis of Chard, indeed! Then I must offer you both my felicitations.'

'We have no need of them,' the Marquis said. 'And your behaviour since you have come into my house has given me to think that we can easily dispense with your company. Good afternoon, sir! The servants will see you out.'

'But I mean . . .' Sir Hector objected, 'I . . . I must discuss this with you. I am Melinda's guardian.'

'Anything you wish to say,' the Marquis said, 'can be communicated through my solicitors!'

The Marquis faced about and walking towards the mantelpiece stood there with his back turned. For a moment Sir Hector remained irresolute, all the fire and anger gone out of him, for once at a loss how to act. Then, with an oath beneath his breath, which Melinda heard quite clearly, he turned, strode down the room, flung open the door, passed through it and slammed it behind him.

Melinda listened as if to hear his footsteps cross

the hall and be quite certain he had left the house. She stood looking after him and then, very slowly, turned towards the Marquis. He had his back to her, staring down at the fire, and suddenly she was afraid.

'I . . . I am . . . sorry,' she stammered.

He turned then and she quailed before the expression on his face.

'Damn you!' he said, and his voice was like a whip. 'Why didn't you tell me?'

She did not answer and now his tone was sarcastic and icy like a bitter wind:

'I have the honour to ask for your hand in marriage! That was what you wanted all the time, wasn't it? That is why you played hard to get! That is why you kept up this ridiculous farce of innocence—so that you could trap me. It was very prettily done: you very nearly succeeded in getting me to believe that you were what you pretended to be.

'And, now, I must marry you! Not for your sake—don't think it is because I have compromised you—but for my own. Your uncle will talk—of course he'll talk! "My niece, the Marchioness!" I dare not, for my own sake, deny it! Very well, we will be married, properly married this time, which is just what you planned. What a charming wife I shall have! A wife who makes assignations with every man she meets—a bargain with Lord Hartington, a promise to Lord Wrotham—that lecher, the lowest type of outsider that has ever walked this earth, has been a paramour of my wife! Do you think I can ever forget that? Do you think I can ever look at you without thinking of him touching you? A debaucher of whom even the lowest woman on the streets is afraid!'

The Marquis paused and Melinda stood staring at him, her face drained of all colour, her eyes wide and dark with pain.

'When I look at you,' the Marquis continued, his voice low but witheringly clear, 'I find it hard to believe that you are what you are. Yet you are evil; an evil that enchants and traps a man; an evil that, in reality, should be destroyed. But, I must marry you! Marry you because I was green enough to fall into the cleverest trap that was ever set by a shrewd, scheming woman.

'Very well, you shall have my name. But know that in giving it to you, I loathe you for what you are! I wish to God that Thunderbolt had thrown you and that you were dead! And if I could see you dead, I would rejoice because the world was rid of you. You have tortured me and now you would destroy me. Go! Go from my sight! I cannot bear to look at you!'

His voice was raised almost to a shout, and with a little cry that seemed to come from the very depth of her being Melinda turned and ran from the room. He heard her running across the hall and up the stairs and then sat down in his chair and covered his face with his hands.

Some time later a footman came into the room bringing the lighted oil lamps. The Marquis did not stir; only when the butler announced: 'Captain Gervase Vestey, m'lord!' did he turn his head.

'Drogo! It's delightful to find you up,' Captain Vestey said. He put his hand on his friend's shoulder, then sat down on the other side of the fireplace. 'You'll soon be as good as new,' he said. 'It was really the blast that knocked you out. Even when I saw you lying on the ground I knew it was only a surface wound. Melinda thought you were dead.'

There was silence for a moment and then the Marquis said in a strained tone:

'Melinda! What was Melinda doing there?'

'You haven't heard?' Captain Vestey asked. 'She saved your life. I suppose she was too shy to speak about it, but she shot Wrotham in the arm as he turned on the count of nine. I always knew he was yellow-livered, but I never thought to see a man deliberately cheat in such a manner.'

'Melinda—shot him—in the arm!' the Marquis repeated almost as if he were feeling for words.

'A jolly good shot it was, too,' Captain Vestey smiled. 'My God! That girl's a sportsman, there's no doubt about it! But, unfortunately, she was just a second late. When Wrotham fired, the bullet caught you on the side of the head; you were still moving away from him, you see.'

'You mean, if it had not been for Melinda he would have killed me?' the Marquis asked.

'You can bet a monkey to a halfpenny he would have,' Captain Vestey replied. 'He's a killer! And now we know why all the other fellows he has fought have died.'

'Melinda didn't kill him?' the Marquis asked.

'No! Might have been a good thing if she had. At the same time, there would have been trouble about it,' Captain Vestey replied. 'But she shattered his right arm. I've just heard that it's been amputated.

Serves him right and what is more he won't dare show his face in decent society again. Freddie and I will see to that!'

The Marquis said nothing and after a moment Captain Vestey said:

'Have you ever heard of such courage as that girl has? After we had left Chard, she drove up with old Travers, hid in the bushes and had the whole thing planned out. As it happened, I was jolly glad to have Travers there. In the state you were, we would have had trouble lifting you into the phaeton. Melinda was splendid through it all. You know, Drogo, she loves you!'

'Nonsense! She does nothing of the sort!' the Marquis said angrily. 'But I had no idea that she had been present at the duel. I must speak to her about it.'

Captain Vestey looked at his watch.

'Well, she ought to be down to dinner at any moment,' he said. 'I suppose she told you that she had asked me to dine with you both? You won't be changing, Drogo? And if you take my advice, you'll go to bed the minute dinner is over. You ought not to do too much the first day.'

'Ring the bell,' the Marquis said sharply, obviously not having heard a word of what his friend was saying.

'Ring the bell?' Captain Vestey said. 'What for?'

'Ring the bell,' the Marquis commanded.

Captain Vestey rose to his feet. As he did so the door opened.

'Dinner is served, m'lord!'

'Where is Miss Stanyon?' the Marquis enquired.

'Miss Stanyon?' the butler repeated. 'I understand

her ladyship has left the house, m'lord.'

'Left the house!' the Marquis echoed. 'What do you mean, she has left the house?'

'One of the footmen told me that she had gone,' the butler answered, a little flustered by his master's tone. 'I believe she left a note for your lordship.'

'Then bring it to me! Why the hell wasn't I given it at once?' the Marquis said sharply.

He had risen from his chair and stood in silence, looking pale and angry, until the butler returned with the letter on a salver. The Marquis snatched it and tore open the envelope. The butler withdrew from the room and the Marquis stood reading the letter until, unable to bear his curiosity any longer, Captain Vestey said:

'What is it? What has happened?'

'Listen, Gervase! Listen to this!' the Marquis said in a strange voice.

'*My Lord,*

'I deeply regret that I have been such a trouble to you. It was wrong of me, I know, from the very beginning to take part in a Ceremony of Marriage which was only a Deception, but I needed the money to buy a cottage in which I could live with my old Nurse and I did not realise there would be so many Terrible Consequences. I had not thought that you would be forced to fight a Duel on my behalf. But I swear to you that I had made no Assignations such as you have accused me of doing. As a joke Lord Hartington asked me to make a Bargain that I would try not to fall in Love and he would try to fall out of Love. And I had never met Lord Wrotham, except on the

evening when I arrived in London and Mrs. Harcourt, whom I encountered on the Railway Station, offered me a lodging for the night. As we entered her House, she introduced me to his Lordship and that was the only time, I swear to you, that I had ever set eyes on him.

'The following morning I came to stay with you at Grosvenor Square. I had never schemed nor, indeed, in my wildest dreams imagined that you would Marry me, and I have no wish to ruin your life or do anything that would not be for your Happiness.

'Therefore, my lord, you will never see me again and Captain Vestey has told me that if I am Dead you can claim the Money and there will be no more difficulties.

'I should like to thank you for your many kindnesses to me. I have been very happy, at times, and I would only ask you to forgive me the Discrepancies in my Behaviour.

'Yours respectfully,
'Melinda Stanyon.'

The Marquis's voice seemed to falter as he read the last two words and when he raised his eyes from the letter they were blazing.

'Do you understand, Gervase?' he asked. 'She was innocent! Do you see what she says? Ella had picked her up that evening at a railway station. I have always been told that the woman worked that way, but I never believed it.'

'Oh, it's true enough,' Captain Vestey said. 'April told me that she meets the trains, offers the country girls who arrive a bed for the night and takes them round to her house. After that there's no escape.'

He saw the look on the Marquis's face and added:

'April told me that she usually keeps them under drugs for the first two or three nights until they are amenable. I daresay Melinda had no idea of what sort of place she was in.'

'I am absolutely certain she did not,' the Marquis said. 'But how was I to know? She came from Kate's.'

'She kept saying she didn't know who Kate was,' Captain Vestey interposed.

'She never had a chance to meet her,' the Marquis said slowly. 'You went round there the very night she arrived, and after Ella had bought her a wedding-dress she was brought here to Grosvenor Square.'

He suddenly put his hand up to his face to cover his eyes.

'My God! When I think what I said to her! The way I treated her! She looked so pure, but I couldn't believe it.'

'And what do you think has happened to her now?' Captain Vestey asked.

The Marquis gave an exclamation.

'She has left the house! Where would she have gone? My God, Gervase! If it's what I think!'

He almost ran down the room, pulled open the door and walked into the hall. The butler was waiting outside.

'Where has Miss Stanyon gone?' he enquired. 'Does anyone know?'

'Not exactly, m'lord,' the butler replied. 'But when your lordship seemed surprised at her absence, I made enquiries.'

'What have you found out?' the Marquis asked. 'Quick, man!'

'Miss Stanyon told no one where she was going,' the butler replied, 'but she asked the link-man outside the way to the Embankment.'

The Marquis turned towards the front door.

'Wait, Drogo! Wait for the carriage!' Captain Vestey shouted.

'You bring one,' the Marquis said over his shoulder. 'I'll take the first thing on four legs that will get me there.'

Before the footman could precede him, he pulled open the front door and was out into the street. He looked wildly up and down and then saw a hansom coming slowly round the corner. He waved and the man drew up beside him.

'A guinea if you'll get me to the Embankment as quickly as possible,' the Marquis said, throwing himself inside. 'A guinea, no two, if you like; only get me there.'

The cabby, thinking he had a drunk for a passenger, whipped up his horse.

'Quickly!' the Marquis cried from inside. 'Quicker! Quicker!'

The horse achieved quite a remarkable speed as they proceeded through Berkeley Square, up Berkeley Street and down St. James's Street, but despite the frequent crack of the cabby's whip the horse was tiring as they reached Parliament Square and turned down along the Embankment.

'Now, drive slowly,' the Marquis commanded, and the driver pulled at the reins and the horse slowed down to a trot.

The Embankment was dark as the lights were far between; there were few pedestrians and the Marquis leaned out, his eyes on the parapet. Then, quite suddenly, he saw her in the darkness between two street lamps. There was no mistaking that small, slight figure, the golden hair, from which the shawl which must have covered it had dropped away.

'Stop!'

The cabby reined in his horse and the Marquis jumped out. He took his purse and flung it at the man, who caught it deftly and gave an astonished whistle when he saw what it contained.

The Marquis, who was now no longer in a hurry, stood for a moment watching Melinda. He saw her raise her face to the sky and then look down at the dark, swirling water beneath the parapet. Very quietly he approached her.

'Melinda!' he said, and she started at the sound of her name.

When she saw who it was, she put out her little hand as if to ward him off.

'No . . . no! You must not . . . stop me,' she pleaded. 'It is just that . . . there . . . there were people about . . . and . . . it looks so cold and . . . dark.'

'Melinda!' the Marquis said again and his voice was very tender. 'How could you come here to do such a thing?'

'I have to,' she answered. 'Do you not see I have to? It has all become such a . . . muddle. I have upset you. I have . . . ruined your life and . . . I did not . . . mean to do so.'

He put out his hands and took hers in his warm grasp.

'It's all been a terrible misunderstanding, Melinda,' he said. 'Can you forgive me? Can I make you see that I only spoke to you as I did because you had tortured me beyond endurance? You drove me mad with jealousy. You see, I have loved you from the very first moment that I saw you!'

He felt her start, then she drew her hands away from him.

'Is this . . . a joke?' she asked. 'Because . . . because it isn't . . . very kind . . .' Her voice broke on the words and the Marquis's arms were round her.

'Kind, Melinda? Who wants to be kind?' he said. 'I love you! I adore you! I have wanted to tell you so since I first knew you but there was something preventing me.'

She was trembling within his arms; but now she moved a little and asked:

'Was it . . . Lady Alice?'

'What has Alice to do with it?' he asked roughly. 'I told her that day when she came into the Library that everything between us was finished. It was because I had seen you that I knew that I wanted none of her nor of her like.'

'But, I do not understand,' Melinda whispered.

'I know that now,' he said. 'And I know that that night at the party, when you looked so shocked, I should have taken you away. But, instead, imbecile that I was, I behaved like a cad to you. I can only ask you, Melinda, in all humility, to forgive me.'

'Of course, I forgive you,' Melinda said quietly. 'But, you do see, I must go away—I must . . . die. There is nothing else that can . . . help matters because, as you have said, Uncle Hector will talk. He may even insist on putting the news of . . . of our . . . marriage into the *Gazette*.'

'I shall put it in myself,' the Marquis said. 'Do you not understand, Melinda? I am asking you, begging you on my knees if necessary, to marry me. I want you for my wife. I have never wanted anyone else as I want you; and, if we can start again, I know I can make you happy.'

His arms tightened around her. She did not speak but he could feel her trembling. After a moment, with a touch of his old masterfulness, he put his fingers under her chin and turned her white, frightened face up to his.

'You have not answered me, Melinda,' he said, and no one had ever heard such tenderness in his voice. 'Will you marry me?'

'I cannot . . . comprehend what has occurred,' Melinda faltered. 'Why have you changed? What did I do that made you so angry with me? I do not understand!'

'It is something that I hope you never will understand,' the Marquis answered. 'I want you to promise me, Melinda, that we will, neither of us, never again speak of the past. It is over; it is done with. It is something in which you should never have taken part and which would never have happened except that I was an obstinate fool and so lacking in principles that I wonder that you can ever trust me in the future.'

'But, you know I trust you,' Melinda said impulsively. It is just that I want you to be happy.'

'And why do you want that?' the Marquis asked.

'Because . . .' Melinda began, and then her voice died into silence.

'Because, what?' he asked.

In answer she hid her face against him. He felt her quiver and knew it was no longer from fear.

'Because of what?' he insisted. 'Please, say it, Melinda. I don't deserve to hear it and yet I want to above all things in the whole world.'

'Because . . . I . . . love you!' Melinda whispered.

And now he swept her closer in his arms and his lips were on hers. Just for a moment he felt her tremble; then she surrendered herself and they were joined in a sudden ecstasy that was beyond words. They both knew only that the world was golden and full of light; that something that had never happened before to either of them had caught them up on the wings of joy.

Then, far away in the distance, as if it came from another planet, they heard Captain Vestey shouting. Reluctantly, as if they could not bear to separate, their lips parted one from the other; but still they looked into the darkness of each other's eyes. Slowly they turned their heads to see the carriage waiting and Captain Vestey came running towards them.

'You have found her, Drogo! Oh, thank God, Melinda, he has found you!'

'Yes, he found me,' Melinda said softly and felt the Marquis's arm tighten around her as he said:

'I have found her, Gervase, and she will never leave me again!'